SUNDAY MORNING SONG

DAYS OF GRACE

∽ 2 ∾

TIA McCOLLORS

SUNDAY MORNING SONG

DAYS OF GRACE

2

TIA McCOLLORS

W

WHITAKER
HOUSE

Unless otherwise indicated, all Scripture quotations are taken from the *New King James Version*, © 1979, 1980, 1982, 1984 by Thomas Nelson, Inc. Used by permission. All rights reserved. Scripture quotation marked (NIV) is taken from the *Holy Bible, New International Version*®, NIV®, © 1973, 1978, 1984 by the International Bible Society. Used by permission of Zondervan. All rights reserved.

SUNDAY MORNING SONG
Days of Grace ~ Book 2

Tia McCollors
www.tiamccollors.com
tia@tiamccollors.com

The author is represented by MacGregor Literary, Inc., of Hillsboro, Oregon.

ISBN: 978-1-62911-172-8
eBook ISBN: 978-1-62911-173-5
Printed in the United States of America
© 2014 by Tia McCollors

Whitaker House
1030 Hunt Valley Circle
New Kensington, PA 15068
www.whitakerhouse.com

Library of Congress Cataloging-in-Publication Data
McCollors, Tia.
  Sunday morning song / Tia McCollors.
    pages ; cm.—(Days of grace ; Book 2)
  Summary: "With her abusive ex-husband behind bars, Quinn Montgomery is ready for a fresh start for herself and her young son. But will her heart heal enough to welcome the affections of another man?"—Provided by publisher.
  ISBN 978-1-62911-172-8 (softcover : acid-free paper)—ISBN 978-1-62911-173-5 (ebook) 1. African American women—Fiction. 2. Single mothers—Fiction. 3. Man-woman relationships—Fiction. I. Title.
  PS3613.C365S86 2014
  813'.6—dc23
                                    2014026816

1 2 3 4 5 6 7 8 9 10 11   21 20 19 18 17 16 15 14

1

I dabbed concealer under my left eye to hide the fading bruise. It was barely recognizable without makeup, so with my self-taught skills, I could easily hide my mark of shame. If anyone noticed, I'd offer one of my well-rehearsed excuses, such as: "I missed the baseball Devin threw to me." Or the simplest explanation: "Just call me clumsy." I tilted my head toward the light of my makeup mirror, then feathered a light dusting of translucent powder across my face. *There.* I was once again the picture-perfect wife who was half of the picture-perfect couple adored by everyone at Light of the World Ministries.

"Amazing Grace, how sweet the sound...."

I could only faintly hear the high alto voice as it drifted from the speaker system in the kitchen. Santana listened to "Amazing Grace" every Sunday morning while he cooked breakfast, which meant that for the last eleven years, I'd been welcomed by the same voice when I sat down at the table. The morning meals rarely varied, and today, we were having my nine-year-old's favorite. Devin never tired of eating French toast, scrambled eggs, and turkey sausage. And whatever Devin wanted from Santana, he got—the overpriced video-game system, the latest shoe craze, or quality time. Devin was wholeheartedly devoted to his father, while I was devoted only by a marriage license. After the first punch, my love for Santana had slowly started to seep out of my heart. Every slap ripped a slit in my soul.

This was only the second time Santana had touched my face. He'd never left marks above my neck until after the miscarriage three months ago. Santana had been praying for a baby girl since Devin's fifth birthday. He prayed; I protected myself. I'd told him it would happen in God's timing, but every morning when Santana left for work, I pulled out the birth-control pills that I'd been taking religiously for almost five years. Even having just one child was overwhelming, and I'd known from the beginning that I wouldn't be ready to expand the family anytime soon.

At first, I'd found joy in being a stay-at-home mother to my newborn son. I didn't want to miss Devin's milestone moments—the first time he learned to grip his own bottle, his first word, his first teetering step. I pureed homemade baby food, used nontoxic cleaning products, and did everything I could to be the perfect mother. But I could never be the perfect wife. As Devin grew in height, Santana grew in criticism. I went from being the wife by Santana's side to the slave under his feet. I hoped that after some time, I'd be able to return to my job at the bank; but the years passed, and everything changed. For the worse. Leaving me trapped, unappreciated, and broke. Having another baby would only hinder my return to corporate America. Santana had no idea what it meant to sacrifice one's dreams and exchange them for dirty diapers.

"Maybe it's God's will for us to have just one child," he'd said, before he'd finally suggested that we check my fertility.

I'd given him false comfort in the assurance that, based on my yearly exam, all was well.

Unfortunately, it only took one day for me to stray from my regular routine, and the cover was pulled from my deception. Heavy downpours were stalling traffic, which meant that I'd be late picking Devin up from baseball practice if I stopped by the pharmacy. I'd planned to make the quick pit stop after getting Devin instead but was distracted by his request to stop for a strawberry milkshake. It slipped my mind. For two days.

Santana happened to be home early from work when the drugstore's automated refill line called with a reminder that I hadn't picked up my prescription. Santana never answered the home phone. Never. Why had he done it that day?

"What prescription do you have at the pharmacy?" Santana asked that evening as soon as I took one footstep from the car. He was standing in the garage, pumping air into the tires of Devin's dirt bike. I remember the toothpick dangling from his lips. Evidently he'd been eating the leftover chicken fajitas I'd been planning to devour. It didn't matter. I felt my appetite crumble.

"Go inside and change your clothes, sweetheart," I urged Devin when he jumped out of the car. He gave his father a high five and dropped his backpack on the garage floor.

Santana waited until the door slammed shut and Devin's footsteps pounded up the stairs and into his bedroom above the garage.

"I know you heard me."

"Hmmm," I said, picking up Devin's discarded book bag. "I was trying to think what it could be. It's probably Devin's cream for his eczema. It's been flaring up again. I noticed some patches on his back."

My gaze darted around the garage for something to use for protection—or as a weapon. I wondered if I had it in me to make contact somewhere on his body, full force. A floating noodle for the pool. A shovel and a rake hanging on the tool rack attached to the wall. A wooden chair I'd been sanding. One day, it would be *my* day to break free.

"Liars can never look you straight in the face," Santana said. He let the toothpick fall from his lips. "I called the pharmacy to see if it was something urgent I should pick up. So, are your birth-control pills urgent or not?"

He lifted the front of Devin's bike like he was popping a wheelie and slowly let it fall to the floor to check the bounce of the tire. He let out the kickstand, then turned to look at me. It was like the calm before the storm. Rage fired in his eyes like the devil himself was challenging me.

"How long have you been taking them?"

"I—I was having severe cramps," I stammered. "Dr. Greer said it would help. Something to do with hormones and all of these crazy changes a woman's body can go through." I tried to look and act as dramatic as possible, but Santana didn't fall for it. He had a knack for reading people, and all he saw in me was weakness.

"I don't believe that's what you used them for. You're a liar." Santana pointed an accusatory finger at me. "You knew I wanted another child, and you blocked it. You let me believe it was God's doing and not yours. You're a liar," he said again.

Devin dashed out of the house and jumped on his bike. "Can I ride to the end of the cul-de-sac?"

"You've got a math test tomorrow," I reminded him. I couldn't let Devin leave.

"Go ahead, Son," Santana said, overruling me. He held the bike steady while Devin climbed on, his face transitioning easily from anger when he looked at me to admiration when he gazed at our son.

No! I screamed on the inside. Having Devin home was the only way to delay what I knew was coming next, behind the closed doors of 1147 Pine Lane. Devin's long legs pumped the bike pedals like he was running for his life. I wanted to chase after him, but instead I let my mind and my body go numb.

"Get in the house. We need to talk," Santana said.

That was the first time the mark of shame had appeared on my face.

It was another year before I was pregnant, and of course, Santana blamed me for the fact that it took *that* long. Nevertheless, eight weeks into the pregnancy, I miscarried. My emotions collided with one another. I grieved my loss, but I was also relieved that I wouldn't bring a child into our world, especially a daughter. Every little girl deserved to be a Daddy's girl. But how could I teach her to love and respect a man I'd grown to hate?

The thought made me run my hand over my stomach.

"...That saved a wretch like me...."

"Are you almost ready, Mom?" Devin peeked into my bathroom.

"Almost, baby. Are you ready to eat breakfast?" I dropped my brushes into my makeup case and folded the towel I used to protect the wood finish of my vanity.

"Just about. I was trying to get my tie knotted right."

Devin walked over, and I slid the knot down so I could pull the tie over his head. Then I tied it around my own neck before giving it back to him. The Windsor, half-Windsor, the four-in-hand knot. I'd learned them because Santana had insisted I know how to knot his ties to perfection so they'd be ready on Sunday mornings or whenever he had to accompany our pastor to various events.

"There," I said. I adjusted Devin's lapel to cover the tie.

Devin admired himself in my mirror. "Casket sharp," he said with a gleaming smile.

"Don't say that," I gently scolded him. "You know I don't like that phrase. Say something like 'sharp as a tack.'"

Devin shrugged. "Ummm...okay," he conceded. "Whatever you want, Ma."

Almost ten, Devin was handsome, and I'm not just saying that. He'd started his birthday countdown on a small dry-erase board attached to the refrigerator where I jotted reminders. He would turn ten in fifteen days, and he was ecstatic about entering into the double digits. His face had already matured from the photo he'd had taken at the beginning of the school year. It was less pudgy now, so my fingers couldn't get a good grip to squeeze his cheeks like they used to. A light dusting of dark hairs covered his upper lip, and I was certain his voice had started to change. How had the time passed so quickly? It seemed like just yesterday that I'd signed him up for his first T-ball team and watched him run the bases in the wrong direction during his first game.

Devin was looking through his dad's cologne collection. As far as I was concerned, the only thing a boy his age needed was an antibacterial soap, some baby powder in the sweaty places, and a good, strong deodorant. It was Santana who'd suggested he wear cologne on Sunday mornings. "The ladies like a man who smells good," was the advice his father had given him.

Devin wasn't a man, and he certainly didn't need to be concerned about ladies or even girls.

"You go ahead down. I'll be out in a few minutes," I said. "We don't want to be late."

"Please don't be late," he said, his cheery disposition suddenly fading. "It puts Dad in a bad mood."

"I'm coming, sweetheart," I assured him as I shooed him out of the bedroom, but not before he sprayed cologne on the front and back of his neck.

"I once was lost but now am found, was blind, but now I see."

Children always know when something isn't right. Devin was one of the reasons I had yet to make my escape. I needed to be in a position where my son could come with me. How could I leave when I didn't have the finances or a plan to make it work? I'd watched countless talk shows about women in abusive relationships. They, too, had been isolated from their family and friends. The women looked just like me. They looked like the women I saw in line at the grocery store, in the pews at church, or in the bleachers at their kids' baseball games.

I put on a pair of small pearl earrings, clamped on a pearl necklace, then collected Santana's monogrammed garment bag of his suit jacket, tie, and an extra dry-cleaned shirt. I slipped my feet into my fluffy new bedroom slippers. My other ones were worn out, and high heels weren't allowed on the hardwood floors in the kitchen.

"You look gorgeous," Santana said when I walked into the room. He pulled me into an embrace and nuzzled his beard against my cheek. It was scratchy, but it wasn't the only reason I flinched. I pulled away slightly.

"You're a little prickly," I said. He'd decided to grow out his beard, and the five o'clock shadow had taken over his face. "Thanks for breakfast."

"You're welcome, baby." Santana unplugged the griddle and used the spatula to scoop the turkey sausages onto the sunshine-yellow oval serving platter he always used for breakfast.

Santana lowered his voice to add, "Devin doesn't know this yet, but he's going to a baseball game after church with the Knight family. It'll just be me and you for a few hours. You know what that means."

Yes, I knew exactly what was on his mind. I shuddered at the thought of having sex with Santana. A husband and wife were supposed to make love. Yet it has been years since I'd been able to call it that.

"I hope I'm feeling better by then," I said. "I still have a headache. It feels like the makings of a migraine."

Santana set the breakfast platter in the middle of the table, then lifted his hands to the sides of my head. He used his middle fingers to exert pressure at my temples. I closed my eyes and pretended that he was the same man I'd married—soft, gentle, caring—instead of the monster that had emerged.

Santana was whispering, and it took me a moment to realize he was actually saying a prayer for my chronic migraines. He actually asked that God would reveal the root cause. How about the fact that he'd pushed my head into the wall? God didn't have to tell him that. I was a firsthand witness.

"Amen," he said before kissing my temples.

"Ewww," Devin said, his usual response to Santana's displays of affection.

"I can do that," Santana told him. "She's my wife."

Devin had already stacked three pieces of French toast on his plate. He overturned the syrup bottle, and the gooey maple liquid ran over his plate until it was a pool of brown.

"That's enough, Devin," I said, taking the bottle from him. "Isn't this the same boy who carried on at the dentist's last week when you had to get that cavity filled? Do you want to go through that again?"

"Hell, no," he said.

I whipped my head in his direction, and the headache pain pulsated. "What did you just say?"

"I'm sorry," he said, his expression already apologetic. He slumped down in his chair. "It just slipped. I didn't mean to say that."

"Well, if it 'just slipped,' it means you've been cursing on a regular basis somewhere else. That's not acceptable, Devin. Not at all." I looked to Santana to back me up. I'd never heard Devin say a curse word, and I wasn't about to excuse it.

"Don't say it again," Santana said, slurping down some orange juice.

"Yes, sir," Devin answered, then busied himself with his breakfast. Between his smacking and Santana's slurping, I was already irritated.

"Is that how we're going to handle it?" I asked Santana softly.

He shrugged. "Every child tests the water every now and then. The boy can't live in a bubble. He's in public school, and not everybody there or on his team is saved and sanctified. He hears worse than that when we go to the barbershop."

I put my fork down. "Just because he hears it doesn't mean he has to say it." I held up my hand when Santana tried to spoon some eggs onto my plate. I could tell by looking at them that there was too much pepper. I hated pepper in my eggs.

"No dairy this week for me," I said. "I want to see if cutting it out will help with my headaches."

Santana furrowed his brow, then pushed away from the table. "I'll fix you some hot green tea." He opened the top cabinet, where he kept a bottle of acetaminophen. He popped open the bottle and shook two pills into my palm. "I've got to get you feeling better."

"I'd feel better if I knew my son wasn't cursing," I said.

"It was one word. Let it go," Santana said sternly, like he was talking to his son and not his wife. "Your son's got to live in the real world. The only thing you're concerned about is correct grammar and good manners. Devin needs book smarts, but he needs street smarts, too. He can't be a real man without them. Trust me—I know."

Of course you know, I thought. *You know everything.*

I ate breakfast in silence while Santana and Devin talked about the upcoming car show. The ride from our home to church was more of the same, but I pasted on my smile when we stepped out of the car and entered through the side entrance of the church. Devin disappeared into the room where the youth ministry met, Santana went into Pastor Lloyd's office, and I went immediately to my seat at the right of the pulpit.

My reserved seating area faced the congregation. I could see everyone, from Carol Pearson, the local late-night news anchor and faithful church member, to Sister Whitman, who had been the adult Sunday-school teacher for the last twenty years. Every Sunday, Deacon Cooper nodded off during the sermon. And my eyes always seemed to find Janae Brown, my husband's every-now-and-then mistress.

2

I saw the way Janae eyed Santana when she thought I wasn't looking. In her dreams, she probably thought she could take him away. In my dreams, I wished she would. But Santana had an image to uphold, so he couldn't afford to destroy the picture he'd worked hard to paint. Ours was a classic redemption story. A hustling drug dealer finds God, repents, and is forgiven, then goes on to build a reputable life with a lovely family. The only thing we didn't have was a picket fence. And instead of a dog, we had a goldfish.

I'd conditioned myself to ignore Janae, but there was no way I could ignore the pounding in my head. Sitting near the musicians, especially the drums, only exacerbated things as the service began. To cope, I mentally tuned out. I registered Pastor Lloyd approaching the podium and opening his Bible, so I robotically opened mine, flipped to the Scripture he'd referenced, and followed the lead of the congregation whenever they laughed, shouted "Amen," or raised their hands in praise.

After the benediction, I waited in the last pew while Pastor Lloyd greeted the congregants. Santana stood proudly at his side, assisting his beloved mentor as needed.

"Quinn, you look lovely as always," Pastor Lloyd said to me once he'd prayed for the last waiting member. "This man must be treating you like a queen." He pounded Santana on the back. "A sure sign of a good man is a great-looking wife."

I wondered what he'd say if I washed off this department-store cocoa-brown foundation.

I smiled. "Thank you, Pastor." In my peripheral vision, I could see Devin talking to Cheyenne. I'd heard through the grapevine that they had a crush on each other, hence the reason for him trying to bathe in cologne.

"So, how did you enjoy the sermon?" Pastor Lloyd asked.

"It was powerful as usual," I said.

"Amen. God was still speaking to me early this morning and even up to the time I stood up to minister," Pastor Lloyd said, unclipping his cuff links. "The amazing thing about God is that a hundred people can all hear the same words coming out of my mouth, but God speaks to their hearts in different ways."

"He's that kind of amazing God," I said, trying to force my heels back on. It seemed like my feet had swollen in the short twenty minutes that I'd had them off. I couldn't wait until July, when Pastor Lloyd would declare his annual "casual Sundays" for the entire month.

"What did God speak to you today?" Pastor Lloyd pushed. "I'm interested in knowing, since I've heard quite a few different testimonies."

I froze, unsure of what to say. I couldn't say that I remembered a single Scripture, a single moment of inspiration, or a single reason why I'd waved my hand in praise in the first place. I tried to pretend that I was deep in thought for the perfect answer, when in fact I had no answer at all. Thank God, Devin ran up, lifted Pastor Lloyd's arm, and draped it across his shoulder. "Guess what I just found out?"

"What's that?"

"I'm going to the baseball game this afternoon," he said. "Right, Dad?"

"So much for the surprise," Santana said, sending his son a half smile. He was more focused on me as he dropped Pastor Lloyd's cuff links into the inside pocket of his suit jacket. His eyes pierced the distance between us. Being married to Santana was like sleeping with a ticking time bomb. It was only a matter of time before he exploded. I could tell I'd lit his fuse.

"Dad, did you pack a change of clothes for me?" Devin asked, unaware of the unspoken accusations between his father and me.

"You know I did. Your bag's in the trunk," Santana said. "There's a new glove in there, too, in case you get lucky enough to catch a fly ball."

"I'll be that close?" Devin asked. "I can't believe it. Thank you."

"Don't thank me. Thank Mr. Knight." Santana reached into his pant pocket, pulled out his car keys, and tossed them to Devin. "I don't have to tell you to be on your best behavior."

"Yes, sir," Devin said.

I squeezed Devin's shoulder. I never had to worry about his behavior. He was the son every mother dreamed of, and he'd been a huge source of my joy since the day he was born. Devin was, without a doubt, the best thing that had happened from my union with Santana. Now, my stomach turned at the thought of what might happen to me at home while he was overstuffing himself with chili dogs, nachos, and a 64-ounce Sprite.

If I could find a way to distract Santana, maybe he would forget about how I'd supposedly embarrassed him.

When I looked back at Pastor Lloyd, he was holding a money clip. He slid a twenty-dollar bill from the wad and pressed it into Devin's hand.

"You don't have to do that," I told him.

"Of course I don't. But I want to. Every boy needs some spending change in his pocket when he goes out. It's a man law."

I smiled. "I definitely don't want to break the man law."

"Thank you, Pastor Lloyd," Devin said. "Don't worry, I'll spend every dime of it."

"I know you will," Pastor Lloyd said with a grin.

Santana helped the pastor out of the coat of his three-piece suit. He folded it over his arm, then offered Pastor one of his favorite candies— the peppermints that melted in your mouth. Pastor Lloyd's breath always smelled minty fresh. Unfortunately, he'd also recently required a ton of dental work because he always was always chewing gum or sucking on hard candy. Evidently he—like Devin—hadn't learned his lesson.

"Do you mind if I steal your husband for about ten minutes?" Pastor Lloyd asked me.

"Not at all. Take your time," I answered quickly. I was relieved that Pastor Lloyd had forgotten about the sermon review he'd requested. I picked up Santana's Bible from the back pew. "I'll meet you at the car."

I walked hand in hand with Devin to the parking spot designated for Pastor Lloyd's staff. Church was the only place Devin still abided public displays of affection. When he'd turned eight years old, I'd been banned from kissing him on the cheek when I dropped him off at school. I wasn't even allowed to show too much giddiness at his baseball games.

"What are you and Dad going to do while I'm gone?" he asked.

"Oh, I don't know. We'll think of something. Maybe we'll go to the movies. We'll definitely grab something eat."

"Can we have lasagna tomorrow for dinner?"

"How did this conversation jump from our plans to what you want to eat for dinner tomorrow?"

"Because you said the word 'eat,' and that's the first thing that popped into my mind."

"I think it's because you're greedy," I said.

"And a growing boy," Devin reminded me. "Actually," he amended, "Dad says I'm a young man."

"Well, does this young man have a young lady he likes?" I asked when I noticed Cheyenne across the parking lot.

"What do you mean by that?"

"You're a straight-A student headed to being an all-star baseball player and a chess-playing whiz. You know exactly what I mean by that."

"Cheyenne?"

"Now you're coming to your senses. Yes, Cheyenne."

"She's nice. And pretty."

I tried not to react. I'd have to get used to my son talking to me about girls now and in the future if I wanted him to remain open and honest with me. As I said, he was a nice-looking young man, and he had the brains and personality to match. There were bound to be little girls—some sweet, others not-so-innocent—vying for his attention.

"She definitely is," I said. "I just want you to focus on books and baseball for now."

"We're just friends," Devin assured me.

"Oh, okay," I said, not wanting to press the issue. I'd give him the third degree another time. If I taught Devin nothing else, I planned on teaching him how to respect and honor the females in his life.

Devin opened the front passenger door for me, then went around to the driver's side. He slid into the front seat and started the car so the AC could begin to cool it off. It was one of the duties his father had given him—cool it off when it's hot outside, warm it up when it's cold. Devin popped the trunk to get his duffel bag, waved good-bye to me, and then hurried inside just as his father emerged through the side door. His father—*and* Janae.

Janae's tight skirt left nothing to the imagination. Even though Santana was wearing a dark pair of shades, I didn't have to wonder what his eyes were watching. Another one of the pastor's aides, Marvin, was two steps behind them. His eyes were focused straight ahead, probably from fear that his wife was watching him. Elyse was as sweet as strawberry pie, but I'd heard stories about her. I'd never witnessed anything myself, but it had gotten around that she didn't play games when her husband was involved. She was the cut-your-tires, smother-you-with-a-pillow kind of crazy when it came to Marvin.

Santana didn't even bother to acknowledge me as the three of them headed toward Janae's car. I lowered my window slightly so I could try to pick up the conversation, but the only thing I heard was talk about her car not being able to start. Marvin popped the latch from inside the car, and Santana lifted the hood. He did his assessment as Marvin turned the ignition.

"Dead battery," Santana said.

Janae acted like Santana had saved the world. I could've told her it was the battery.

"I'll get my truck and my jumper cables," Marvin said, then jogged off to the monster truck all the boys at church admired. At every outdoor function, Marvin parked his truck in the middle of the parking lot, where it became the official hangout spot for the boys who were strong enough to lift themselves onto the back of the bed, which Marvin cushioned with stacks of quilts and pillows. He also kept his personal cooler of beverages stocked. At the end of the day, he'd make the boys clean his truck of crushed soda cans, empty potato-chip bags, and crumpled napkins; but when the next function came around, he'd do it all over again.

I figured Santana and Janae were pretending to study the horsepower under Janae's hood. Their voices had lowered, so I couldn't pick up their conversation anymore. The mystery car trouble had been solved, so I knew they weren't talking about an empty gas tank, spark plugs, or an alternator. Santana would never admit to having a relationship outside our marriage, but I didn't need him to confess to what I already knew.

Janae threw her head back and laughed. Nothing Santana said was ever *that* funny. Yet Janae hung on his every word. I could tell by the way she seemed to lose herself in him. Maybe it was my thoughts about Janae that caused her to look my way. She didn't try to hide her flirtatious behavior. I hoped one day she got what she deserved. That woman had *no* idea. I lost sight of both of them when Marvin pulled up in his truck, blocking my view. It was probably for the best.

It only took a couple of minutes for them to get Janae's car up and running. Pastor Lloyd appeared at the side door of the church. He'd changed into a pair of slacks and a blue and white striped button-down shirt. He disappeared behind Marvin's truck, too. Now I was trying to spy on four pair of legs.

I opened the church bulletin to see what was going on in the coming days and whether Pastor Lloyd had any speaking engagements. The happiness of my week was usually based on how many evenings Santana spent assisting Pastor Lloyd. The more he was out of the house, the better. As long as I had his dinner plate fixed and waiting in the microwave before I went to bed, it was usually a silent night. Unless homework had kept Devin up past his bedtime, he was typically in his room and knocked out no later than nine o'clock.

I flipped to the calendar on the back of the bulletin. There was a men's meeting on Tuesday, a church administration meeting on Thursday, and on Friday night, Pastor Lloyd was the guest speaker for a church holding a revival. From the looks of things, this was going to be a relaxing week. I might even get to dabble with my painting.

Tap. Tap.

Pastor Lloyd rapped on my closed window. I think this man's smile was permanently etched on his face, or at least it had been over the last ten years that I'd known him.

"Me and my better half want to have you and Santana over for dinner soon. She wasn't feeling her best this morning, so I confined her to her bed with some vitamins and some good old-fashioned orange juice. It's probably just a cold, but sometimes rest can be the best medicine."

"Give her my regards and tell her I asked about her," I said, making a mental note to call and check on Sister Lloyd later in the week.

"I will. Take care of yourself. We'll see you next Sunday."

"And we'll discuss a date to have dinner."

"Good. I'll let the wives handle everything. My wife is excellent at those kinds of things." Pastor Lloyd beamed. "In fact, my wife is excellent at most things."

"She sure is," I agreed. Pastor Lloyd lifted his wife on a pedestal, whether she was around or not.

Sister Lloyd was definitely hospitable and thoughtful. She took great care to make sure that the women at Light of the World Ministries had auxiliaries and programs that catered to their needs. I'd had the privilege of helping her plan the annual women's tea. Santana had volunteered me, of course, but once I'd gotten involved, I'd found it to be fulfilling. An outlet.

This year, in particular, Sister Lloyd and I had worked more closely together during the three months leading up to the event than we ever had before. So close, in fact, that I'd felt a pull to confide in her. Santana never laid a finger on me while we were in the planning phases of the tea. For those three months, he was the perfect husband. For those three months, he was the sweet, spontaneous man who'd taken me to the courthouse one afternoon when we were supposed to be only meeting for lunch, and I'd been so crazy in love that I'd said yes without a second thought.

But I knew his façade wouldn't last forever. Some evenings, he returned home with a different look in his eyes. They'd be glazed over. He'd sniff a lot. He was fidgety, but he'd disappear into the guest room and lock himself inside. I was growing more suspicious that the demon of drugs had emerged from hell to snatch him back under.

One night, while riding along with Sister Lloyd to the office supplies store to pick up the printed programs for the tea, I had nearly disclosed the abuse to her. Then I'd gotten choked up. Literally. I'd coughed uncontrollably. It had felt like a hand was gripping my throat. And then the visions had started. I'd seen what would happen if I told. It might get better—maybe even stop for a short time—after Santana and I started counseling, because that was undoubtedly what the Lloyds would suggest. I doubted Sister Lloyd would hold my confession in confidence. She'd tell her husband, because she'd feel it was the best measure to take. The more I thought about it, the more it seemed like a bad idea. Sister Lloyd was gentle, kind, and soft-spoken; there was nothing wrong with that, but I needed a woman who could help me take a stand. I needed someone who was stronger than me.

Santana slid into the front seat and tossed his jacket in the back. He unknotted his tie, pulled it over his head, and dropped it on my lap. "Have you thought about the sermon yet?"

He still hadn't let it go. The tie taunted me like a noose. He could choke me. *One day, he's going to kill me*, I thought. I closed my eyes but saw a light piercing through the darkness of my closed lids. "*The* LORD *is my light and my salvation; whom shall I fear? The* LORD *is the strength of my life; of whom shall I be afraid?*"

I didn't know how. I didn't know when. But I knew my time was coming.

3

"My head was pounding all through the service," I said. "I couldn't think of much else. Even the bright lights were too much for me."

Other wives would receive compassion, but it was only in Santana to critique me.

"Maybe you should be in children's church next time. I guess you have to be entertained with skits and coloring pages if you want to remember anything. And what about apple juice and graham crackers instead of the Communion elements?"

I blew out a long breath.

"Excuse me. Did you say something?" Santana seethed. He yanked the car in reverse at the same time that he sent Marvin a peace sign.

"I apologize," I said, turning to look out of the window. "I can't control these migraines. The medicine I took this morning didn't work."

"It's probably those birth-control pills you were taking. I bet you didn't think about how much they threw your body out of whack. A woman's body isn't meant to take in a drug like that for God knows how long, and it probably made a lasting effect on your body."

What a hypocrite. An ex-drug dealer lecturing me about the effects of drugs on my body.

"The pain is excruciating, but I pushed through the service today anyway," I said, hoping to garner some kind of sympathy. "Even Sister Lloyd missed church for a cold. Don't I get any credit?"

"No, you don't. And if you want to compare yourself to Sister Lloyd, then maybe you should learn to keep your mouth shut. You don't see her mouthing off to her husband."

"Few people know what really goes on behind closed doors." My words had come out before I'd had a chance to censor them. I couldn't believe they were my own.

Santana's grip tightened on the steering wheel. "You might want to shut your mouth while you're ahead," he warned me.

I sunk back into myself. The bravado seeped out of me. I was going back home, where there would be no one to defend me. We pulled into the driveway of our immaculate brick home that we'd had built from the ground up. Before the builders had laid the foundation, we'd written our dreams on a piece of paper and buried them there. That's where my dreams and prayers were—still buried in the dirt.

Santana shifted the gear into park but didn't activate the garage-door opener.

"I have some business to take care of," he said.

I didn't bother to ask any questions, since I knew I wouldn't get any answers. Besides, Santana needed a chance to cool off, and I would relish the opportunity for some time alone. My watercolors were calling my name. For over a week, I'd dreamt of a place that looked like paradise, and I knew the vision wouldn't leave my mind until it had found its way onto canvas.

I waited, expecting Santana to come around and open my car door. When I realized he had no intentions of getting up from behind the wheel, I pushed the door open and headed inside. Santana was at the end of our street before I'd found the house key in my purse.

I kicked my shoes off in the foyer and put on a pair of fresh socks taken from the basket we kept by the front door. The house still smelled of breakfast. I set my Bible and purse on the front demilune table and went into the kitchen for my stash of takeout menus. Who eats Chinese takeout on a Sunday afternoon? A wife who's been abandoned at home. I didn't even bother to change out of my Sunday best before I shot around the corner to a nearby shopping center, where my favorite Chinese restaurant was located. I walked out minutes later with one carton of vegetable lo mein, two spring rolls, and two fortune cookies. Once home again, I changed into a pair of my comfortable jeans and an old Richard Petty racing T-shirt that a former bank colleague had given me as a birthday gag gift, and happily enjoyed my lunch with no one else to cater to.

It amazed me how Santana's presence in the house could totally change the atmosphere. Being home alone was so peaceful.

After dropping the chopsticks in the empty carton, I picked up my set of paintbrushes and rolled them back and forth between my palms, slowly and then faster, like I was trying to ignite a fire. When the heat from the friction warmed my skin, I dropped the bristled ends into a cup of water to soften them. Then I pushed back the drapes framing the guest-room window so that I could take advantage of the natural light. I had a perfect view of the freestanding hammock that I'd positioned under our towering oak tree in the backyard. Near it lay Devin's red dirt bike. He'd had it out back to test the makeshift wooden jumping ramp that he and his buddy from down the street had built.

I blocked out Charlotte, North Carolina; I blocked out my house and the horrible things that Santana had said to me; and I noticed for the first time that my migraine had subsided. The only thing left in my vacated mind was my vision of paradise. I mixed blues, a soft green, and two different shades of white until I had the perfect tint for the water. Like always, I started with the ripples of the current. With every brushstroke, I could feel the water moving between my toes. The mist blew into my face as the wind lifted my hair. I brushed the horizon in shades of pinks, purples, and oranges until, an hour later, my blank canvas had been transformed. If only I could step inside the canvas and escape. But I couldn't.

Sleep called. I answered. I cleaned the paintbrush bristles but left the paint on my palette to harden, then stretched out across the full-sized bed that we'd bought especially for guests. Except that we never had any. Nothing compared to a nap on a Sunday afternoon. I didn't wake until Devin tapped lightly on my door. I hesitated before I forced my eyes open, wondering if it were the pesky woodpecker that returned every spring to attack the fascia board near the roof.

"I'm home, Ma," Devin said softly.

I squinted. "Hey, baby. What happened? Why are you home so early?"

"It's almost eight o'clock," he said, looking puzzled. "After the game, we went out to eat, and then we went to the batting cage." He held up a gloved hand with a baseball cradled inside. "I caught a fly ball at the game. Can you believe it?"

"What are the chances of that?" I mused, pushing myself up to get a better look.

Devin beat the inside of his glove with the ball. "It's like it came right to me. Everybody around me was cheering and jumping all over me. I know I'm going to the Major Leagues one day. I just know it."

"I know it, too. And don't forget about your Mama."

"I'd never do that. Never." Devin turned the brim of his baseball cap to the back. "Do you need anything?" he asked.

"Some more sleep," I yawned.

"Where's Dad?"

"He had to run out," I said, not wanting to think about his father and what he might be doing. "He'll be back." *Unfortunately.*

"Can I go down to Aaron's house? I'll call first."

"It's too late," I told him. "You should probably jump in the shower. You've been baking in the sun. Go look at yourself. It looks like Daddy's been flipping you over with a spatula on the grill."

"It was burning up out there. I drank, like, three sodas."

No wonder he was so hyper. "How are you going to sleep if you're pumped with sugar and caffeine?"

He frowned. "Spring break starts tomorrow. I don't have to worry about sleeping. I don't really have to go to bed now, do I?"

"I completely forgot about spring break," I said. "You don't have to go to bed right now, but you still need to take a shower. Then maybe you can settle down with a good book. Didn't you check out the last book in that series you like when we went to the library?"

"Yes, but I don't want to read. Can I play my video game?"

I hesitated, but I was too exhausted to object. "An hour," I stressed. "And if I'm still asleep, you're on your honor to turn it off without my having to ask."

"Yes, ma'am." He tossed the baseball up in the air so that it spun.

I closed my eyes as Devin padded back down the hall. Even from the guest room, I could follow his moves—to the kitchen and into the pantry. *Click.* He'd probably pushed the door closed with his foot. Then I heard the whir of the ice dispenser, followed by the clank of ice cubes as they spilled into a glass. The refrigerator door opened and closed. There were a few more clanks and then a moment of silence before I heard the television. Before I could belt out a warning, the volume fell to a soft murmur, and I fell into my second round of sweet sleep.

⌒

The harsh glare of the bedroom lights permeated my dreams. Santana rushed into the room like he was a thief ransacking the house of a family away on vacation. He yanked open and slammed shut every drawer of the bureau in the guest room. The only things we kept in there were our off-season clothes. He bent down and peered under the bed.

I bolted upright. "What's wrong?" I asked.

He knew that all our important documents and everything else of value were under lock and key in our fireproof safe in his office. He was acting wild and belligerent. He turned, and for the first time, I noticed the redness of his eyes. They had that glazed-over look. The devil had returned.

"Shut up, Quinn," Santana bellowed. "Just shut up."

"Maybe I can help you," I said.

"You know what I'm looking for?" he screamed. He yanked the comforter off me and tried to lift the mattress from the box spring. I jumped off, tripping on the goose-feather pillow that had tumbled onto the floor. It broke my fall. My protective instincts kicked in. I picked up the pillow to shield my body, then scrambled back against the wall.

"I—" Santana's chest heaved as he stared at me with fiery eyes.

I was more confused than anything.

"I am looking for my respect. I'm looking for my appreciation. Can you help me find that, too?"

I was at a loss for words, and that wasn't necessarily a good thing. Not answering could cause him to further erupt. Giving the wrong answer could still cause Santana to explode.

I looked at the clock. 10:42. How had I slept that long?

"Where's Devin?" I asked. I needed to defuse Santana's anger.

"Asleep. And don't worry about Devin. Worry about yourself. What was Pastor Lloyd's sermon about today?"

No words. My breathing was short.

Santana caught sight of my new painting. "Oh, so you were working on a little paint-by-number instead of getting God in you?"

Santana yanked my canvas off the easel and punched a hole in it.

Tears fell from my eyes. My hands begin to shake uncontrollably, until my entire body trembled like an earthquake.

"Whom shall I fear?"

Santana mistook the tears for fear. He had no idea. I'd known my day was coming, but this morning when I'd awakened, I hadn't thought today would be the day.

A roar escaped my throat as I pounced on Santana like a lion. I couldn't stop my arms from flailing, my legs from kicking, or my teeth from sinking into any part of his body that I could reach. I clawed at his eyes. I wanted to rip them out so he could never look at me with disgust again.

"You dumb b----!" he yelled. "What's wrong with you?"

I'd caught him off guard, but it gave me the upper hand for only a few moments. Santana gripped the hair at the nape of my neck and slung me against the wall. The pain spiked from my hip through my spine and up my backbone. It was enough to slow me down but not to take me out.

I pushed myself up, grabbed the leg of the easel, and swung it toward his head. *God, give me strength. I need help.* It seemed wrong for me to pray for help in a violent situation, but God was the only One I knew to call on. I never meant for him to send Devin.

"Dad! Mom!" Terror was etched into his young face. He looked like a toddler again.

"Get out, Devin," Santana yelled. "Now, Son."

Santana wiped a hand across his face. I'd broken the skin, and there was blood pushing through the claw marks I'd left behind. His body heaved as he stared at me, as if wondering which way I'd come at him next.

"Get out, Devin," I panted. My mouth was dry. I looked at him only briefly; I had to keep my eyes on Santana. But one second was all it took for my eyes to speak to my son. I turned back to Santana and sneered, "I will not let my son grow up like this."

"Grow up like what? With anything he wants? And you live better than anybody you know."

"It isn't about stuff. I couldn't care less about any of it when I'm living with the devil. You, Santana Montgomery, are the devil."

"If you want to see the devil, I'll show you the devil. You should be grateful for a man like me. You haven't had to pick up a pinkie finger since you married me. You've been living on my dime for ten years, Quinn."

"No, I've been living under your foot for ten years," I screamed. Saliva flew from my mouth with every word. "And today is the last day."

Santana inhaled a deep breath that filled his chest and made him tower over me. "That must mean this is your day to die."

4

Santana and I shifted back and forth like we were doing a choreographed dance. My movements dared him to make the first lunge. His small step in my direction challenged me to initiate the attack.

"I'm already dead," I nearly whispered. "You've taken my life and my happiness. You've stripped me of my dreams. No more."

"I didn't do anything to you," Santana scoffed, all cockiness. "You did all that to yourself."

He was delusional. And now I realized what else. He was high.

Slowly, Santana unbuckled his belt. He slid the black leather out of each loop, then took a solid grip of one end and snapped it in the air like a whip meant for the slave that I was. No, the slave that I *used* to be. Sooner or later, some slaves find the courage to fight back. And although the courage was in me, the speed wasn't. When Santana dove toward me, I was no match for his muscle and strength, and though I fought with everything that I had left, he managed to loop the belt around my neck. The breath was leaving my body.

"What do you have to say now?" he screamed. "You can't get the words out, can you, Quinn?"

He was right. My words were choked into my throat. But prayers don't have to be uttered aloud. I unleashed a silent plea to heaven: *I will not die. I'll live. God, send an angel. Send someone to protect me. Rescue me, Lord Jesus.*

My vision blurred. It became gray, then faded to black. Shadows raced around me. I couldn't follow them because I didn't know if I would return. Leaving this earth would mean leaving Devin behind. I would not leave my son with the devil.

I could feel my lips moving, but I didn't hear any speech. "*The* Lord *is my light and my salvation; whom shall I fear? The* Lord *is the strength of my life; of whom shall I be afraid?*"

I could smell Santana's cologne and a hint of perfume that wasn't mine. The heat of his breath blew onto my face.

"What do you have to say now, Quinn?" he whispered in my ear. He purposefully scrubbed his rough beard against my cheek. It scratched like sandpaper.

"*Yea, though I walk through the valley of the shadow of death, I will fear no evil; for You are with me....*"

The more I quoted Scripture to myself, the more my spirit strengthened. The light returned. At first, it was the size of a pinhole, but it gradually opened until there was an angelic glow. Even so, my breaths grew shallower. I counted the breaths leaving my body and prayed that help would come before I took my last one. *Eight...breathe...seven...breathe...six...breathe....*

I struggled to open my eyes so that I could look Santana in the face. I wanted him to know that, despite what it looked like, he wouldn't win. If God chose to bring me home, I'd still get the victory. My eyelids fluttered, and the tension of the belt around my neck loosened slightly. Then it slackened more. It dropped completely.

"No, Son," I heard Santana say, calmly.

I weakly raised a hand and shoved two fingertips between my neck and the leather belt. I felt the burning welts. They were wet with blood. The color slowly returned to my vision. When my eyes were focused enough for me to see the room, I realized that Santana was backed up to the wall beside me. And he was staring down the barrel of a gun.

5

Two years later

Do you mind if I ask you a question?"

"Not at all," I told the lady who was examining her figure in the three-panel mirror. "I'm not exactly a fashionista, but I'll give it a shot."

We were the only two women in the dressing room. I would've rather slipped back behind the curtain to finish trying on my array of skirts. I'd brought in every cut, print, and length imaginable. Sometimes the very one that looked great on the hanger was the one that made me look like a fashion disaster. Too big, and I looked like my great-aunt Clara. Too tight, and I looked like I was trying to be a teenager again. I was "getting my girlie back," as I called it, and was making it a point to have something other than T-shirts and yoga pants in my wardrobe.

The woman faced me straight on, her feet together. "I know this is going to sound crazy to you, but does this dress make my knees look chubby?"

I must've frowned. I'd heard it all, from "chicken-wing arms" to "cottage-cheese thighs" to "turkey necks." But I'd never, absolutely never, heard of chubby knees.

"Actually, it doesn't," I answered truthfully. The hemline flirted about an inch above her kneecaps, and when she twisted at the waist, the fabric danced in soft, golden billows. "It looks really nice."

She took one last, lingering look. "I guess you have no reason to lie," she said. "You don't know me from Mary Jane."

"I'd want someone to tell me the truth," I said.

"Then, truthfully, you look great," she said. "I mean, Angela-Bassett-arms and Tina-Turner-legs great."

"Thank you," I said.

"Do you have any kids?"

"A son."

"See, there? You had a baby, and everything snapped back into place, didn't it?"

"Actually, my son's twelve, so it's been a while."

"And my son is eleven, and I'm still talking about my baby weight."

We shared a laugh. To me, she was an average-sized woman. She could use a little tightening here and there, but couldn't we all?

"So, how did you do it?" she asked me. "One of these days, I'm bound to come upon a formula that actually works for me."

It crossed my mind to invite her to one of the classes I taught at the gym, but I didn't know how to bring it up without offending her. My step and tone classes were growing in popularity, and I'd soon have a sizable pool of clients who might want me as their personal trainer—if and when I ever decided to do that again. Still, sharing my passion for exercise and fitness with others was sometimes taken as criticism.

"I just make sure I burn off more calories than I consume," I said, wrapping it up as simply as I could. "And I work out—cardio, body sculpting, strength training. I actually teach classes at one of the local gyms."

"See? You lost me right there." She reached behind her dressing-room curtain, pulled out two skirts, and hung them on the rod of items shoppers didn't intend to buy. Then she slapped her backside and pointed at me. "If I could get this to look like that, it would be a miracle."

I laughed. "It doesn't take a miracle, just hard work." I knew, because I'd put in two years of relentless work. If a man ever decided he wanted to lift his hand against me, he'd regret even the thought of it for the rest of his life. Besides being able to defend myself, there were other benefits. I felt as healthy as I had in my twenties, had dusted off my tennis game, and was training for my first half-marathon.

"You should definitely get that skirt," she told me.

"I think I will," I said. "And if you ever change your mind about exercise, you can find me at Warehouse Fitness in downtown Greensboro. It looks like a warehouse from the outside, but inside it's set up like a fitness boot camp and obstacle course. Have you ever heard of it?"

She seemed to cringe at my words. "As a matter of fact, I have, and I won't be going back there."

"Bad experience?"

"You could say that," she answered.

I didn't press for details, since I didn't want to taint my view of my workplace. I hadn't had any problems there since being interviewed and hired by Lance, one of the owners, almost a year ago. He'd taken a chance on me, a newly trained and certified exercise instructor, because of the fact that I'd moved from Charlotte. He made the Queen City his home most of the month, but every other weekend, he took the short hour-and-a-half ride to Greensboro to meet with his partner and catch up on gym business.

Since my weekends were reserved for time with Devin—whether he wanted to laze around, go to the batting cages, or invite one of his new neighborhood friends over for a friendly video-game competition—I rarely crossed paths with Lance. In fact, I seldom dealt with anyone outside of the other instructors at the gym. My life revolved around my son, as it should. It was just the two of us. Devin was the reason we had this new life, because he'd saved me from my old one.

"I've signed up at several different gyms over the years, but I always end up doing the same thing I'm doing now," the woman explained.

"Which is?"

"Nothing. I start. I stop. I jump on the wagon. I fall off. One of these days, I'm going to stick to it. You and your legs have inspired me."

I laughed again. "And you've given me one more reason to help people who want to exercise but don't want to do it in the traditional gym setting." I'd been trained to keep a stack of business cards in my purse so that I could produce one at a moment's notice. "We should keep in touch," I said as I handed her one.

"Definitely." She glanced at my card. "Nice to meet you, Quinn. I love that name. I'm Zenja Maxwell. I don't have a card on me, but I'd love for you to take my number. Make sure you remember I'm the lady with the chubby knees."

I pulled out my phone so Zenja could give me her number. I'd never seen myself as the type to initiate leads for business, but a woman had to do what a woman had to do, especially if she hadn't had a paycheck directly deposited into her own account for nearly twelve years.

I'd considered going back into the banking industry, but I desired more flexibility for Devin's sake. When I did the math, I realized the positions I'd qualify for wouldn't provide the income I'd need to live past paycheck to paycheck. I knew I couldn't initially provide Devin with the luxuries he'd enjoyed before, but he had what he needed the most—a safe, healthy, happy mother. If I had to work my manicured fingers to the bone, I would. But fitness training was only part of it. I was also a consultant for a company that specialized in female-friendly self-defense products, such as stun guns shaped like lipstick tubes and Mace in pink leather cases.

"Multifaceted. How interesting," Zenja said when she flipped my card over to read about the other side of my business—self-defense classes and weapons for women. "Quinn, you're the woman I've been looking for. Would you be willing to teach or demonstrate some self-defense moves to a group of about thirty or forty women? And you'd be more than welcome to set up a table of your products. For free."

"Of course I'd be interested," I said. "If you get me the date, I'll check my schedule to see if I'm available."

"Actually, will this Friday work for you?"

I already knew that my schedule was clear. Devin might have had plans in mind, but we could postpone them for the opportunity to get some pocket change on the side.

The workshops and product sales were always the most lucrative part of my business. I found that out the first time I taught a workshop to a group of residents at a senior living facility. I'd expected men and women with canes and in wheelchairs, but most of them were active, energetic, and downright frisky—especially Mr. Al. With the proceeds from that venture alone, I'd been able to furnish my entire bedroom. When we'd first moved to our apartment, I'd slept on a mattress on the floor. I'd allowed Devin to bring his furniture, but only because I felt guilty for uprooting him from the only friends, church, and city he'd ever known.

"My girlfriend Caprice started a couples' ministry called Friday Night Love," Zenja went on to explain. "The husbands and wives typically do things together, but this week, we're changing it up a bit. The men are having a chef come to demonstrate quick, easy meals they can prepare for their families, and the women will see a presentation by a police officer about protecting ourselves—how we can be proactive instead of reactive when it comes to preventing robberies and other crimes. Things like that." Zenja flipped through some outfits hanging on the return rack. "I was thinking we could get you to show us how we can physically defend ourselves."

I nodded. "I'll give you a call in the morning to confirm," I said. "And if you get the chance, you can scan the code on the back of my business card—it'll take you to my promotional video on YouTube."

We both disappeared into our dressing rooms across from each other and pulled our curtains closed. "You've built an impressive business, from what I can tell," Zenja said.

"I'm trying," I said, wriggling out of the skirt. "I haven't been here that long. It takes time, but God has truly blessed us."

"Us? Meaning, you and your husband?"

"Me and my son," I quickly corrected.

I usually pretended that Santana had never existed. Someday, I would have to face him, but with a twelve-year sentence keeping him in jail, I wasn't worried about crossing that bridge anytime soon. Although he and Devin exchanged letters, my son wasn't ready to visit his incarcerated father, and I certainly wasn't going to force him to do so.

Devin had testified against Santana and his violent tendencies and explosions. My son knew more than I'd given him credit for. On the other hand, the defense had called him to be a witness for how Santana behaved as a father. Everyone knew Santana adored his son and wanted a Montgomery man to carry his legacy. *Some legacy.* There were women who prayed for their sons to grow up to be like their fathers. I prayed that Devin did *not*.

The sounds of our clinking hangers replaced our voices as we tried on one outfit after another.

"Is anything working for you ladies?" called a froggy voice that I knew belonged to the sales associate with the sunburned cheeks.

"Some, but not all," I said, emerging from the dressing room with the three skirts I'd decided to purchase.

"I can help you find some more suitable choices, if you'd like."

I looked at my watch. "Actually, I need to get going. I'll buy these now and come back later."

I followed her to the register, where she took a lifetime to meticulously fold my skirts and then wrap them in tissue paper. "Make sure you come back before our great sale is over."

Time was ticking away. Devin's football practice ended in thirty minutes, and it would take me that long to make it back across town. I couldn't leave without my skirts, though. I needed clothes that properly fit my ever-changing figure. I'd started rebuilding my wardrobe on the day Santana had begun serving his sentence. I'd happily donated a closetful of his Sunday suits to a nonprofit organization geared toward helping impoverished men find a job and feel better about themselves. I didn't want to own anything that personally coordinated with Santana's designer suits, and I didn't care how much of his money he'd spent on our high-priced wardrobes. I was finally getting to a happy place. There were some things that just couldn't be bought.

"We're your number one place in town for seasonal makeovers," the sales associate was saying. "I know the temperatures are still soaring, but the fall collections coming in are some of the best I've seen in a while, and I've been in retail for almost fifteen years."

"Don't worry, I'll be back," I assured her.

I had to check my phone to remember the name of the lady in the dressing room. "Don't forget to phone me tomorrow, Zenja," I called in her direction.

"Definitely," her voice floated over the door. "Nice meeting you, Quinn. I hope we can work it out for Friday. Do you think you can be ready for us in three days?"

"I'm always ready," I said, then speed-walked to the car.

Rush-hour traffic was already starting to build, but fortunately, it was nowhere near as bad as Charlotte. After sitting through two rotations of a traffic signal in an attempt to make a left turn, I realized that the only way

I'd make it to pick up Devin in time was if the green lights were on my side the rest of the way.

They weren't.

Not only did I get caught at traffic lights on the surface streets, but there was a backup on the highway. I'd rarely met with traffic snags since moving to a smaller city. It was a nice reprieve to live at slower pace. Greensboro was large enough to keep you busy but small enough for that hometown feel.

After some time—too long—I was able to inch past two vehicles parked along the shoulder; from the looks of it, they'd been involved in a fender bender. The highway finally cleared, and I floored the gas pedal. I was so focused on getting to Devin's school that I didn't notice the police officer waiting at the speed trap until it was too late. I lifted my foot off the gas instead of tapping the break as flashing blue lights trailed me.

"Great," I said, slapping the steering wheel. The last thing I needed was a ticket.

I slowed down, pulled onto the shoulder, and braked to a stop. The evening sunshine beaming through my back window blocked my vision. I reached into the glove compartment for my registration, then pulled my license and insurance card from my purse. The officer was taking forever to get out of his patrol car. I guess he was running my license plate to make sure I wasn't a criminal at large, or someone with outstanding warrants. No worries for me. The biggest crime I'd ever committed was realizing I had a bottle of nail polish at the bottom of my shopping cart at Target when I was loading my bags into the car but then being too lazy to take it inside to pay for it.

Five minutes passed before the officer approached my window. I let it down slowly and tried not to show my agitation. While some women use their bosoms to distract officers as they tried to talk their way out of tickets, I didn't have that option. The only thing I had to offer was shapely legs and an attractive smile—or so I'd been told. I smiled and hoped that the officer would show me some mercy.

6

The officer was wearing sunglasses that looked like a flashback to a cops television show from the seventies. I hated it when I couldn't see a person's eyes.

"Ma'am, may I see your driver's license and registration?"

I handed them over without saying a word.

"Did you realize you were speeding?"

"I'm late picking up my son from practice," I explained, not confessing to my violation. I knew I'd been going at least fifteen miles per hour over the speed limit.

"You were going fifteen over," he confirmed.

"I apologize, Officer. My mind was on getting to my son."

"I'm sure he'd want his mother to arrive safely, even if she's a little late," he said.

I wished he'd take off those sunglasses. "Yes, sir. You're exactly right. It's best to err on the side of caution," I said, trying to win him over with sugar. "Again, I apologize."

"Did you know your left brake light was out, as well?"

"I had no idea," I said. I heard the cash register ring in my head. *A speeding ticket. A brake light. A possible increase on my insurance premium.*

"I'll be back in a moment, ma'am." The officer watched as a line of traffic changed lanes before heading back to his patrol car.

"Excuse me, Officer?" I stuck my head out the window before he could walk away. "Do you know how long this is going to take?" I asked in my sweetest voice.

"I'll be back in a moment, ma'am," the officer repeated.

I kept the smile on my face, but I felt like acting six years old and sticking out my tongue at him. I waited eight long minutes until he returned with a yellow carbon copy of a citation.

"I'll let you go with a warning this time," he said. "I really shouldn't be doing this, since you were being Danica Patrick out here. Do you know who that is?"

"I just moved from Charlotte. Everybody knows who she is."

"I moved from Charlotte not too long ago, myself," the officer said. "I thought your face looked familiar." He slipped off his sunglasses for the first time and hung them on his front shirt pocket. "Where did you work when you lived in Charlotte?"

"I didn't," I said. I wasn't about to volunteer any information to aid in his probe of my personal history. On the slightest chance that he knew me through Santana, I didn't want him to make the connection.

I tried to look at him without getting pulled in by his eyes. The sunglasses had hidden their intensity. Not only was he a man in uniform, but he was a *fine* man in uniform.

"Thank you for the warning," I said, folding the citation and sticking it in the side pocket of the door. "If we're done, I really need to get going. Slowly. Under the speed limit, even."

"Don't forget to take care of that brake light, Ms. Montgomery."

"I'll get it done, Officer."

He tapped the hood of the car as he walked away.

I know the men in blue—or black, in this case—are called to protect and to serve, but I never wholeheartedly trusted police officers. They seemed to think they were above the law. Policemen were the ones who abused their wives and got off. They were the ones who pocketed confiscated items and used them for their own benefit. When they were supposed to be patrolling the neighborhoods for drug rings, they were secretly involved in the distribution. As handsome as he was, he was probably hiding a secret.

When I arrived at the football practice field at Devin's school, he was waiting with the coach near the gate of the lower field. At least he wasn't the last child there. Two other boys were perched against the gate, both with ear buds stuffed in their heads.

"Sorry, Coach," I said through my window as I pulled up to the curb. "Bad traffic."

"No problem," he said with a smile. "You weren't the only one. A couple of other parents are caught in it, too."

I popped the trunk so Devin could throw in his athletic bag, shoulder pads, helmet, and sweaty cleats. He tossed his backpack on the backseat. I didn't see how he could carry that thing; it was stuffed like he was going on a camping trip.

"Hey, Ma," Devin said, collapsing into the car. He reclined his seat.

"You look tired," I said. "And you smell hot."

Devin looked at me like I had something hanging out of my nose. "How do you smell hot?" he asked.

I laughed. "One day when you have kids, you'll understand."

"I don't think I'm ever having kids."

"Where did that remark come from?"

"They're too much work."

"Well, I'm glad you acknowledged that. And the next time I ask you for help with something, I'm going to remind you about what you just said."

Devin shrugged. "That's fair." He unzipped the cooler of snacks that I always kept stashed on the floor of the passenger side when I picked him up from practice. He pulled out a pack of cheese-and-peanut-butter crackers and used his teeth to rip the plastic open.

"Ma, when do you think I can get a phone? I think I've gotten more responsible. I couldn't even call to see where you were."

"That's when you ask the coach or another adult if you can borrow their phone," I said.

Did I need to remind him that he was the same boy who'd forgotten his lunch that very morning, and that I'd had to take it to him since he refused to eat the "overcooked turkey burgers that tasted like cardboard" at school? His words, not mine. Was this the same boy who'd forgotten his baseball cap at the barbershop last week?

This was a never-ending conversation. At least once a week, Devin would plead his case for getting a phone. I'll admit, I was a paranoid parent when it came to technology. I wasn't up to speed on the latest gadgets, which meant that if Devin wanted to, he could use his phone in ways I couldn't imagine.

I didn't think he would—I wanted to believe that he *wouldn't*—but he was a growing young man subject to peer pressure, societal influences, and his own curiosity.

"I don't think you're old enough to have a phone," I finally said. "Phones aren't toys. They're expensive, they give children access to things they shouldn't have access to, and you have to be *very* responsible. And even if you have the best intentions, someone can steal it from you."

"Everybody has one except me," Devin said, catching himself before he started to whine. He knew I didn't like to listen to whiny boys. "You tell me all the time how mature I am."

"You are," I agreed. "But mature people still make mistakes, and if you make big mistakes with a phone by doing things you think are fun or are no big deal, you could wind up in serious trouble."

"What do I do if there's an emergency?"

"Go to the school office and use the phone, or ask one of your friends to borrow theirs. Most of the time, if you're not at school, you're with me. I just don't think we need to worry about it right now."

"For Christmas?"

This boy just wouldn't stop. Devin always made valid points, but a special on 20/20 had built a stronger case. A young teenager had been tried, convicted, and sentenced to eighteen months' jail time for child pornography after receiving a text message with a photo of a girl from their school—shirtless. The picture had been passed around until the girl's mother had caught wind of it and had begun a circle of lawsuits.

"What would you like for dinner?" I thought I would silence his pleas by changing the subject.

Devin shrugged. He was sulking now. I didn't know if his attitude change was the natural progression in his preteen years or if it was the result of a missing father figure.

I couldn't pretend that Santana's being in jail wouldn't eventually affect Devin as he progressed through the stages of life. He'd bottled up most of his emotions in the days after Santana's arrest. But after a visit from Pastor Lloyd, he'd exploded in an emotional breakdown of anger, hurt, and embarrassment. I'd let Marvin take him under his wing for some time. I trusted his judgment, and Devin had needed a strong shoulder to cry on.

Devin had carried a heavy burden. He'd secretly called 9-1-1 before bursting into the guest room and holding his father at bay with the gun. He'd testified of the screaming and fighting he'd heard late some nights when we thought he was asleep. He'd noticed the bruises that I tried to conceal with foundation, yet he'd said nothing. It pained me that he'd endured so much in silence.

"How about pizza and wings?" Devin finally said, his voice barely audible.

I frowned. Cheese and fried wings weren't at the top of my nutritional list, but I also knew that he wouldn't settle for the spinach, kale, and cranberry salad I was craving. So, I let him order what he wanted from the pizzeria near our apartment complex, and when we got home, I threw together my elaborate salad with items I kept stocked in the fridge.

During dinner, Devin still wasn't his usual, chatty self. I knew he was disappointed about the phone situation, but he'd soon get over it. It wasn't the first time he'd had to, and it certainly wouldn't be the last. After his dinner and homework were done, Devin went to get ready for the next day. It was now his responsibility to iron his own clothes, as well as sort and fold the clean laundry. The only things I didn't make him touch were my undergarments, since he'd already expressed how "grossed out" they made him.

While he did his work, I did mine.

Around eight thirty, Zenja called to confirm my presentation at the Friday Night Love event, which meant that Devin would be my handy assistant.

"Ma," Devin said as he walked into my bathroom, where he found me plucking stray hairs from between my eyebrows. The hairs there grew like kudzu. "I apologize for my attitude."

I put down my tweezers and turned to face him. "That's okay, baby," I said. "We're all entitled to have a rough day every now and then. And I accept your apology."

Devin gave me a sideways hug. He watched me for a moment, and I knew he was about to ask me a question. His mind was always processing something. It was a computer that never had the chance to reboot. Out of the blue, he asked, "Do you ever think about Dad?"

Even though two years had passed since *that day*, Devin didn't need to know the thoughts that I had about his father. "Why do you ask?" I said, wishing I could deflect the question.

"Because sometimes when I'm playing my video games, I think about the competitions we used to have, or when I look at myself in the mirror, like I just did when I was in the bathroom, I think I look like him a little."

"You do look like your dad," I admitted. "And you should think of the good memories involving him. You had some great times together."

"I know. I try, but he did evil things to you."

My inclination was to tell Devin that he should forget he had a father. I wanted to tell him that all the love he had for his father should be showered on me. I wanted to tell him that if he wanted to pretend that he didn't have a father at all, it would be alright with me. But I couldn't. Santana would have to face his own demons and work through his relationship with his son when the time arrived.

"The only thing you can do is ask God to help you forgive your dad," I replied. "I actually think you've forgiven him in your heart, like I have. But sometimes you can't forget things. And that's okay. I've made the best decision for me. Your dad and I will never be together again. I'll relate to him and refer to him only as the father of my child, but that's absolutely it. Yet that doesn't mean we shouldn't pray for him. He still loves you, you know?"

"Yes, ma'am. I know," Devin said. "Is it okay if I write him a letter to tell him about being on the football team?"

"That's fine," I said. "Give it to me when you're done, and I'll put it in the mail."

I had certain rules when it came to Devin's correspondence with Santana. They were to communicate strictly via handwritten letters, and Santana couldn't know our address. I used our old PO box in Charlotte as the return address, and any letters that Devin received from Santana were picked up by Marvin's wife and mailed to me at another PO box in Greensboro. In the year before I left Charlotte, she'd stepped up to be the kind of woman I needed in my life. Along with God and Devin, she'd been my strength.

When Santana's letters arrived for Devin, I reviewed them before passing them along. Now I was the one in control.

"I think I'll write it on Friday," Devin said. He'd become distracted by the towel bar over the sink, one end of which had detached from the wall. He was trying to fix it with the screwdriver I'd left on the sink.

"Speaking of Friday," I said, "I need you to be my assistant."

"Doing what?"

"Helping me with a self-defense presentation at a church. I want you to man the table and watch over my products."

"Why? Do you think the church people are going to steal your stuff?"

"No. That didn't even cross my mind. But I always like to have someone man the table because that's the professional thing to do. Even though I don't want you to demonstrate the products, you can always tell the people what you know."

"I am a good salesman," Devin boasted. "Remember that last time I helped you? We walked out with our pockets full."

I swore I saw dollar signs flash in his eyes. He'd been willing to help then because I'd offered to pay him by the hour, including time for packing, unloading, setting up, and breaking down the display. Devin had earned enough money to buy a new video game.

"You do have the magic touch," I acknowledged. "Plus, who could resist a cute little face like that?"

"Can you increase my hourly pay?" Devin asked. He rubbed his hands together.

"Don't push it."

His face lit up. "I'll even wear one of those bright-pink T-shirts with your company name on it."

"I happen to love those T-shirts, and they're part of your work uniform, anyway." I said. "They're supposed to get people's attention."

"They attract people *and* insects," Devin said, then retold the story for the hundredth time. While helping me distribute promotional materials at a street fair, he had been harassed by every type of buzzing insect with wings. I had yet to convince him that the shirt wasn't to blame but rather the cologne he'd practically bathed in before leaving the house. Bad habits die hard.

"If the shirt attracts people, it attracts sales, too," I added. "And if we make sales, then I can keep food on the table, clothes on your back, and shoes on your big feet."

Devin lifted his bare foot and playfully kicked me in the backside. His feet were long, wide, and flat like his father's.

Three days later, dressed in a neon-pink shirt, Devin trudged along beside me with those Fred Flintstone feet and helped set up a display table in the church's multipurpose room for what Zenja's friend Caprice called Friday Night Love.

7

Caprice Mowry, the founder and facilitator of Friday Night Love, wore her hair in the same style that I would if I'd had the guts. It was a cute wash-and-go that could probably be easily styled with a little mousse and a comb-through with her fingers.

I'd originally let my hair grow past my shoulders because Santana preferred it long, and I'd kept it that way for so many years because I could never commit to one of the trendy styles. I'd bought every hair, fashion, and style magazine in the grocery store checkout line, but I'd always resorted to my ponytail.

"Thank you for allowing me to come tonight," I told Caprice.

"It's my pleasure," she said. "I told Zenja I was so glad she went shopping for a new dress because you're exactly who we need tonight. I think the ladies are going to be informed, empowered, and well-fed. Did she tell you the men were taking a cooking class?"

"She did," I said. "And it's all the better that the wives get to do a taste test afterward."

Caprice grinned. "If Chef Daniel has them cooking even half as good as he does, then I'll be the first in line."

The doors to the multipurpose room burst open and admitted a group of men. One propped the door open, while several others hauled in white Styrofoam coolers and packing containers. I assumed that the man trailing them was Chef Daniel, dressed as he was in the full regalia of short-sleeved chef's coat, black-and-white checkered trousers, and chef's hat. I couldn't help but notice the red high-top sneakers that completed his look.

"It looks like it's going to be quite a production," I said. "My son may need to go and join them. He's good for boiling a hot dog and making a grilled cheese sandwich, but that's about it."

"Hot dogs and grilled cheese can take you a long way," Caprice said, then shook her head. "He's in the same boat as my godson, Kyle."

"It'll make my life a whole lot easier when Devin picks up some cooking skills."

"And my husband, too. Hopefully Chef Daniel can get our men to keep it hot in the kitchen, just as they expect us to keep in hot in the bedroom."

"Hilarious," I said. "I'll leave that to you married folks." The last thing—and I mean the absolute last thing—on my mind right now was what went on in the bedroom.

An alert that sounded like a train whistle blared from Caprice's phone, and she checked the screen. She pursed her lips and rolled her eyes. "Please excuse me. My sister's asking for my help in the back. If you need anything, just stop anyone passing through this way. They should be able to help you, or they'll come find me."

"Thank you," I said. "I'll just finish setting up. I assume we'll all be somewhere in that corner for the presentations." I pointed to a large square of blue rubber mats lining the floor.

"Yes. My husband is going to send some of the men to set up folding chairs, as well. We're going to start with one of our local police officers, who is also a member of the church. He's going to talk about how to burglar-proof our homes, among other safety tips."

"Perfect," I said.

Even though my apartment was on the second floor, activating the pre-existing alarm system was one of the first things I'd done when we'd moved in. Inside, on the wall by the front door, I'd also hung a small plaque bearing the words of Psalm 121:7 (NIV): "The LORD will keep you from all harm—he will watch over your life." I knew my alarm system could alert 9-1-1, but even before that, I could call on Jesus.

While Caprice hurried away to assist her sister, Devin and I started to unpack the three cardboard boxes of the nonlethal weapons I'd brought along: bejeweled pepper sprays, stun guns that looked like lipstick tubes, and an expandable pink baton like the ones mall security guards kept clipped to their belts. I'd recently invested in small safes that looked exactly like soda cans. Ingenious.

"This is cool, Ma," Devin said, flipping over the fake soda can. "I saw one in the fridge and thought you were just trying to save your soda for a special occasion."

I smiled and pressed my pointer finger against my lips. "Don't talk so loud," I whispered. "One day I'll show you some more of my secrets."

"You have more secrets?" he asked incredulously. "Don't show me. I want to figure things out for myself."

"Be my guest," I said. "But I doubt you'll ever figure them out. I'm a pro."

"If I find all your hiding places, can I get a phone?"

That boy and this phone infatuation were going to wear me out. "No," I said, because I didn't want to give him any reason to snoop through my personal belongings.

He shrugged. "At least I tried."

Devin divided a stack of postcards and fanned them out on opposite ends of the table. We worked in an easy flow, enjoying the gospel music being piped in through hidden speakers above us. It was a nice blend of cross-cultural music—different races celebrating their unique cultures yet praising one God. There was even a Latina-influenced song, which can make even the stiffest, most introverted person think he has rhythm.

"Come on, Ma," Devin said, pulling my hand to salsa with him.

"Alleluia," I sang along with the music.

Devin held his hands high so that he could twirl me under his arm. When I twisted back out, I noticed we had company. It was the police officer who'd pulled me over. He gave us a personal round of applause.

I stopped and fanned a hand in front of my face. "I guess we got carried away," I said.

"Oh, no. It looked like you were having fun." He gave a smile of recognition. "Ms. Speedy Gonzalez, is that you?"

How embarrassing. "Quinn Montgomery is more appropriate," I said, feigning sternness as I folded my arms across my chest.

"I should write you a ticket for those dance moves," the officer teased, pushing his hands into his pockets.

"I thought I was doing pretty good."

"You were alright. You have to know how to swivel the hips," he said. He put one hand across his abdomen and raised the other in the air. His attempt was more reminiscent of a rusty tin man. I wasn't the one who needed the ticket for questionable dance moves.

"I might have to send you in front of the judge for that one," I said. I leaned forward to get a closer look at his name badge, then looked at Devin. "Judge, what do you say about Officer L. Gray?"

Devin held up his hands. "I'm not getting into this one. I can't choose between my mom and a police officer."

"Of course you can," I said. "When in doubt, always go with your mama."

"She's right," Officer Gray said. He picked up a canister of Mace disguised as a pink bejeweled lipstick case. "You've got some dangerous stuff on this stable."

"Not too dangerous. Just enough to stun somebody so a woman can have time to get away."

The officer picked up my card and looked at it before sliding it in his shirt pocket.

"You aren't going to use that to track me down for a ticket, are you?"

"Naw, I wouldn't do that. But what about your brake light? Did you get that replaced?"

My facial expression told on me. "Are you on or off duty right now?"

"It depends on what you say."

"Well, I'm not going to stand in a church and lie," I said. "I didn't get it changed, but at least I bought the replacement bulb. Unfortunately, I didn't have time to let the guy at the auto parts store replace it, and I haven't taken the time to figure out how to do it myself."

"You must be a busy lady, Ms. Montgomery."

I nodded toward Devin. "He keeps me busy."

Devin slid our empty boxes under the table, then extended his hand. Santana had always taught him the importance of looking a man in the eye and giving a confident handshake. "I'm Devin," he said.

"And I'm Officer Gray, but you can call me Mr. Levi. Good, strong grip."

"Thank you," Devin said. "My dad taught me."

Officer Gray looked at me. "Your husband taught him well."

"We're not married anymore," I quickly said. I guess it was habit for me to correct anyone who assumed I was still tied to a husband. "But yes, his father did teach him well," I added for Devin's sake.

Officer Gray studied the items on my table a bit more while we finished setting up.

"So, you're Levi, like the jeans?" I asked.

He chuckled. "Yes, but it's short for Leviticus."

"Like in the Bible," Devin said.

"You got it," Officer Gray said. "Leviticus is the third book of the Bible, part of the Pentateuch. The priests were chosen from the tribe of the Levites."

He was referencing the Bible like a scholar. I knew you shouldn't judge a book by its cover, but I never would've expected that from him.

"You know your Bible history," I said. "Does that mean you're a man of the cloth, too?"

"Oh, no," Officer Gray said. "I serve God in other ways, but that's not one of them."

Officer Gray—Levi—was charming. I stole glances at him while I pretended to work on making my display table more appealing. His intriguing eyes captured my attention, but he also had an "almost" dimple, like God had started to push his pinkie into Levi's left cheek but then changed His mind. That would've made his face look even more childlike. His head was round like the Gerber baby, but there was nothing else pudgy about him. The sleeves of his uniform hugged his arms like a custom fit, and I could actually see the belt around his waist, since there wasn't a bulging belly to hide it. I guess I hadn't noticed all that before, when I was worried about getting a ticket.

I turned my gaze from him. This was not the time or the place to check out Officer Leviticus Gray. Besides, I knew the deal with police officers—they didn't make the rules, but they liked to break them, no matter how handsome or Scripture-savvy they were.

More and more couples entered the room, signifying to me that the program was about to start. I checked my watch. "Would you happen to know where the ladies' room is?"

Levi pointed in the opposite direction from where we were standing. "It's down that side hallway, all the way at the end," he said.

"Thanks."

"I have some time to spare," he added. "Why don't you let me change your brake light?"

"Oh, you really don't have to do that, Officer Gray."

"Call me Levi. And it's no problem. All I need is your keys." He extended his hand as if he wouldn't take no for an answer.

"The bulb is in the glove compartment. Thank you again," I said as I searched for my keys in the bottom of my bag.

"You're welcome."

I lifted my tote bag and shook it. No jingle.

Devin reached into his pant pocket. "Oh, here you go. I forgot I had them." He tossed them to Levi, who snatched them easily. "Nice catch."

Once Levi was out of earshot, Devin turned to me. "How do you know him, Ma?"

"He stopped me the other day for speeding when I was on the way to get you after practice," I admitted. "I didn't get a ticket," I rushed to say. "He just gave me a warning."

"It's like I've seen him before," Devin said as he handed me a stack of extra brochures.

"Some people have familiar faces," I said. And it was hard to forget a face like his.

Within five minutes, I'd returned from the restroom, where I'd freshened my face with a light touch of bronzer and tamed some stray hairs in my ponytail. Levi returned with my keys, and I thanked him again before he took off to help the men arrange the folding chairs.

I tried to keep my eyes off him, but I kept finding myself glancing his way. Our gazes connected more than once. He wasn't wearing a wedding ring, but that didn't mean anything. Some married men didn't. Even if he wasn't married, he was probably in a serious relationship. He carried himself like the kind of man that women wanted to snatch up.

By a quarter to seven, the multipurpose room was buzzing with couples. I watched their happy interactions, but I couldn't help wondering if any of them were putting on a fantastic show, just like I'd done for years. There was bound to be at least one woman here who'd survived a push or shove. One who'd been called out of her name on the evening ride to the church. It was a habit I hadn't broken yet—I always assessed a crowd in search of a woman who might be hurting.

I was mentally rehearsing my bullet points on self-defense basics when a pink blur rushed past me, then doubled back. "Excuse me, Ms. Montgomery?"

"Yes?" I said, standing. "Quinn is fine."

"Beautiful name," the woman said. She was dressed in light pink, from her shirt to her socks, and was wearing metallic silver athletic shoes and lots of noisy silver bracelets. "I'm Carmela, Caprice's sister, and I'll be assisting you if you need anything."

"Nice to meet you, Carmela," I said. "Are you ready for me now?"

"We're going to start in about five minutes, but Caprice will give a little welcome and do a group prayer first before the couples break off into their separate areas. We're actually going to let Officer Gray start things off for the women."

"How long do you think Levi is going to speak?"

Carmela paused, and I noticed the flicker in her eyes go dim for just a second. "Oh, so you know Officer Gray?"

"We've just gotten acquainted," I explained. There was something there. Maybe Carmela was the woman I'd been suspecting.

Carmela snapped back into her role as Helpful Holly. "I told *Levi* that he had about twenty minutes to speak, and I've allotted ten minutes for questions. You'll have thirty minutes for your hands-on presentation and ten minutes for questions. Does that sound okay?"

"Whatever you'd like," I said.

Carmela walked the length of my table. Like Levi, she picked up the bejeweled pepper spray and held it at arm's length. That would probably be one of my best sellers tonight.

"Now this is some bling," she said. "If you have to spray somebody, you might as well look cute doing it."

"If you have to use it, I'm not sure whether you'll be worried about how cute you are."

"True," Carmela said, picking up a brochure. "Are you looking for consultants? I'm always eager to expand my business opportunities."

I handed her my card. "You should check out the Web site and read more about the company and the openings they have available," I suggested.

"It's been hard work, but over the past year, this business has supplemented my income as a fitness instructor."

Carmela held up her hand. "I'm not trying to do the fitness thing," she laughed. "I just want to sell some blingy pepper spray and pink stun guns."

"This business is definitely for the female entrepreneur who wants to be her own boss, set her own schedule, and build her own brand. Keep my card. After giving it some thought, if you think you're still interested, call me."

"I will," Carmela said, affixing the card to the clipboard she was carrying. Then she reached into the miniature backpack dangling over her shoulder, pulled out a bottle of water, and handed it to me. "I have a seat reserved for you in the first row."

Devin had started working on a letter to his dad, but then, unable to concentrate, he'd resorted to a handheld video game. He'd seen my presentations and demonstrations enough that he could do them with his eyes closed. And of course, I'd taught him every self-defense move I knew. He barely responded when I told him I was going to my seat.

Carmela led me to the front row and situated herself between me and Levi. Caprice followed the schedule that Carmela had mentioned, and before long, the men were off to try their hand at cooking honey-glazed salmon, roasted asparagus, and home-style mashed potatoes.

"Good evening, ladies," Levi said, commanding the attention of the entire room as soon as he stood up. "I'm Officer Levi Gray from the Greensboro Police Department, and tonight I'm going to talk to you about some safety measures that will keep your *home* safe and keep *you* safe. I know that you are women of faith—I'm a man of faith, as well—but in addition to prayer, there are some preventative measures we should take to keep ourselves out of the way of danger."

"Amen," Carmela said. She started to clap until she realized she was the only one applauding.

Did she just say "Amen"?

Levi cleared his throat before continuing. Over the next twenty minutes, he gave me more than enough to think about. Although we were still living in an apartment, Devin and I had added a home purchase to the vision board we'd made when we first moved to Greensboro. We'd set a goal—five years to find a nice home in a safe neighborhood. My second priority, after safety, was a great school district. Devin's priority was the location in terms of the house's proximity to parks and other recreation areas.

Regardless, we both loved Greensboro enough to make it our home. The crime rate was low compared to other nearby cities. But that didn't mean we shouldn't prepare for unfortunate circumstances. I vividly remembered when the home of one of my coworkers at the bank was burglarized. It had taken Jalisa three weeks to be able to spend the night at her own house again. She's struggled to get over the fact that someone had entered her home and rifled through her personal belongings.

Levi finished his presentation, but the ladies' questions took up twenty minutes instead of the allotted ten. It was worth it to me just to be able to watch his handsome self for an extra ten minutes. I knew a good-looking man when I saw one. Santana hadn't taken that from me.

When the questions were finished, Caprice stood and started a round of applause for Levi. Carmela's claps were the most enthusiastic, of course.

"I don't know about you ladies, but I feel more empowered already," Caprice said. "And, just like Officer Gray stressed, we have to be aware, especially in this day and age, when neighbors don't look after one another as they should." Then Caprice motioned for me, and I joined her at the front. "And in the unfortunate event that we should come across a danger-ous situation, my new friend, Quinn, is going to show us some techniques to take some fools down." She flexed her muscles with a smile before saying, "Quinn, the floor is yours."

I introduced myself to the group and talked a little about my background before giving an overview of my company. As far as they knew, I'd built this business because, one, as a single parent, I needed a flexible schedule, and, two, God was pushing me toward entrepreneurial pursuits. Both were true. Of course, it all had begun when I'd decided I wanted to be able defend myself if someone tried to inflict bodily harm on me. After being choked with a belt, hanging on to my life, I was naturally passionate about my cause.

When it was time for me to demonstrate some of the self-defense moves, my eyes landed on Levi. "Officer Gray, could I get your assistance for a moment, please?" I asked.

"Sure." He twisted the cap back on the bottle of water he'd been chugging and came to stand beside me.

"Now, Officer Gray is a sturdy man—"

"Yes, he is!" Carmela bellowed.

The ladies laughed, and some of them murmured their agreement, as if afraid their husbands might be listening.

"If he wanted to muscle you down or hurt you in any way, he probably wouldn't have to exert much force or energy," I continued. "But there are ways that you can escape from the grip of men three times your size—even bigger men than our officer, here. If nothing else, you can stun him, giving yourself a chance to run away."

Officer Gray adjusted his stance so that he seemed larger and more intimidating. His face transformed from pleasant to stern. Too easily. I'd hate to see him angry.

"Ladies, I'm going to show you the most vulnerable places to attack an aggressor. It's all about getting away by any means necessary. You kick the groin, you gouge the eyes, you bite, you fight like your life depends on it." I stopped for a dramatic pause. "Because it probably does."

Levi pretended to rough me while I demonstrated moves to escape from choke holds, bear hugs, wrist grips, and sexual assaults. I finished by saying, "Of course, the best type of self-defense is prevention, ladies. Now, If I'm not mistaken, I think there's still enough time for you to approach the mats and practice some of the moves I've just shown you. But I'll hand the floor back to Caprice."

Caprice stood and clapped her hands over her head. "Alright, women of God. This is the part you've all been waiting for. We're not dressed like this for nothing. Let's practice! But don't hurt anybody," she teased. "After we work up a sweat, our hubbies will be waiting to feed us a gourmet dinner."

At a tap on my shoulder, I turned to face Levi. "I'm impressed," he said. "You really know your stuff."

"You doubted me?" I said, tucking my shirt into my yoga pants.

"I never said that."

Carmela appeared out of nowhere, buzzing around Levi like a bumblebee to a flower. She tugged softly at his bicep. "Can we borrow you over here for a minute?"

"If you need to," Levi said, slight hesitation in his voice.

"Yes, we definitely need to."

"Have fun," I told him.

I walked among the groups of ladies, assisting them with their techniques. Although the session was drawing to a close, I could've done this all night. Devin, however, couldn't. I noticed that he was struggling to stay awake. Fortunately for him, the foot traffic after Caprice closed the session was more than enough to keep him occupied. On top of that, he received compliment after compliment from the ladies on how cute he looked in his pink shirt or how much of a gentleman he was to be helping his mother.

His handsome face surely helped my sales, since I not only sold out of all my products but also took eleven preorders for additional items that would be delivered directly to the women. As expected, the lipstick pepper spray and soda-can safes were big hits.

Zenja was finally able to make it to the table once the crowd thinned out. "I hope you're glad you found me in the fitting room," I told her. "I know I am. It's truly been a blessing."

"The blessing has been ours," Zenja said. "I'm telling you, this session has been a real eye-opener. Thank you for sharing your wisdom with us." She scanned the empty table. "And it looks like we emptied your inventory. That's a good thing."

"That's a great thing," I said. I pulled the pink overlay and black tablecloth from the table, then snapped them out so I could fold them.

"The school district where I work is always organizing educators' conferences, and I'll definitely keep you in mind when they're looking for new ideas," Zenja said. "I know that my teachers and staff would love a presentation like this."

"I'd appreciate that," I said. "Word of mouth keeps my business growing."

"And here's your impromptu partner," she said as Levi walked up. "You two make a great team."

"I thought so, too," Levi said.

I nodded in agreement.

"Can I help you take anything to your car?" Levi offered.

"Actually, I don't have anything left. There's just a small box of promo items, and Devin can handle it."

"Cool." He glanced around, as if he wanted to offer to help me with something else.

Zenja looked from one of us to the other with a curious eye, and I would have sworn I saw the hint of a smile. "Did you want to come and grab a plate of food?" she asked me. "It smells delicious in there."

"Oh, no, I'm fine," I said, even though she was right—it smelled like a full-scale restaurant had opened in the cooking area. I wouldn't have minded a taste, but as a guest, I didn't want to look greedy. After all, they'd bought every product I'd brought; I didn't want to help myself to their food, too.

"If you change your mind, feel free to come and join us," Zenja said. "I'd better go find Roman. My baby can lay it down in the kitchen, anyway. We'll be in touch."

Levi was lingering. I knew what that meant. I might have been out of the dating game for over a decade, but a woman knew when a man was attracted to her. I still didn't know how to feel about it. I was flattered, but it was probably too soon. The last time I'd trusted a man, I'd ended up spending ten years in solitary confinement.

"Here, sweetheart," I said, handing Devin a small cardboard box of marketing material. "You can go ahead and take this to the car. I'll be out in just a minute."

Devin looked at me, then shifted his gaze to Officer Gray. "Yes, ma'am," he said, then padded away, barely lifting his feet from the ground. That was the reason he always had scuff marks on his shoes.

Levi turned the empty table on its side and folded the legs. "Zenja's right—we were a good team tonight," he said. "Would you mind if I contacted you for other events? People call for officers to give presentations all the time, and I've become the designated speaker."

"Sure," I told him. "I'd appreciate that."

"Would you mind if I called you sometime for something unrelated to work?"

"Such as…?" I asked, knowing full well what he was alluding to.

"A matinee. Breakfast."

Officer Gray was asking me out. He'd been the first to ask me since my divorce had been finalized. I'd known it was bound to happen sooner or later. I didn't count the times I'd been asked out at the gas station by the old men offering to clean my windshield while I waited for my tank to fill. I also didn't consider the married man at the grocery-store deli who tried to woo me by adding extra fish fillets to my order at no charge. I accepted the fish, but I wasn't accepting his advances.

I didn't realize I'd been mulling it over for so long until Levi spoke again.

"I won't be offended if you say no," he said. "My ego might be a little bruised, but I'll recover."

"No, it's just…" I stammered. "I'm not sure how Devin would react."

"That's why I asked you for the times that I did. He'd be in school, and you wouldn't have to worry about explaining anything."

"Can you give me some time to think about it? I'll let you know when— and if—you can call me."

"So, you're going to do me like that?" he laughed. That "almost" dimple deepened in his cheek.

I shrugged. That was a sure way to quickly weed him out of my life. If Levi wasn't serious, I wouldn't hear from him anyway.

"That works for me," Levi finally said, extending his hand. I expected a rough, businesslike shake, but he put his other hand on top of mine and held it gently between his. Then he bowed slightly. "Nice to meet you, Ms. Quinn. Expect to hear from me soon." And with that, he turned and walked away.

Why did I watch him?

8

LEVI

Levi had always been respectful and aware of women's feelings, but there were some women a man just couldn't be too nice to. They were the kind of women who took every gesture as a come-on and every word as a compliment or flirtatious gesture. They were women like Carmela Garrett.

The first time Carmela called his name in the parking lot, he pretended not to hear. Standing by his patrol car, he leaned over to his walkie-talkie, as if the dispatcher were calling out something important, and hoped she'd find someone else to harass. But from what he knew about the Friday Night Love event that had just concluded, Levi was the only single man around. He was Carmela's target.

He had to give it to her—as much as it bugged him, the woman didn't give up easily. No wonder she made a good living, networking and marketing dozens of products.

"Officer Leviticus Grayyyyyy." She sang his name like it was the sweetest thing she'd ever heard. "Leviiii. Wait up before you go back out to protect and serve our great community."

Levi paused and got his face together before turning around. "Hi, Carmela," he said. "How are you?"

"I'm excellent, fabulous, and highly favored," she said. "I can tell you're doing good. Looking good, at least, all up in your uniform and whatnot. You know what they say about a man in uniform."

"Even a prison uniform?" he asked.

She pushed his arm playfully. "You are just too much."

Levi opened the door of his patrol car and slid into the seat, hoping she'd get a hint that he was ready to go.

She didn't.

"As a committee member for Friday Night Love, I wanted to take the opportunity to thank you for your service tonight." She handed him a gift card to a local restaurant. "I know it's not much and you wouldn't accept any money from us, but I said the least we could do is treat you to a meal. With your schedule I bet you don't get home-cooked meals very often."

"I don't do so bad," Levi admitted. "I cook a lot myself."

"Really?" Carmela leaned against his patrol car. "I do, too. Maybe we can do a potluck sometime when you're off."

Maybe not, Levi thought to himself. How could he bow out of this one without hurting the woman's feelings? One date. One date three months ago, and now he couldn't get rid of her. He didn't even consider it a real date. They'd met for coffee, and he hadn't been able to endure her chatter for more than an hour.

"If you can catch me awake," Levi decided to say. "I have to catch up on my sleep so that I can be focused and on top of my game. You can't afford to be caught slipping on a job like this."

"Well, you let me know. I'll be more than willing to cook you a feast and drop it off to you. No problem."

"Thank you," Levi said evenly.

That would never happen. There was no way she'd ever get his address. It was the nice and bubbly ones that always turned out to be crazy.

"As a matter of fact, I'm working with a sister here at the church to try and get a food and distribution deal for a new line of spices that she's working on."

Here we go again, Levi thought. He smiled and nodded his head as Carmela outlined all she planned to do to get the ball rolling, or, as she put it, "Get things cooking." Carmela was still giving her pitch when Levi noticed Quinn walking to her car. There was something about her. She had a softness, yet a strength. A bravado and a beauty. Save for a little shine on her lips, both times he'd seen her, she hadn't been wearing any makeup, and she still looked stunning. That was true beauty—when you could still catch a man's attention without a face full of makeup.

Quinn tooted her horn as she passed.

Levi's heart sank. *Good-bye, Carmela,* he wanted to say. He didn't want to give Quinn a reason to turn him down. Attracting a woman had never been a problem for Levi. For many he just didn't sustain a natural attraction past their physical beauty so he quickly moved on. There was no use wasting his time or theirs. Women got too emotionally involved, too quickly. Levi didn't have time for that.

Other women couldn't handle his long hours or the dangers that were inherent in police work, but he was doing what he loved. The woman God had for him would have to carry a certain grace and confidence when he was away long nights or days. When he walked out of the house and left his family behind, she'd need to know that not even the gun in his holster could fully protect him. They'd have to rely on God for that. She'd be the kind of woman who prayed for *him* as much as he'd pray for *her.*

"There's nothing like a good Cajun spice blend," Carmela was saying when Levi came out of his thoughts.

He turned the key in the ignition and revved the engine. There had to be a way he could arrest Carmela's mouth. Lock it up. Throw away the key.

"Time for me to get out of here, Carmela. I'll see you around."

"Yes, you will. I'll be looking for you at church," she said with a wink.

Levi slammed the door and shut himself in the silence. The only sound was the soft hum of the air-conditioning working to cool him off. Even though it was autumn, temperatures were still pushing 90 degrees. He hoped they would taper off soon. He'd been born and raised in the South, but he preferred the cold in the winter months. The world seemed to slow down, and women tended to dress like they had some sense, bundling up with bulky sweaters, blue jeans, and leather boots instead of revealing more than he wanted to see. Make that *should* see. He was a man, so he couldn't totally ignore it; but he wasn't going to run behind every piece of skin. At one time, it had been a pleasure for him, but he'd lost the taste for half-naked women. The only half-naked woman he wanted to stare at was his wife. Whenever that would happen.

Levi drove his patrol car to his townhome and parked it in the driveway, since his truck and motorcycle occupied all the space in the garage. He doubted the knuckleheads who'd vandalized it last week would be back. Probably a group of bored teenagers with nothing better to do. He'd been awakened by an early-morning call from his neighbor who'd noticed the eggs and whipped cream as she'd left to take her children to school. Luckily, that was all it had been. He'd rinsed it with the hose and then run it through the car wash down the street. For the most part, his neighborhood was quiet, save for the occasional loud party or holiday cookout. Someday, when he had reason to, he would search for a place with more square footage; but right now, he had everything he needed.

Just as he entered the house, his cell phone rang. A picture of his son, L.J., one front tooth missing, flashed on the screen.

"Hey, boss man," he answered with no hesitation.

"What's up?"

"Excuse me?" Levi said.

"Hi, Daddy," the boy corrected himself.

"Check your manners, Son. You know better than that. That's for your friends at school, not for Daddy, okay?"

"Yes, sir."

"That's more like it. How was school today?"

"It was good. We got to eat outside. Ms. Saxon gave us blue Jell-O with little red gummy fish and worms inside. It looked gross, but it was good."

"Maybe we can try that the next time you come and see me."

"Coooool. And can we put some gummy worms in a cup with some whipped cream and mashed-up Oreos, too? It makes it look like dirt."

Levi could hear the thrill in his voice. "Whatever you want," he said.

Sweets were a rare treat for L.J. His mother rarely fed him junk food; when he had a good week at school, she rewarded him with Fig Newtons, poor boy. The only time he got a sugar high was when he was with his dad. And they enjoyed every minute of it.

"And you know what else happened at school today?" L.J. asked.

Levi chuckled to himself. His son's mouth was just like Carmela's—it never stopped moving. But Levi loved that L.J. liked to unload on him.

"What?"

"I got an award for math."

"That's good stuff," Levi said. "I'm proud of you. You know your daddy was good in math, too. You get that from me."

"Mommy said I got my big head from you, too," L.J. said.

"A big head means a big brain," Levi said, biting his tongue from commenting further. He didn't bad-mouth Brandy to his son, not even in a joking manner. Levi's own mother had cut his dad so much with her tongue that Levi had grown up hating a man he'd never met until he turned twenty-one.

Brandy had been one of those girls who showed more skin that brains. Levi had fallen for it during one of his weaker moments. Looking back, he never should've gone out that night. One night had changed things for him. One night had made him a father. Even though they'd mutually agreed to go their separate ways after finding out about her pregnancy, Brandy had continued acting bitterly toward him. They weren't meant to be, but evidently, L.J. was. And Levi refused to stay out of his son's life. Brandy had moved from Charlotte to the D.C. area, but Levi was as involved as an out-of-state parent could be.

Brandy had gotten married three years ago, although Levi couldn't say if it was happily. Knowing Brandy, she'd done it for the money. Of course, Levi had given her the go-around when he'd learned that another man would be living with his son and thereby having more hands-on time raising him. But Rich had passed every test and was more cordial to Levi than Brandy. Brandy had her own issues, plain and simple.

"Daddy, do you think you're ever going to have a wife?" L.J. asked.

"Boy, what are you talking about?" Levi said as he unbuckled the heavy belt that held his holster. He untied the laces of his steel-toed shoes and left them under the kitchen table. He couldn't wait to get out of this polyester shirt.

"My friend Andrew has another mommy," L.J said. "His daddy got married, and he was in the wedding. He said he got to wear a tux and everything. What's a tux, anyway?"

"A tux is a real nice suit that men wear on special occasions."

"I didn't wear a tux when Mommy got married."

"You wore a suit, didn't you? Like something you'd wear to church."

"We don't go to church that much," L.J. said.

That was no surprise. Levi wished that Rich and Brandy would go to church on as many Sundays as they grilled out or invited people over to watch football. Sunday was their time to chill, and there was nothing Levi could do about that. That's why he made it his business to instill godly principles in his son. Levi had planted the seeds. The fruit would show up in due time.

"Can I wear a tux when you get married?" L.J. asked.

"If you want to."

"I do. But you have to get married before I leave for college, because if you don't, I won't have time to come down there and be in your wedding."

"I hope it won't be that long," Levi said. "But if you're in college, you'd better come anyway. Because if you don't, I'm going to give you a knuckle sandwich."

L.J. laughed. "You tried one time, but you couldn't even catch me."

"That's right—you're too fast for me," Levi said, recalling the last time he'd seen L.J. It had been about three months since he'd last picked him up in D.C. and brought him to Greensboro for a week. Levi had taken off an extra two days just to recuperate from having his son with him for seven days straight. There was no way he could ask for full custody right now. Not with L.J. still so young. Levi would give it a few years, until he was around the age of Quinn's son. Maybe thirteen?

"Oh, I have to go now. Mommy said it's time for me to go to bed."

Levi glanced at the microwave in the kitchen. It was after nine thirty. "You should be in bed already," he said.

"It's Friday night. I get extra time. But I'll call you back tomorrow."

"Not too early, now. I need to get some sleep," Levi told him.

L.J. had memorized Levi's phone number at the age of three, and he'd always called whenever he felt like it. Brandy had finally broken his habit of sneaking off to call in the wee hours of the morning.

"Okay, four thirty," L.J. decided.

"No. At least wait until your mommy wakes up, and *after* you've eaten breakfast," Levi told him.

"Okay. I'll wait and say my prayers in the morning. We need to pray together."

"What do you want to pray about?" Levi asked. He couldn't hang up the phone without making sure his son's concerns were addressed. If there was something bothering him, he needed to know about it.

L.J. huffed. "Finding you a wife, Dad. Remember?"

"My bad, boss man. I forgot."

"That's why we have to ask God to help you. He makes the best choices, anyway. Isn't that what you told me?"

"That's exactly what I said."

Levi shoved some leftovers into the microwave and nuked them. Those seeds were starting to sprout after all.

9

It was only Sunday evening, and although I'd found myself anticipating a call from Levi, I hadn't thought he'd contact me so soon. Tuesday or Wednesday, maybe. But he hadn't wasted any time.

"How's your day been?" Levi asked.

"Pretty good. I'm prepping for the week now," I said, turning up the temperature and steam on the iron so I could take the wrinkles out of Devin's jeans. Even though he was supposed to iron his own clothes, I'd given him a break so that he could take care of washing his smelly football practice uniform and getting his helmet, shoulder pads, and snacks packed in the trunk of the car.

"How about you?" I asked Levi. "Did you scale any buildings or jump off any bridges while chasing criminals?"

He chuckled. "This is Greensboro, North Carolina, not New York City. It doesn't usually go down like that. I had only a few speeding tickets, two domestic violence disputes, and a break-in."

"So, do you have to miss church every Sunday?" I asked.

"Not anymore. This was actually my last Sunday on duty. They changed my schedule so that I'm off Sundays and Mondays."

"I know you're glad about that."

"I am," Levi said. "There's something about Sundays."

There *was* something about Sundays. They had been the worst for me. "It takes a special person to be a police officer. I don't see how you do it," I admitted. "It seems like it would be draining."

"It is, sometimes," Levi acknowledged. "But, at the same time, it's fulfilling to serve others. Except for the traffic tickets. I never feel good about those, but they have to be issued. I always pity the people I have to chase down with that flashing blue light and siren."

"Did you pity me, then?"

"When I stepped up to the car, you looked so gorgeous, I couldn't bring myself to give you a ticket."

"Is that so?" I asked.

"Honest truth."

"So, the women you think are beautiful get to drive away without tickets?"

"No. That was only for you. First time I've done it."

I'd probably be a fool to believe him, but I did anyway. "Well, thank you again."

"You can thank me by letting me take you to breakfast tomorrow."

"How is that a thank-you?" I asked.

"Because I'd get to see your beautiful smile again."

Maybe my smile had gotten me out of that ticket, after all.

"You're spreading it on thick," I said. "I think you've made me blush."

"Then, mission accomplished," Levi responded. "What do you say?"

He waited patiently while I weighed the options in my mind. Again. Really, there wasn't an option that could compete. Mondays were mundane. After dropping Devin off at school, I typically returned home to eat a breakfast of scrambled egg whites and oatmeal, then hit the treadmill for a thirty-minute walk. Then I showered, put on some exercise gear, and waited for the Step & Tone class I taught at noon. Maybe a change would be good.

"Sure," I finally decided. "I'd love to meet you for breakfast. Is eight thirty too early?"

"Not at all," Levi said.

I could hear the smile in his voice, and I was surprised that I had a cheesy grin on my own face. He gave me directions to a spot he said was small and quaint but served some of the best breakfast food Greensboro had to offer. "Small and quaint" probably meant it was a hole-in-the-wall, but I didn't care about the furnishings or the building as long as they had a high health-department inspection rate and good food. There were plenty of places with gleaming tables and chairs and bland food.

The next morning, my assumptions were proven correct.

Our breakfast was brought to us by a woman old enough to be my grandmother. Her hips were as wide as our table, but so was her welcoming smile. She and her sisters owned the spot, all of them sharing the middle name Mae. The restaurant had been in the family for a little over sixty years and had been a favorite hangout of civil-rights activists when they'd passed through in the 60s. To everyone else, it may have been a hole-in-the-wall, but to the "Mae" sisters, it was a legacy.

"And this is why I come here," Levi said, tearing into one of the fried chicken wings he'd ordered along with a waffle the size of his plate.

My meal was even more appetizing because of the company sitting in front of me. Eye candy. Even dressed in something other than his uniform, he didn't disappoint.

Steam was still rising from my shrimp and grits, but I wanted to enjoy it to the fullest while it was piping hot.

"Your hair looks nice," Levi said, wiping his hands with a napkin. "You had a lot of hair combed up in that ponytail the other day. Is it all yours?"

I laughed, then sobered. "That's a rude question to ask a woman," I said. "But for the record, yes, it's all mine. From the roots to the ends."

"That's nice to know. It's not like I would care if it wasn't, because it looks so good, but *au naturel* is better than dyed and processed with chemicals."

"I'm not even going to go down this road," I said, taking a sip of my orange juice.

"Well, consider it a compliment," Levi said.

"I thank you. And my hair thanks you."

He had no idea of the measures I'd taken in order to get these curls. As soon as I'd hung up the phone after his call the night before, I'd plugged in the curling iron. Most days, there was no reason for me to wear my hair any other way than up in a ponytail or pushed back with a headband. By the time I finished my classes at the gym, any curls would've dropped, anyway. But since I was going out to eat with someone other than Devin, I'd pulled out my grown-lady game and, for the cost of beauty, slept with those horrible, pink foam bendable curlers. I'd looked like Medusa, but the price had been worth it.

"So, tell me about yourself," Levi said. "What do you enjoy, other than fitness training and teaching self-defense?"

"That's about it," I admitted. "Right now my life revolves around my business and Devin. It's just the two of us. We're homebodies."

"You need to get out more," he said. Just like Devin, he was a syrup dumper. I had a feeling he had a sweet tooth.

"I know some of the other mothers of boys on Devin's school football team and spring recreational baseball team, but they're just acquaintances. I didn't feel a connection with any of them, so I didn't push it."

"And you've been here how long?"

"Just a little over a year." I shook my head. "The time's flown."

"Do you have a church home?"

"I've been visiting a lot of churches, but we haven't settled on one place yet. I know that's horrible. I used to live and breathe church. Devin misses it. But the churches I've been visiting are a little too old-timey for him, if you know what I mean. He's used to the services being more contemporary."

"You'll know the place when you find it. It'll feel like home," Levi said. "I've been at Grace Temple for about a year. Of course, until this recent schedule change, I couldn't attend every Sunday. I'd visited twice, and the third time, I became a member. They're like family already. Especially Caprice Mowry and her husband, Duane. We hang out from time to time. They throw some serious Sunday dinner parties."

"Zenja Maxwell and Caprice are best friends, right?" I asked. "I think that's what Zenja told me."

"Yes. Zenja is married to Roman. He's a bad brother who can play a mean saxophone. In fact, he can play any instrument you put in front of him. The next time he's performing somewhere, I'll have to take you. They're good people."

"I'm just forewarning you…I doubt I'd go."

"Why?"

"Because I don't have anywhere to take Devin."

"Do you have a friend he can stay with?"

"Only acquaintances," I reminded him. Sometimes, men didn't get it. Mothers were protective of their children, and I was probably one of the most shielding moms out there.

"Not even for a few hours?"

I shook my head. "People have the tendency to put on a good front. They show you the side they want you to see, but there are so many unspeakable things they do. You'd be surprised."

"Believe me, I know," Levi said.

He lifted his hand, and one of the Mae sisters appeared by his side. He asked for a glass of ice water, which he probably needed to dilute the sugar rush he was undoubtedly experiencing from all that syrup.

When she left to get his water, he said, "I don't get to see my son very much, but I'm still particular about the people he's around. His mother knows how I am. It happens to work in my favor that he runs his mouth and ends up telling me about everything and everybody."

"You have a son?" I hadn't considered that possibility. "How old?"

"Six. His name is L.J., and he thinks he runs everything. I call him my 'boss man.' That's my boy. I miss him like crazy."

"Where is he?"

"D.C. I get him for about a week in the summer, but other than that, it's usually up to me to ride up there when I have a few days off. It's not far, so I don't mind the drive. I tune in to a good talk radio station or pop in one of my pastor's CDs and roll out. Driving the speed limit, of course."

"I don't believe you," I joked. "I know you men who walk the thin blue line have some kind of special code or privilege if you get stopped."

"If we did, I'd never admit to it," Levi said.

"I knew it," I said.

Levi was very easy to talk to. He had a relaxed way about him. After thirty minutes of conversation, it was obvious he was totally in love with his son. Because L.J. was his namesake and his only child, he felt he had a responsibility to make sure he had everything he needed—not just in terms of finances but also in emotional and spiritual support. If Levi's actions truly lined up with his words, he fit my definition of a real man.

"Tell me one thing that a woman first meeting you would be surprised to know," I prompted him. He clearly wasn't shy about asking me whatever question came to his mind, so it was my turn to put him in the hot seat.

Levi thought for a moment. Our empty plates had long been cleared, but none of the Mae sisters made a move to rush us out of the tiny establishment. It had been bustling with the before-work crowd when we'd first arrived, but now there were only two other tables of diners. Now I realized why Levi had fallen in love with this place. It was easy to do when you felt like you were eating at your own kitchen table.

"I'm a history buff," Levi finally said.

"Really? How so? Your family's history? African-American history?"

"Everything," Levi said. "Since moving to Greensboro, I've done some research on the exhibits of the civil rights movement. Everybody knows about the four boys from A&T who staged the sit-in at the lunch counter in Woolworth's, but not many people know there was a stop in Guilford County for the Underground Railroad. There's more history here than people realize." He reached his arms above his head and leaned back in his chair in an exaggerated stretch, then rested his palms on top of his head. The muscles in his arms bulged. I wasn't the only one who'd put in some time at the gym.

"What would I be surprised to know about you?" he asked me.

"Oh, I'm not that interesting," I said. "I paint, but that's not very unique. Plenty of people do that. On canvas," I added. "I thought I'd better clarify that before you invited me over for some home-improvement projects."

"I already had the paint color picked in my head," Levi said. He fiddled with his napkin. "What are you working on now?"

"Nothing. I haven't painted in a couple of years. When we moved, I packed up my supplies and most of my paintings and put them in storage. I have a few of my favorite pieces in the apartment, but everything else is collecting dust."

"Clean them off. Find your brushes. Paint something."

"Maybe I will," I said. I remembered the canvas I'd last painted, ripped through by Santana's fist. He'd punched his arm through my paradise.

I looked at my watch and couldn't believe the hour hand was inching toward eleven. It felt like I'd just walked in the door and found Levi in the corner nook where he'd been waiting.

"I must say, you've shattered my stereotypes of police officers," I confessed. "The ones I've come across usually act like pit bulls. Like they have something to prove."

"I bark, but I bite only if I have to," Levi said.

"I don't even want to know what you mean by that," I told him.

"Lighten up. I'm kidding."

I looked up and noticed two of the Mae sisters watching us like we were the highlight of their morning. One of them, with her hair twisted into a bun at the nape of her neck, gave me a thumbs-up. The other one swung an apron at her and pushed her toward the kitchen.

"It's been a joy seeing this side of you," I said to Levi. "I've enjoyed myself."

"We'll have to do it again," he said, scooting his chair away from the table.

"Maybe. Give me a call," I said, knowing I was being a flirt. I actually *did* want to see him again, so I was flattered that he'd suggested a repeat. At least I knew he'd enjoyed himself, hopefully as much as I had. I unhooked the strap of my purse from the back of my chair and looped it over my arm.

"Maybe?" Levi said, lifting one eyebrow. He pulled out my chair for me. "You force me to pay for your breakfast, and then you say 'maybe'? You may need to go in the back and wash some dishes."

He took out his wallet and left $30. We'd eaten a hefty breakfast, but I didn't think it had been thirty dollars' worth. Either he was just a big tipper or he was trying to impress me. Either way, it worked.

Santana had been stingy. I'm all about being budget-conscious, but whenever he'd given me money, he'd wanted an account of how I'd spent every penny. Literally.

"If I haven't been a gentleman, then you need to give me a chance to redeem myself," Levi said, holding the door open for me. We bid good-bye to the Mae sisters, and Levi promised them he'd see them again next week.

"Time will tell." I pressed the button to unlock my car, and Levi had my door open before I had a chance to reach for the handle.

"You've started my week off in a good way, Quinn," he said. We simultaneously leaned in to give each other a sideways hug. I could tell that he gave good hugs—the kind that made a woman want to linger in his arms. I know I could've stayed there.

"I'll give you a call," Levi said once I was in my car.

His Ford truck was parked a few spaces down. It reminded me of Marvin's truck, except that Levi's had standard-sized wheels, while Marvin's were over-sized, making the truck look capable of crushing every car in its path.

I bumped and dipped my way through the pothole-filled parking lot and headed downtown. The drive to Warehouse Fitness was quicker than I'd expected. I floated into the gym, greeted the receptionist at the front, signed in for my lunchtime class, and went to the locker room to change into my workout gear. With a number of large businesses around us, the lunchtime classes were popular. From what the women in my class had told me, it was the only time they could find to work out. It was either lunchtime or no time.

As usual, Ginger, one of my regular participants—and an overzealous one—was already waiting in the room.

"Wow!" Ginger said when I walked in. "What's the special occasion? Your hair looks gor—ge—ous!"

I pulled my hair into a high ponytail on top of my head and secured it with four hairpins, hoping to preserve some of my curls. "Is the change that obvious?"

"Yes. And you're glowing. Like 'you've been with a man' glowing."

"You're ridiculous."

"I might be ridiculous, but I'm right. Tell me I am. I know you're a good Christian woman, so don't go lying on me."

I sighed. "You're right, but it was only for breakfast."

"First it's breakfast, then lunch, then dinner, then dessert." Ginger paused and shook her hips. "Then there's the after-dessert activities. But take it from me—that can't happen for at least three months."

"For me, it's not until three carats," I told. "And marriage vows."

"You can't be serious," Ginger said, admiring herself in the mirror, as she often did. Since the beginning of the year, she'd put herself through a number of fierce high-impact workouts and managed to melt away over forty pounds. Now she was trying to tone her "jiggles," as she called them.

"I'm very serious. If I'm ever in a committed relationship that will lead to marriage, that's the first thing I plan to make clear. In fact, I'll make it clear before we get in too deep."

"I didn't think people did that anymore. It's so old-fashioned. Surely, God doesn't expect you to buy a car without taking a test drive."

I shook my head. "I'll just have to trust that the machine God sends to me will work fine."

"Better you than me," Ginger said. "I don't have that kind of willpower."

We slid to the floor at the same time and began our stretching routine. Ginger might have been a soft and fluffy woman at one time, but she'd always been more limber than I would ever be.

I pulled my legs into a butterfly stretch and used my elbows to push them down gently until I felt a soft pull.

"Look at it like this," I told her. "Whenever you sleep with a man you're not married to, you're not only sleeping with him but also with everyone else he's ever slept with."

Ginger scrunched her nose. "That's nasty."

"And *he's* sleeping with every man *you've* ever slept with."

"I don't even want to think about that. In fact, there's no one worth remembering."

"My point exactly. Which means they probably don't remember you, either, even though you gave away a little piece of yourself to them."

Ginger stretched her legs in a *v* and leaned over to her left side. "Well, when you put it that way, you totally put a damper on my groove. I was getting together with my man tonight."

"Sorry," I said, not really meaning it. At least I'd killed her plans for one evening. I couldn't speak for what would happen after the shock wore off.

A group of ladies from a nearby check-processing center walked in wearing matching shirts. They'd just completed a thirty-day weight-loss challenge. The group had begun with nine participants, and the number had dropped to four by the end of the second week. I bet the other five wished they'd stuck with the program, since the inches had finally started dropping off their coworkers.

"So, what does he do for a living, this mystery man?" Ginger asked.

"He's a police officer."

She made a face. "No can do. I'd never be involved with a police officer again. They're arrogant and think they're above the law. They want to run things on the street and in the home. And I know—from experience—that they can be some bugbears. They'll flip the script on you like Dr. Jekyll and Mr. Hyde if you don't do what they want you to."

I didn't bother telling her that I'd been thinking the same things *before* I'd spent time with Levi today. He'd changed my outlook, at least about himself. But now my concerns returned and intensified with each word Ginger spoke.

"Now you're your own woman, and you make your own decisions," Ginger said after she'd totally clouded my thoughts. "But as for this chick"—she poked her finger in her chest—"no, ma'am. Fool me once, shame on you. Fool me twice, shame on me." She pointed to an old, discolored scar on her knee. "It started verbally, before he had the audacity to push me on the sidewalk. I walked away, wanting to leave before the argument escalated, but he couldn't let it go. That was the first and last time. I don't understand these women who stay in abusive relationships for years. They're weak."

"You never know a woman's situation," I said, somewhat defensively.

I swallowed the lump in my throat and was thankful that another rush of lunchtime exercisers entered the room. I couldn't go there.

I got up and clipped the wireless mic to the back of my pants. Then I adjusted the bass of the music loud enough for it to reverberate through my insides. The deep thumps bounced in my eardrums and knocked out my thoughts of Levi for the time being. Maybe God was giving me a warning through Ginger. She'd spoken nearly the same thoughts that I'd been grappling with. I only wished I'd had someone to shine that same light when I'd met Santana.

10

He was tall. He was dark. And he was handsome. The walking cliché. I found myself watching for him. Every Friday afternoon, he arrived no earlier than 3:45 and no later than 4:15. He walked into the bank, shook hands with our security guard, and patiently stood in line with the other patrons. We often made eye contact as I processed deposits, drew up cashier's checks, and collected payments for bank credit cards. If another teller was available when he was next in line, he'd let the customer behind him take care of his or her business first so that I would be his teller. Every Friday. We both acted as if our interactions were strictly business, and I'd never been the kind of woman to make the first move. Finally, he did.

"Cashing my checks used to be the happiest part of my Fridays," he told me one day.

"What changed?"

"I still like getting my money, but seeing you puts the icing on the cake."

I nodded as he slid his license under the opening in the bulletproof glass that separated the tellers from the rest of the bank. I was giddy inside, but I wouldn't show it. I could tell he was more mature. If I'd had to guess, he was at least ten years my senior.

"I don't live on this side of town, and I don't work nearby," he went on. "I'm here every Friday because of you, Ms. Hudson. I drive thirty minutes out of my way, and every mile is worth it."

"Is that so?" I asked, not looking up at him. My coworker Joi watched everybody like a hawk and seemed to tell everybody's business but her own. I was, and always had been, a private person.

His check was made payable to the order of Santana Montgomery. I swiped it through the machine to verify its authenticity, then pulled up his account to make sure he had enough funds to cover the cash. As always, his account was in the five digits. It was padded enough for me to know that he wasn't living paycheck to paycheck. When he came into my branch, he never touched the checking account. He merely cashed the check at hand and asked for it in bills no larger than fifties.

I counted out his bills aloud, stacked them, and slid them inside an envelope. Fifteen hundred dollars, and never a dime above or below.

"Is there anything else I can do for you today, Mr. Montgomery?" I asked.

"Call me Santana," he said with a grin. He pushed the bank envelope into the inside pocket of his gray business suit. "You can let me take you to dinner."

I peeked at Joi, who was impatiently waiting for the elderly Mr. Linwood to finish counting out his various coins. He usually found himself in my line to make his exchange for quarters he could use at the Laundromat. I turned back to Santana.

"I'm flattered—"

But he turned and walked away.

He didn't just do that, I thought. *I hope he doesn't bring his rude behind back in this bank.* I quickly turned my frown into a cordial expression as another customer stepped up to the counter.

When I walked to my car after work that day, I thought to myself that Santana Montgomery wasn't necessarily rude, just overconfident.

I recognized every car in the parking lot except for a black Mercedes-Benz with its windows tinted just as dark as the shiny paint job. The driver's window lowered slowly as I passed.

"Did you think about my offer?" It was Santana Montgomery.

"I don't recall your *asking* me anything," I told him. "You made a *statement.*"

"Can I take you to dinner *tonight*, Ms. Hudson?"

Yes, he was a regular bank patron, but I didn't really know this man. It was safe to flirt inside the four walls of the building, but things were different now. He could easily be a well-dressed serial killer.

"I can sense your hesitancy," he said, as if reading my thoughts. "And you should feel that way. There are a lot of nuts in Queen City. But I'm not one of them." He flashed a million-dollar smile. "Why don't you follow me to one of my favorite dinner spots? It's in the public eye. Well lit. No funny business, I promise."

Another coworker, Jalisa, took a stroll around his car. She pulled a piece of paper out of her purse and wrote down his license-plate number. Then she stepped to the front, casually lifted her cell phone, and snapped a close-up of Santana's face. "That's for the six-o'clock news, if necessary. I got you, girl."

"Well, dang," Santana said. "What else do you need—my license and registration?"

Jalisa extended her hand, but I pushed it out of the way.

"She's kidding," I said.

"No, I'm not. But for you, I'll let it slide."

"I'll follow you," I told Santana after some thought. "But if you look in your rearview mirror and see that I've disappeared, don't take it personally."

He nodded. "That'll work."

He kept a steady speed on our ride from the outskirts to downtown Charlotte, and when we were separated by other cars, he was careful not to leave me stranded at a traffic light. Meanwhile, I tried not to make it obvious that I was freshening up my makeup. At various stoplights, I dabbed my oily forehead and nose. Then, at a stop sign, I smoothed a fresh coat of pressed powder on my face and filled in my lips with a soft peach-tinted gloss that I'd gotten as a free gift at a department store makeup counter.

The dinner invitation had worked out in my favor. The Caesar salad I'd had for lunch had virtually disappeared, and my stomach had started to give me clues that it wanted something more filling. I hoped his special spot was worth the drive downtown.

I parallel parked behind Santana in front of a high-rise office building. Men and women in business suits flitted in and out of the tinted revolving doors. I waited until he exited his car to be sure this was the right place.

"We're here," Santana said. He'd peeled off his suit jacket and unbuttoned the top of his well-starched white dress shirt. "You didn't make a run for it, after all."

"I'm too hungry for that," I said with a grin.

"Then you won't be disappointed." He opened my door and held my hand while I stepped out of the car.

We entered the building, and the security guard at the front desk stood up as if the president of the United States had entered.

"Can you call up for me?" Santana asked.

"I've already got you covered, my man," the security guard said, clipping a walkie-talkie on his belt. "I'll take you up now."

We walked to a bank of elevators and waited for one to descend to the ground floor. When the doors slid open, three women exited, dressed in matching polo shirts with a company logo. *Casual Friday*, I thought. At the bank, we wore red shirts and khaki pants every other Friday. Thankfully, today wasn't one of those days.

The mirrored walls inside the elevator allowed me to check my appearance. At five feet eight inches, I was considered a little above average height for a woman, but I looked dwarfed standing beside Santana. He was probably six foot five and solid as a rock.

"Are you okay, Ms. Hudson?" he asked. He gave my shoulder a light squeeze with his big hand.

"Why so formal, Mr. Montgomery? Since I've followed you all the way down here, Santana, I think we can be on a first-name basis."

"I like how you say my name," Santana said. "Say it again."

I rolled my eyes and toyed with the curls around my face as I watched the numbered buttons light up with the elevator's ascent.

We didn't stop until we reached the rooftop, fifteen floors up. Santana was right about its being well-lit. The setting sun looked so close that I almost wanted to reach up and see if I could touch it.

It hadn't seemed that breezy when I'd stepped out of the car, but now the wind softly lifted my hair and blew it across my face. I peeled away a few strands that stuck to my lip gloss.

"You aren't saying much," Santana said.

"Because I'm in awe," I said, surveying the setup.

There was a single table for two covered in a white tablecloth that flapped in the wind. In the center was a square glass vase filled with purple flowers. Nearby, a server was waiting with a covered plate.

"You did all this on the chance I'd agree to follow you here?" I asked. "You took a big risk."

"I don't mind taking risks," Santana said. "You never know unless you try."

"And if I hadn't come?"

Santana took my hand and led me slowly toward the table. I was willing to enjoy the scenic view of the rooftops and the other buildings that towered around this one, but I didn't want to go anywhere near the edge. He'd done good getting me up this high.

"If you'd turned me down, I would've eaten alone," he said with confidence. "Good food is good food, even when you're by yourself. But of course, it's always better to have someone to share it with, as well as for conversation."

Santana pulled out my chair, and once I'd sat down, he seated himself across from me. The server uncovered the plate to reveal a platter of stuffed mushrooms. *Heaven!* I could eat stuffed mushrooms every day.

"Would you believe, I love stuffed mushrooms?" I asked, forgetting that I was fifteen floors up.

"So, my choice was on point?"

"Bull's-eye," I said.

"That's only the beginning," Santana said.

And that was the first day of our whirlwind romance.

⌒

Had I known the Santana then that I knew now, I never would have taken that trip up the elevator. I couldn't have fathomed that the man who'd wined and dined me would pound, shove, and push me against the walls so hard that I'd puncture the Sheetrock.

That's why I'd been so slow to trust anybody of the opposite sex again. Even so, I was disappointed but not surprised when two days passed, and Levi still hadn't called me. I'd thought our conversation was intriguing enough for a second call. I'd figured we'd hit it off enough to warrant another conversation. At least, he'd acted that way. It just proved what I'd always known—that women could never tell what men were thinking, and vice versa. Women made big deals out of small things; men made small deals out of big things.

"Ma," Devin said, "here's the letter I want you to send to Dad. I finally finished it." He handed me two folded pieces of paper. They were covered from front to back with his microscopic handwriting. It looked like little ants crawling across the page.

"Okay, baby. I'll take care of it tomorrow."

"Are you mad at me for writing to him?"

"Of course not," I assured him again. No matter how many times he asked, and regardless of how I was feeling at any given moment, I would never disrespect Santana in front of him. I had my moments when I questioned every choice I'd made and beat myself up for letting him suck the life out of me, but those were the times that I crawled into God's arms. I cried and let Him dry my tears.

I knew Devin still battled conflicting feelings. It would be that way, his therapist had said. I was supposed to help him direct his emotions and work through them, instead of telling him how he ought to feel. Santana had been a wonderful father—I couldn't take that away from him, regardless of the abuse. I could, however, make sure that the ugly dragon of abuse wouldn't rear its head in my son. So far, it hadn't, and I prayed it never would.

I briefly scanned the letter. *Schoolwork.* Devin talked mostly about how social studies was the most boring subject ever. *Football.* He couldn't wait for the first game. The practices were more intense than anything he'd ever done in baseball, but he was going to stick it out this first year because he didn't want to be a quitter.

That was part of the case, but I also knew football players were some of the more popular kids at his middle school. I always encouraged Devin to be his own man—a leader instead of a follower—but I had to loosen his reins enough for him to feel his own way through his new school. Until now, he'd been with the same friends, in the same neighborhood, his entire life.

I refolded the letter and stuck it in the top drawer of my nightstand. Devin stretched across the foot of my bed while I studied my online consultant's catalog, with the intention of ordering a new inventory of self-defense products. I didn't have any future workshops booked, but I had some leads to follow up on.

Devin flipped over on his back and stared at the ceiling. "Ma, do you think you'll ever get married again?"

I stopped and looked at him.

"I was just thinking about it one day. I think it would make you happy."

"Right now, I'm happy with just you and me," I said. "You're my main focus right now. But if I happen to meet someone I like—and who likes me—I wouldn't take things a step further until I was sure you were okay with it. Is that really what you're worried about?"

"Nope. I was just curious," Devin said. He'd propped one foot on top of his other knee and was now intent on pulling sock lint from between his toes.

Boys.

"It's getting late," I said. "Go ahead and take your shower so you can get that toe jam off my bed." I used my feet to give him a little push that catapulted him off the bed. He hit the floor with a thump.

"Ouch," he said, cradling his shoulder as he flopped back and forth like fish out of water.

Where was his Oscar? He was pure drama.

"You get hit harder than that on the football field," I said, ignoring his theatrics. "Get up, boy."

"I'm just kidding," he said before doing some crazy karate-looking move to flip himself off the bedroom floor. "Is there anything you need from the bathroom before I shower?"

"Why?"

"Because I'm locking the door. I don't want you coming in."

I'll admit, I had a bad habit of going into the bathroom when Devin was in the shower. At least I always knocked first. Recently, he'd become more protective of his bathroom time. He didn't want me coming in at all, claiming he needed some personal space. *Please.* He could have all the personal space he wanted when he had a personal bank account to pay his personal bills.

"I already know what you have," I yelled after him. "I changed your diapers and cleaned your bottom, remember?"

That didn't sway him one bit. He was starting to sprout hair—and I don't mean just on his chin. And girls? The last time I'd picked Devin up from football practice, one of the cheerleaders had been swarming around him in short shorts and a tank top. The only innocent-looking thing about her was the high ponytail on her head, tied with a yellow bow with blue polka dots. I had locked her face in my memory.

Devin lifted his shirt and started to examine his stomach. I didn't know what he was looking for. A six-pack? Maybe it was in there somewhere, it just hadn't been taken out of the bag yet. I did notice, however, that his arm muscles were becoming more defined.

"Ma," Devin said, flexing his bicep, "Coach Johnson is having a cookout for the team at his house on Sunday after church. Can I go?"

"I haven't heard anything about it," I said.

"He said he would send out an e-mail this evening."

I picked up my phone and pulled up my e-mail. It was the first message at the top of my inbox, sent about fifteen minutes prior. I opened it and read the details with Devin peering over my shoulder.

"See?" he said. "From three to six. We can go to church, come home and change, and then you can drop me off later at Coach's house. Everybody is going to be there. Coach Johnson is the youth pastor at his church, and some of my teammates go there with their families. He's safe, Ma."

"Unfortunately, Devin, just because somebody is a minster at a church or works with a team of students doesn't mean he's safe to be around. And I'm not just talking about Coach Johnson. That goes for anybody."

Any news station could confirm that fact. Just yesterday, they'd run a story about a minister in Boston who'd been molesting the children under his care for years. I was angered and disgusted. If it could happen in Boston, it could happen in Greensboro. No city was an exception to the rule.

By the look on his face, Devin's hopes had deflated.

"I'll think about it," I told him.

"Alright," he said, his shoulders still slumped. "I'm getting in the shower."

Devin had barely gotten the water running when my cell phone rang. I recognized the number as Levi's. *Perfect timing.* I could've answered on the first ring, but I didn't want to give the impression that I'd been waiting for his call, even if I had been.

"Quinn?"

"The one and only," I said. "How are you, Levi?"

"Tired," he said. "How's your week been going?"

I could hear the drain in his voice.

"Regular week," I said. "Same old, same old."

He sighed. "I wish I could say the same. There must have been a full moon, because Greensboro has gone nuts."

"Really?" I said. "I don't make a habit of watching the local news unless I'm checking the weather forecast, so I have no idea what's been going on in the city."

"I don't blame you. I don't know where you live, but the problems probably haven't been on your side of the city. They've been concentrated in one of the rougher parts of town. You'd be surprised how quickly a small argument can set off a chain reaction of foolishness."

I wasn't surprised at all. Unbeknownst to him, I'd lived it. I'd triggered Santana's chain reactions of anger by doing simple things like accidentally leaving the milk on the counter overnight or mistakenly putting an empty glass jar in the trash instead of the recycle bin.

In the background, I heard banging around, maybe of pots and pans in the kitchen. Lots of banging.

"But I didn't call to talk about the Greensboro Police Department," Levi said. "I wanted to see if you'd like to get together on Sunday afternoon. I'm not quite sure what we'll do, but I'll think of something by then."

"I'd love to," I said without a second thought. My mind hadn't even processed the question.

"Well, that was a lot easier than last time," Levi said. "I'll have to thank the Mae sisters for whatever they slipped in your food."

"Maybe that's what it was," I said. "I'd better stay away from that place."

"I don't know…I saw how you were eating those shrimp and grits. That's going to be hard to do."

"What can I say? I'm a sister who loves good food."

Things couldn't have lined up better with the football coach having his cookout this Sunday. Devin would be thrilled that I was going to let him attend. He had Levi to thank for that.

"I can swing by and pick you up, if you'd like," he offered.

"I don't like to let strangers know where I live," I told him. I wasn't sure how he'd received it, but I was serious.

"I can't blame you for that. In fact, you *should* be wary like that. But the more time we spend together, the less of a stranger I'll be."

For the past two years, my prayer had been for God to help me protect my heart. It was in His care, under lock and key, and only a man after God's own heart would have access. I wasn't saying that Levi was that man. I wasn't saying that there was a relationship brewing between us. But I had realized that I was finally open to love again. Love didn't come without chances. Love didn't come until you were willing to open up your life—sometimes to a stranger.

"Your son is more than welcome to come along," Levi said. "Maybe we'll grab some sandwiches and have a picnic at the park. I can bring my football and throw it around with him."

Even though it was a nice idea for an outing, I still wasn't ready to take that step with Devin.

"It just so happens that Devin has a cookout to attend with his teammates this Sunday," I said. "It starts at three o'clock. After I drop him off, I can meet you, around three thirty. You let me know the place."

"Sounds good," Levi said. There was more banging and the sound of water running, which made it hard for me to hear him. "You should think about visiting Grace Temple on Sunday. Service starts at eleven."

"The thought had crossed my mind. I just might do that."

"Maybe I'll see you there," Levi said. "In the meantime, I'll let you know where to meet me by Saturday."

"That works for me," I said.

We said good night, and after our call, I felt better about Levi than I had ever since Ginger's discouraging comments at the gym.

I folded up the letter Devin had written to his father and addressed the front of a pre-stamped envelope. I'd already memorized the address of the penitentiary and his inmate number. Every now and then, I wondered if Santana felt any remorse. I mean, if he really felt it with a repentant heart, not just as a rehearsed speech he'd presented to the judge. He'd been confined from the outside world before, while serving sentences for drug possession and distribution, but that didn't mean jail was something a person ever got used to. He hadn't had a son before. He hadn't had people who appreciated and depended on him.

We'd been one year into our marriage when I found out about Santana's drug history. He hadn't only sold drugs but had used them, too. I believed

Santana when he told me that that part of his life was over. I guess the demons had returned and were too strong for him to fight. When I was packing to make the move to Greensboro, I'd discovered what he'd probably been looking for *that* night—a bag of cocaine.

Drug addiction didn't just change the life of the addict; it changed the life of everyone around him. I knew firsthand, for my father had fought the same demons. My grandmother—God rest her soul—had cried many tears for the sake of her son. It was only her prayers that had sustained her, even after my father had died. She was the one who had taught me how to pray. And she had always stressed the importance of praying for my enemies.

So, that night, before I fell asleep, I prayed for Santana.

11

I remember this church," Devin said as we pulled into the parking lot of Grace Temple on Sunday morning. "This is where we came to when you did your last self-defense class."

Devin had been the most delightful person to be around ever since Friday night, when I'd told him that he could attend the cookout at Coach Johnson's. On Saturday morning, he'd voluntarily vacuumed the entire apartment, loaded the dishwasher, and cleaned his football equipment out on the patio balcony, all without my having to ask. I was beginning to think I should let him out of the house more often.

"Hey, Ma—there's that police officer that almost gave you a ticket," Devin said as we entered the building. "What was his name again?"

"Mr. Levi," I told him. My heart raced at the sight of him, but I tried to look and act as casually as possible. Levi didn't seem to have noticed us, so I steered Devin in the opposite direction.

"Let's go find a seat on this side," I said, nudging him to the right doors of the sanctuary.

"But don't you want to go and say hey?" Devin asked, looking over his shoulder.

"No, I'm fine. We're here for the service; plus, he's busy talking to someone. Maybe we'll run into him after church is over."

"I hope so. He's pretty cool. And I want to let him see that I don't always wear pink shirts."

I playfully popped him on the back of his head, and a woman passing by said, "I had to give my son one of those this morning, only I wasn't playing."

I grinned at her. "They need one every now and then, don't they?"

"Ma," Devin said with a tone of surprise. "You don't know that woman. She might think you're crazy."

"Mamas understand each other," I told him. "Every mama has a little drop of crazy in her. We need it to do deal with our children."

A wide smile spread across Devin's face. "So that explains it."

I popped him again.

The service at Grace Temple turned out to be more than I'd expected. The praise and the sermon alike lifted me to a high place of worship. I could see why Levi had joined on his third visit. If this was the usual Sunday-morning worship, I wouldn't want to miss a single service.

Before Pastor Jones began his sermon, he dismissed all children age eleven and older who wanted to attend the youth ministry service in the multipurpose room. I nudged Devin's knee.

"I can go?" he asked incredulously.

"Go ahead. I'll meet you there afterward."

"Cool," he said, standing up without hesitation. He probably wanted to leave before I changed my mind. I'd let out his leash a little bit more. It wasn't as scary as I'd thought.

I never saw Levi during the church service, but I didn't intentionally look for him. I knew he'd be a distraction to me, no fault of his own. When my eyes weren't steadied on the pulpit area, I stared at the hair of the woman in front of me and contemplated telling her about the small piece of lint stuck behind her ear. I made it through the service without flicking it off.

After the service, I filed out with the rest of the congregants and stopped briefly at a kiosk decorated with purple balloons, where I picked up a flyer about an upcoming women's retreat in the Blue Ridge Mountains. It had been years since I'd been to the mountains. Then I followed a stream of parents back to the multipurpose room, where our children were herded together by age group like packs of buffalo.

The voices of children and parents competed with the surround sound of the Christian rap videos playing on the giant screens around the room. In one corner, a group was dancing and had started their sanctified version of a soul train. The scene took be back to my high-school dances, when I'd been known for my skills in recreating any and every move from the popular music videos. Not only could I freestyle, but it was easy for me to learn the choreographed steps of Janet Jackson, one of my favorite entertainers at the time. *These kids don't know a thing about real dancing,* I thought.

I looked for Devin's bright yellow polo shirt and blue slacks, and finally found him in a smaller group, chatting in another corner. And right behind him was the girl whose face I'd locked in my memory. Again, her hair was gathered in a thick, flowing ponytail, this time tied with a light pink ribbon that matched the pastel floral-print dress that fell just above her slightly bowed knees. She wore a single strand of pearls around her neck and small pearl stud earrings. She looked like she'd walked straight off the prairie. I still had my eyes on her. Tomorrow she'd be back in short shorts again.

Noticing me, Devin waved, then said something to the group. The cheerleader leaned in and gave him a quick hug from the side before he jogged over to me.

"How was it?" I asked.

"They had music videos and a step team, and we connected by video chat with a man in South Korea."

"Wow," I said. "I guess that means you liked it."

"I definitely want to come back here," he said. "They even asked some Bible trivia challenge questions. Guess who was one of the winners." He pulled a Chick-fil-A gift card out of his pocket.

"Way to go!" I said. I wasn't surprised. From the time he was old enough to attend church with the adults, Devin had always paid close attention to the messages. He didn't come just to socialize, even though he liked that, too. Every year for Christmas, I gave him an age-appropriate devotional book. He read from it every night.

"Did you see anybody you knew?"

"Yep. Dylan and Heaven were there, and they're in my class. And I know Payton because she's a cheerleader."

"Now which one was Payton?" I asked innocently.

"She had on a dress," Devin answered.

That about narrows it down, I wanted to say. If I hadn't known who it was already, it would've been like pulling teeth to get a more detailed description from him.

"Do you talk to her a lot?"

He shrugged. "Not that much. I only see her after football practice, when everybody is waiting to get picked up. She's in Mrs. Ortiz's class."

"Oh, okay," I said, done with my digging for now. "Is there anything you want to do before we go home? We have a while before it's time to go to Coach Johnson's."

"You cooked lunch, right?"

I nodded. "I put beef stroganoff in the Crock-Pot late last night. It should be done when we get home."

"Oh, there's Officer Gray again," Devin pointed out. He called out to Levi before I had a chance to protest. Levi turned at the sound of his name.

Wow, what a work of art, I thought as he approached us. I knew I'd been wise not to seek him out during the service. I would've forgotten all about the reason for being there.

"What's up, Devin?" Levi said, giving Devin a high five. "I almost didn't recognize you without the pink shirt. You look sharp. Pants pulled up, no underwear showing—I like that."

"My mama doesn't play that way," Devin said.

"Good mama," Levi said. He turned to me. "Nice to see you again, Quinn."

"You as well," I said. It felt so strange to act like we hadn't crossed paths since the Friday Night Love presentation. I knew that he hated Chinese food, that he had stuttered until he was ten years old, and that fabric softener made his skin itch. He knew that I couldn't stand the taste of any red drinks, that I flossed and brushed religiously (and had never had a cavity), and that I'd been a latchkey kid.

"How did you all enjoy the service?" Levi asked.

"I want to come back for sure," Devin said.

I nodded. "We'll definitely be back."

"Great. Pastor Jones's messages always hit the nail on the head. He's a phenomenal teacher." Levi stuck his hand in his pocket and jiggled some change. "I'm headed out before the traffic gets too crazy. It can be a beast getting out of the parking lot, and I have plans later on today."

Levi's words sent a warm rush through me.

"Me, too," Devin said, "at three, so we have to roll out, too."

"Enjoy your day," Levi said. "I'll see you again." Our eyes met. "Soon."

He did not just do that. I glanced over to see if Devin had noticed, but his attention had been consumed with Payton, who was walking across the parking lot.

"Ready, Devin?"

Levi and I were parked on the same row but at opposite ends. He drove past us, impressing Devin with his shiny, expensive-looking rims.

"That looks kind of like Mr. Marvin's truck," Devin said. "That's the kind of truck I want when I get my license."

"And who do you think is going to buy you something like that?" I asked with a little laugh. "Not only do you need your license, but you need a job to make car payments and cover gas and insurance."

"But you said you'd do anything for me, Ma. You say it all the time."

"Let me clarify," I said, starting the car. "I mean that I will sacrifice whatever it takes to make sure you have everything you need to live—the necessities. Maybe you should think more along the lines of a ten-year-old car with good gas mileage."

"Don't worry about it, Ma. I'll take care of it. I've got faith."

"Well, faith will take you a long way," I said. Who was I to crush his dream?

I pulled up to our gated apartment complex and swiped the card for entry. It wasn't the four-thousand-square-foot home that I'd been accustomed to for ten years, but square footage in a home meant nothing if you didn't have peace there.

I'd barely shifted the car into park when Devin jumped out.

"I have my key," he said.

I took my time strolling up the flight of steps to the second floor. I didn't have much to do other than change my clothes. Late last night, Levi had sent me a text message telling me to dress comfortably, so I had a feeling we were going to do the park thing. That was fine with me.

Maybe he'd eventually ask me out somewhere that would require my getting glammed up. I had several outfits in my closet with no place to wear them except church.

Devin basically shoved his lunch down his throat, then disappeared into his bedroom. I stretched out on the couch to watch a movie, but it wasn't long before the movie was watching me doze.

"It's time to go, Ma," Devin said, lightly tapping me on my shoulder.

I stretched and stood.

Devin handed me my car keys. "Do you know how to get there?"

To say my son was anxious would be an understatement. "No worries, baby. I know where the Johnsons live. What's in the bag?" I asked, noticing that he was carrying the duffel he'd gotten when he'd signed up for football.

"Swim trunks and a towel. Jared said Coach Johnson has a pool."

Devin could swim like a fish. I'd started him with "Mommy and Me" swim classes when he was six months old, and from that point on, it had been hard to get him out of the water. It was probably the reason he took thirty-minute showers. Nevertheless, I usually liked to be around when he was swimming. Sometimes, in his overconfidence in the water, Devin wasn't as cautious as he should be.

"The only way I'm letting you get in that pool is if you follow the rules, and you know what they are: No horseplay. No diving in the shallow end. Respect the water. And if an emergency comes up, remember, you are not a trained lifeguard. Call an adult for help. I don't care how good a swimmer you think you are."

"Yes, ma'am," Devin said. He was rocking back and forth with impatience.

"Give me a minute," I said.

Devin slumped on the couch as I went to give myself a final once-over in the mirror. I traded out my silver hoop earrings for some small silver ball studs and slipped my feet into a pair of braided sandals. I wasn't quite ready to give in to cooler temperatures, and thankfully the first days of fall were still cooperating.

"Ma, I'm going to wait in the car," Devin called out.

I spritzed some body splash down my arms, on my neck, and across my shoulders. I wanted to smell good, but I didn't want to have to fight off gnats, if my assumption about the park was correct. For good measure, I sprinkled some baby powder down the inside front of my shirt—one of Grandma's tricks to keep things fresh and dry—and headed out the door.

I walked Devin to Coach Johnson's front door, then went inside to do my personal investigation of the place where my son would be spending the next three hours. The Johnsons' house was amazing—hardwood floors, high ceilings, and the best in furniture and home décor. Other than impromptu parents' meetings on the football bleachers, I hadn't had much interaction with Coach Johnson's wife, Tricia. She was a firecracker in the best way. She had spunk, charm, and hospitality.

"You should stay and hang out with us," Tricia tried to convince me. "The boys are so much fun. And when the testosterone gets to be too much, I slip downstairs to hide, turn on a chick flick, and savor a bowl of macaroni and cheese." She gave my triceps a gentle squeeze. "But then again, it looks like macaroni and cheese hasn't touched your lips in years."

I laughed. "Please. I love mac and cheese. Three-cheese, as a matter of fact. But I enjoy everything in moderation."

"Well, that's good, because we have more than enough," Tricia said. She heaped several scoops of macaroni and cheese into a takeout container. It would be enough for me and Devin for the entire week, but I didn't object. I didn't even mumble a word, except for "Thanks," as she filled another container with baked beans, then wrapped up some beef ribs. She stacked the containers inside a gift bag and tied the handles shut with a red ribbon.

"Are you sure you don't want to stay?" she asked me.

"No, it's best that I leave," I said. "Devin needs some space. And besides, he's been eyeing me for the last fifteen minutes."

"They all do. Don't worry, he's in good hands." She lowered her voice. "I act like I'm washing dishes and cleaning up in here, but I'm being nosey. I know who they're talking to, what they're talking about, and who's doing what."

"I feel better knowing I'm not the only snooping parent," I told her, then picked up my bag of food, grateful that Devin would be fed for the rest of the week. "Thanks again for the food. I'll be back at six, if not before."

"Do you just want to leave the food here?" Tricia asked. "I can keep it in the extra fridge downstairs."

"That'd be great," I said. I realized I didn't want the stuff sitting in my warm car all afternoon.

Tricia saw me to the front door. "Go do something nice for yourself."

"I think I will," I said with a smile.

12

The spread Levi brought out at the park was nowhere near as homemade as the food lined up on the Johnsons' counter, but the turkey subs, diced cantaloupe, and bags of baked chips were just as thoughtful. He'd even taken the time to arrange two quilts in the bed of his truck. And to top it off, he put in a mix CD and rolled down his windows so that we could enjoy some of his favorite sounds.

"Nice music," I remarked.

Levi wiped his mouth with a napkin and finished swallowing a gargantuan bite of his sub before answering. "Roman—Zenja's husband—gave me this CD of his band."

"Definitely keep me posted the next time they play in the area," I told him. "I'd love to check them out."

When we'd finished eating, Levi jumped off the back of his truck and opened the cab door. He unfolded some black fabric about the size of a sheet for a full-sized bed and spread it on a concrete slab nearby. I had no idea what he had in mind.

"Don't ask just yet," he said, seeing my puzzled expression.

I watched Levi line up four paint trays in the grass, then filled each one with a different color—red, yellow, orange, and blue. I rested my arms on the side of the truck bed and watched him whistle and work. Finally I got it. We were going to paint.

Levi walked over and held out his hand to help me out of the back of the truck. "I'm going to roll up your pant legs," he said. He didn't wait for my permission but bent down and turned up the cuffs of my light beige khakis until they were midway up my calves. I was so glad I'd shaved my legs that morning.

"And now your shoes," he said, slipping off my sandals. "Nice toes."

"Thank you," I said. I believed in regular pedicures. They were the little thing I did for myself once a month.

"Last week, you told me you like to dance."

"I did?"

"Yes, you did." Levi set my shoes on the truck bed.

"Must've been the Mae sisters' food again," I said. "I don't remember telling you that."

"Do you remember telling me you like to paint?" He was pulling off his socks and shoes now.

"That I do remember."

"We're going to do both. We're going to paint-dance." Then Levi steered me by the shoulders over to the paint trays.

"I've never heard of such a thing," I said.

"I made it up. I was trying to think of something different." Levi stepped one of his feet into the tray of orange paint, the other in the blue. I followed suit, stepping into the pans of red and yellow. The paint felt like slime as it squished between my toes.

"How are we going to get this off our feet?" I couldn't help but ask. I guess it was the mother in me. I was always one step ahead.

"I've got it handled," Levi said.

"Okay. If you say so."

"You trust me?"

"What other choice do I have?" I asked, my feet still in the paint trays.

Levi laughed as he helped me step out of the paint. This time, he didn't let go of my hands but led me from the edge of the canvas to the middle, our footprints making a colorful trail behind us. Then we walked the perimeter of the canvas, and I let him lead the dance, serenaded by Roman's band.

Our feet painted patterns across the span of blank canvas. The music slowed, causing us to change our rhythm, but we kept our bodies a safe distance apart. We were adults with hormones and feelings, but I could tell he valued his relationship with God as much as I valued mine.

Few words passed between us. In the distance, a man kicked a red ball back and forth with a young boy, and two little girls were involved in a game of tag. They squealed in delight as they ran in circles, around and around and around.

That's when Levi held my hand above my head and twirled me around. "Are you alright?" he asked.

"Perfect," I replied.

But I'd spoken too soon.

It was only an instrumental song, but I recognized it from the first chord. No matter how it was played—strummed on a guitar, whined across a violin, or pecked on a piano—the memories it evoked sent my body into a shiver. The words started to sing through my head.

"*Amazing Grace, how sweet the sound, that saved a wretch like me….*"

I gently pulled away from Levi and walked off the canvas. The dry blades of grass pushed themselves between my toes. Tears tried to escape my eyes, but I willed them not to.

"What happened?" Levi asked, coming to my side. "Did I do something wrong?"

"No, it's not you at all," I assured him. I rubbed my hands down my arms, which were covered in goose bumps, and turned my back to him, facing an oak tree that provided shade to a small swing set.

"Do you want to go sit on the truck?"

"No, I'm fine here. It's the song. It caught me off guard."

"'Amazing Grace'?" Levi asked, confusion in his voice.

I turned to face him, and for whatever reason, I saw safety in his eyes. They pulled my secrets out of me like a tug-of-war…and his eyes were winning.

"My ex-husband used to play this song every Sunday morning when we were getting ready for church. Everything had to be in a certain order. I made sure his suit, shirt, socks, and shoes were ready for the service. I tied his tie the way he wanted it. He made breakfast for Devin and me, but sometimes he wouldn't serve me the same thing he and Devin ate. It depended on whether he thought I was looking fat."

Levi rubbed his hands down the sides of my arms.

I shook my head. "I don't want to mess up our Sunday and what you had planned."

"Please talk," Levi said. "You need to talk about it."

I couldn't bring myself to tell him the worst of it. "For years, I put up a façade for the entire church. He was the pastor's right-hand man, and our lives were supposed to be perfect. But nothing could have been further from the truth."

"I'm sorry," Levi said.

Levi left my side again, and after a moment, the music stopped. Tunes began to rage in my head with the words that Santana would scream as he landed each blow: *"You're an idiot." "Nobody wants you but me." "You think you want to leave me? And go where? You have nothing."*

"Don't turn off the music," I told him. "Just play something else."

So he did. Then he walked back across the canvas, leaving a single trail of orange-and-blue footprints. I could tell he didn't know what to say, so he just hugged me. He hugged me like a big brother hugs his little sister in pain. I didn't have to worry about the lack of space between us, because the only feeling I had rising in me was security.

"You need a new Sunday morning song," Levi said. "A song that God puts in your heart."

He took me back to the paint trays, and I stepped in the red and yellow again.

"You should dance alone," Levi said. "I'm not even going to watch you."

He crossed to the other side of his truck, and once I realized that he really wasn't going to join me, I allowed myself to feel the music.

My first steps felt cautious, but the more I moved my hips, lifted my hands, and ran my feet across the canvas, the more comfortable I became. A breeze picked up around me. The aroma of the world rushed into my nose— the grass, the flowers. It's hard to explain, but I even smelled the pureness of the air. The music lifted me up and carried me to the place where I'd been during worship that very morning.

I hugged myself and tilted my head, letting the sun shine on my face. I swayed back and forth to the sounds of a saxophone. I added a soft sway to my hips as the drums tapped with the tune. The trumpet made me swirl, and the piano set my arms free.

I danced like no one was looking. And soon, even if Levi was watching, or if the man with the kickball and the two little girls playing tag all stopped to stare at me, I didn't care.

13

LEVI

Levi wanted to protect Quinn. He *needed* to protect Quinn. Especially now that he knew who she was. He'd always thought her face was slightly familiar, her son's even more so. And he'd finally realized why.

It had been a Sunday, now that he thought about it. He'd sat on the front porch with Devin while the paramedics attended to Quinn and another police officer dragged her husband to the patrol car. He hadn't been happy that the men in black had broken down his door and rescued his wife from his wrath. He'd cursed out everyone as he'd passed, even the neighbors who'd dared to emerge from their houses because of their alarm. It hadn't seemed like the kind of neighborhood that was used to flashing blue lights and wailing ambulance interrupting their daily lives. That Sunday evening, they had discovered the truth.

Two years prior

"Do you have a video game or something you can play with?" Levi asked the young boy.

"I don't feel like playing anything," he said without lifting his head, his eyes shielded by a baseball cap. The boy had been questioned by Levi's fellow officers. From what Levi had gathered, he'd secretly called 9-1-1, then held his own father at gunpoint until help had arrived.

"How old are you, young man?" Levi asked.

"I'll be ten in three weeks."

"Do you have big plans for your birthday?"

"I did. But I don't think it will happen now."

Levi could've kicked himself. That was the wrong question to ask. "Stay here," he told him. "I'll be right back."

Levi stepped through the broken doorframe and into the house. Every light had been turned on, aggravating his headache. He was fatigued from all the action on his shifts the last few days. The City of Charlotte was going crazy. He'd been looking into joining the police department of one of the surrounding cities but hadn't yet made up his mind about where he wanted to move. That was the good thing about not being tied down—he could pick up and move whenever he felt like it. He'd been in Charlotte for eight years. It was time for a change of scenery.

Officer Stevens was still inside, looking over his report. Things could've been worse. The first officers on the scene had tried—unsuccessfully—to get the boy to drop the gun he'd held on his father. One bullet would've changed everyone's lives. It was only his mother's voice that had finally prompted him to release the weapon.

Levi wandered back outside, where he noticed a baseball and two leather mitts in the side yard. He picked up the larger glove and put it on. One of his homeboys played in the Major Leagues, and that was the only reason Levi watched the game from time to time.

"Wanna toss the ball?" Levi asked.

The young boy lifted his head. "Sure." He jumped up as if launched by an invisible button and clambered down the porch steps.

Not sure of the boy's skills, Levi tossed the ball underhand. When the boy returned it with an overhand throw, Levi figured he wasn't timid with the baseball.

"Am I going to jail for holding that gun on my dad?"

"Nope," Levi assured him. "You're not."

"I just wanted him to stop. I thought he was going to kill my mom. I've never seen it that bad before."

"Does your dad hit your mom a lot?" Levi asked.

The boy wasn't quick to answer, as if he was unsure whether what he said would be held against him or might make matters worse. He threw the ball at Levi with enough speed to hit his glove with a slap.

"My mama looked like she was dying," the boy said. He rubbed his face with his forearm, and although Levi couldn't see his features fully in the cloak of darkness, he knew the boy was wiping away tears.

Levi noticed a woman being rolled out of the house on a gurney, and he purposefully threw the baseball over the boy's head so he'd have to search for it, as a distraction.

"Someone named Marvin is coming to pick up the boy, per his mother's instructions," Officer Stevens came over to say. "She refuses to leave in the ambulance until she knows her son is safely with this man. He's supposed to be on his way."

"She's beat up pretty bad?" Levi asked.

"The fool tried to choke her with a belt," Officer Stevens said. "If her son hadn't gotten the gun, she could've been leaving here in a body bag."

"And in front of his son?" Levi shook his head. "I don't get it. I know everybody has his own demons, but I just don't get it."

"I don't, either." Office Stevens clicked his ballpoint pen and stuck it in his front pocket. "She wants to see him. Take him over for me, will you?"

Levi summoned the boy and put a gentle hand on his shoulder as he walked him to the ambulance. The woman's face was swollen on one side, and there were deep, bloody welts across her neck. Levi had seen the signs of strangulation before.

Her husband hadn't left unscathed, however. She'd clawed skin off his face, leaving a red river of blood on his cheeks, as if he'd had a bad encounter with a cat. Served him right. The woman had finally mustered the bravery to fight back. Levi just hoped she wouldn't return to her abuser, like so many women did.

⟋

Based on what he knew of Quinn's life right now, she hadn't gone back. And she never would. The circle of life had brought that battered woman into his world again.

Levi dumped the paint trays in a black garbage bag, twisted it shut, and carried it over to the brown trash receptacle by the covered pavilion nearby.

He added the bag to the remains of charcoal and crushed soda cans, probably from a recent cookout.

Speaking of cookouts, Levi had decided to invite Quinn over to Zenja and Roman's the following Sunday. She needed to get out of the house and meet some good, godly people who didn't have hidden agendas. Her attending Grace Temple today was a start. He'd noticed her across the sanctuary, worshipping God in a way that made her even more beautiful than she already was.

Levi was just getting to know Quinn, but the draw he felt toward her was undeniable. Her hands had felt so soft when he'd held them during their "paint-dance," and she smelled like an apple orchard. God knew he loved himself some apple pie.

He would go with the flow and let the chips fall as they may. What did he have to lose? A little pride? Part of his ego? He'd lost both before. It came with being a man.

After they'd cleaned their feet with the moist towelettes and old towels he'd brought along, they took a stroll down the bike path before Levi had to send Quinn on her way. She didn't want to be late picking up her son, and Levi could tell that she needed some time alone.

Sooner or later, he'd have to tell her that he remembered that day. It was the right thing to do. If she walked away from him out of embarrassment and chose never to speak to him again, then that was the chance he'd have to take. It was her choice; it was her life. From what she'd shared, she hadn't had much say over her life so far. It was about time she did.

As he drove away from the park, Levi called Roman using the Bluetooth in his truck.

"What's up, man?" Roman said when he answered the phone. "You're not out fighting crimes?"

"Not today," Levi said. "I thought I told you I'm off on Sundays and Mondays now. I know I shared it on the men's prayer call last week."

"Man, I was so sleepy last week, I couldn't wake myself up in time for that five-thirty call. I'm not a morning person, but I do what I can. Praying with all you knuckleheads has changed my life, that's for sure."

"Yours and mine both," Levi said. "I've been tired as a dog, too, but what choice do I have? Gotta eat, so I gotta work."

"Tell me about it," Roman said.

"Look, man, I'm not going to keep you, but I wanted to ask if I could bring a guest with me to the cookout at your house next Sunday."

"You know you don't have to ask me that. But, wait—is it a woman?"

Levi laughed. "Yes, it's a woman. Actually, it's Quinn Montgomery—the one who taught the self-defense class at the church a couple of weeks ago."

"I remember her. So, you're trying to make business into pleasure?"

"We've hung out a couple of times since then. Just kicked it. Nothing serious."

"You must see something in her, because you've never brought a woman over here since I've known you. In fact, you never say that much about who you're dating."

"Man, I've been too busy to date. The police department is my girlfriend, but that wouldn't be the case if your wife and Caprice had anything to do with it."

Roman groaned. "Those two are all about matchmaking. I told Zenja the only marriage business she needs to worry about is her own. Ticked her off. She really went off on me. She got over it, though. I had to show her that night how much she meant to me."

"You like walking on thin ice, don't you?" Levi asked with a chuckle.

"Sometimes I make her mad and I don't even know what I did. Sometimes she does the same thing to me. Part of the reason we argue is because we're so much alike. But there's no way on God's earth I could live without her."

Levi knew the story of Roman's infidelity and the war he'd waged inside himself to make things right. An innocent conversation about six months ago had turned into an all-out marriage counseling session one night at Caprice and Duane's. Despite what he and Zenja had been through, they'd come out of the fire without the smell of smoke, as old folks used to say.

Whenever Levi was around Zenja and Roman, he admired the way they interacted. She would make up his plate at mealtime, not because she had to but because she wanted to. He would leave his spot on the comfortable couch if he'd anticipated a need of hers, or simply to check on her for no other reason than to see if she was alright. Their love was reciprocal. He'd messed up, and he'd said he would spend the rest of his life making it right if he had to. Levi had the feeling it wouldn't take an entire lifetime.

"Don't make a deal out of it to Zenja," Levi told Roman. "She'll make it more than it is."

"If you're bringing a woman over, then it's already more than it is, whether you admit or not."

"We're acquaintances, that's all. But she just moved here, and I know she needs some strong, godly women in her life. The only person she hangs out with is her son."

"Where'd she move from?"

"Charlotte. Like me."

"Cool. Well, she's welcome, and I'm not saying a thing to Zenja," Roman assured him. "She'll find out when she opens the door."

It was all about open doors right now with Levi. If Quinn would give him the opportunity, he was walking into her life.

14

Fate has a way of lining things up just right. Had I gone shopping for skirts on Tuesday instead of on Wednesday, like I'd originally intended, I may have never met Zenja, been invited to Friday Night Love, or been stopped for speeding by Officer Leviticus Gray. I'd never been so thankful for a warning citation in my life. I haven't had a man on my mind since my whirlwind romance with Santana at the age of twenty-two, when I thought I knew what love was about. Now, at thirty-five years old, I'd never imagined I'd have a crush. But Levi had taken over my thoughts since I'd left the park, and even though it was time for bed, he was still holding a coup d'état in my head. I couldn't help it. Any woman would find herself thinking about the man who'd just had her dancing with paint on her feet and then had washed them off afterward. *Lord Jesus, help me.*

This was one occasion when I wished I had a girlfriend to call. There had been a time when I would've phoned Rasheedah, Ty, or E'Lyse, the other three friends who made up what we called the Fabulous Four. After I had gushed about my little park outing, Rasheedah, the hopeless romantic, would have made me recount every move and every conversation with Levi, word for word. Ty would have demanded I find out about his medical history, his career status, and the state of his financial portfolio before I let my heart get too far into it. And E'Lyse…oh, E'Lyse. I'd always thought she was destined to be single forever. If there was something wrong with a man, she'd find it. And if she couldn't find anything, she'd concoct something. She was the type of women who said, "Jesus is the only man I need," and actually meant it. The last I'd heard through the grapevine, almost seven years ago, E'Lyse was planning her wedding, engaged to an HVAC repairman. I missed those girls, but Santana had driven such a wedge

between us, and sparked so many arguments, that the breach was probably irreparable.

Devin walked in the kitchen to say good night. I loved how he smelled
when he first emerged from the shower—clean. Fresh. It was no wonder he
used up so many bars of soap and bottles of shampoo.

"Going to Coach's house was the most fun I've had since I've been here,"
Devin told me.

"Good," I said, trying not to stare at him and make him self-conscious.

Devin's chin was dotted with small white spots of a benzoyl peroxide
cream I'd given him to fight the tiny adolescent bumps that had been popping up on his face. He may have been all boy, but he was still vain. He'd
gotten that from Santana.

"Thank you for letting me go," he said.

"You're welcome. And both of us are going to start getting out more," I
said, testing the waters.

"That's a good idea. You probably get bored hanging out with me all the
time, anyway."

"No, I love spending time with you. Do you get bored spending time
with me?"

Devin looked at me, then turned away, as if by answering honestly he
would crush my feelings. That was answer of a response for me. I'd sheltered
the poor boy by trying to keep him so close under my wing.

"We have fun together, Ma," Devin said, tying the top of the full garbage
bag, "but it's good to do different things with different people."

"You're right," I said. I clicked on the light under the microwave above
the stove, then turned off the rest of the kitchen lights. Devin trailed me
down the hall to our bedrooms, which were almost directly across from
each other.

"Night, Ma," he said.

"Lights out by nine thirty," I told him. "Don't forget to wash that stuff
off your face."

"I'll wash it off in the morning," he said.

"You might want to take care of that now. I'd hate for you to have a hole
in your face in the morning," I joked.

I retired to my room, pushing the door closed enough for it to touch the frame but not to latch. I climbed in bed and kicked off the comforter. My Bible and the devotional book I'd been reading from every night were tucked under the pillow on the opposite side of the bed from where I slept. I had to put something in my head to meditate on besides the reality show that had sucked me in...and besides thoughts of Levi. With a combination like that, there's no telling what kind of dream I'd have.

I'd found that reading from the book of Psalms helped to put my mind at rest, so I flipped to Psalm 103, one of my favorite chapters. Not only were parts of it underlined in red, but other parts were highlighted in pink. I read verses one through five:

Bless the LORD, O my soul; and all that is within me, bless His holy name! Bless the LORD, O my soul, and forget not all His benefits: who forgives all your iniquities, who heals all your diseases, who redeems your life from destruction, who crowns you with lovingkindness and tender mercies, who satisfies your mouth with good things, so that your youth is renewed like the eagle's.

I laid the Bible on the pillow beside me, leaving it open to Psalm 103. If anyone's life had been redeemed from destruction, it was mine. I knew that when it was all said and done, my youth would be renewed like the eagle's. God would restore all the days that had been taken from me. Since leaving Charlotte, I already felt younger and more vivacious. Of course, some of it I credited with my workout regimen; but the biggest reason was purely God's grace. I was ready for the next step, and seeing how Devin was getting some of his extroverted spark back, he was, too.

I reached into the drawer of my bedside table and pulled out the cell phone I'd had when I'd lived in Charlotte. I never used it to make calls because I didn't want to chance being traced, but I'd decided to keep the number in the event that any of the few people I might want to stay in contact with would be able to access me, if necessary. I plugged in the phone to check it for messages when it crossed my mind, which ended up being every couple of weeks.

Initially, the voice mails I received were from former neighbors who'd noticed that I'd pulled a disappearing act once Devin hadn't returned to school. I could read Meredith Sewell like an open book—her message dripped with phony concern, and I knew she would report any and all information to the homeowners' association. Then there was Cheryl Danzey, the team mom for Devin's baseball league. She was probably more concerned with soliciting donations for sponsors, since Santana had been a major contributor. At least six months had passed since I'd last heard from Pastor Lloyd and his wife. The time between their calls had started to lengthen when they realized I wasn't going to return. I couldn't. Not right now. Their messages had always been lengthy and laden with scriptural encouragement for me to forgive Santana and assurances that, even in light of all that had happened, our marriage could be restored. I'd nearly choked the first time I'd heard that line.

No, thank you. I didn't doubt God's ability to restore marriages that had endured domestic abuse, but mine wasn't going to be one of them. The Lloyds knew only half the story—Santana's half. It wasn't worth my time to constantly relive the ten-year period over which he had broken me. I'd already done that with my attorney and in court.

The voice-mail icon lit the screen as soon as my cell phone powered up. One message was an automated woman's voice informing me that I'd won two round-trip tickets to a resort in Arizona; to claim my prize, all I had to do was call the number provided. *Delete.* The next message was from a woman whose voice I didn't recognize. She asked for me by my first and last name, then left a number where I could return her call. She didn't leave her own name, a company name, or a reference number. Fortunately for me, all our bank accounts had been in Santana's name, so I didn't have creditors and bill collectors harassing me after I abandoned the house. In fact, once I'd packed up all of Devin's belongings and hand-picked the personal items I'd be taking with me to start over, I'd gladly handed the keys over to Jerome, Santana's brother. Since then, Santana's business hadn't been mine to worry about.

That being said, my credit was virtually nonexistent, and I'd been approved to rent our apartment only because I'd paid six months' worth of rent in advance, and because the apartment leasing manager had said that something was telling her to trust me. I knew that it wasn't "something" but *Someone.* God's favor was doing more for me than I ever could've done for myself.

After trying two more times to place the voice of the unidentified woman, I decided to worry about it later. I floated off to sleep with no other thoughts except those about God's kindness toward me. Well, I won't deny that I also wondered when Levi would call me. I wouldn't have minded a second dance.

15

Devin and I had completed all our preparations for the coming week on Sunday night, but, as always, I felt like I'd turned into the school's student drop-off lane riding on two wheels. He'd have exactly four minutes to make it to his homeroom before he was counted tardy. It was always a battle for me to get Devin up and moving on Monday mornings, and the result was that I returned home in a frenzy. It took me a good hour, at least, to settle into my place of peace.

Today, I collapsed into my favorite love seat, positioned strategically near the patio door so it would get direct sunlight. I limited my breakfast to yogurt and a banana, since I knew I'd be helping Devin polish off the food I'd brought home from Coach Johnson's house. The mac and cheese was calling my name, so I'd already committed myself to extra time on the elliptical machine after my noon exercise class.

Ring. Ring. Ring. Ring. I'd decided to return the call from the mystery woman. After four rings and no answer, I was trying to compose some kind of vague message to leave when she answered.

"Hello?"

"Hello. My name is Quinn Montgomery, and I'm returning a call. Someone left me a message asking me to call, but that's all the information I have."

A beat of silence passed.

"Hello?" I said, set to hang up. It was probably a telemarketer preparing to give me her well-rehearsed speech on why I should purchase a time-share. I'd planned on disconnecting service to this cell phone in six months, but if telemarketer calls were all I was going to receive, I'd reduce that time to three months.

"Quinn?"

"Yes, this is Quinn Montgomery," I said again. Now I was starting to get suspicious.

Silence.

"This is Janae Brown," she said quickly.

For a moment, I thought I'd misheard her, because the woman I knew by that name would have no business calling *me*. "This is who?" I said again, peeling the silver foil lid off my yogurt.

"Janae Brown," she repeated, then hesitated. "I know you…from when you attended Light of the World Ministries. In Charlotte."

"I know where I know you from." I stood to my feet, as if she'd invaded my home. In a way, she had. "And should I remind you of the other ways that I'm familiar with you?"

"Please don't hang up," Janae begged, her voice almost whiny and sad.

"Why did you call me? We have no business together. And what business we used to have is locked up in jail."

She kept stalling, tempting me to disconnect the call, but part of me still wanted to know why she'd called in the first place.

"I wanted to apologize to you," she finally said.

"No apology necessary," I told her, willing my voice to sound calm and steady, even though my insides were shaking. I stuck a plastic spoon in my yogurt cup and set it on the arm of my chair. "You were only a small part of the problem," I added, "and, as I'm sure you know, I've moved on."

"I never should have become involved with Santana," she rushed on. "I knew that then, but I can see the repercussions of it now."

Hindsight is always 20/20, I almost said. What did she want? A gold medal for staying away from a man who was behind bars? Maybe another woman would applaud her, but the way I was feeling, I couldn't even give her my respect.

"Look," I said. "I'm sure you've grappled with your issues now that the marriage is over, but you should've realized what you were doing—tearing apart a couple—while it was happening. It's easy to apologize and be remorseful now, when your temptation is out of each. You probably don't want him anymore, anyway."

I was standing in the kitchen but didn't remember walking in there. True, it was just a few footsteps away from the love seat, but I still had no recollection of moving. I stopped in front of the wooden knife block and had a vision of myself hurling one at the wall.

"I could be wrong," I continued, since Janae hadn't found any other words to say. Maybe my reaction had thrown her off guard. "Maybe you still want to be with him. To each her own. If so, he's all yours. No strings attached. No vows. No rings. But if I were you, I'd head for the hills while you have the chance."

She sighed. "I wish it was that simple."

"Like I said, I'm not interested in your business or Santana's. Have a great life, and good-bye."

"I had his baby," Janae blurted out. "I have a daughter by Santana. She's almost two years old."

When the vision of throwing a knife returned, I left the kitchen. A scream of anger rose in my throat, tempting me to let it out. What did she expect me to say? "Congratulations"? "Where do I send the gift"? "Awww, here's my address. Send me a picture"?

I know children are supposed to be a blessing from God, but hearing about Janae's daughter was pulling every bit of strength out of me. Yet this woman would not hear me lose it.

"That's what you called to tell me?" I asked. "You call to 'apologize,' but you really wanted to throw that in my face." It wasn't a question.

"No," she insisted, "that wasn't my intention at all. When I called and left the message the first time, I hadn't decided whether I was going to tell you or not. But when you called me back, I thought it meant that I was doing what I believed God was leading me to do."

"Oh, so now you want to bring God into it?" I slung back at her.

She sighed deeply. "I deserve everything you want to say to me and every name you want to call me."

I could tell she was crying now. On top of her sniffling, I could hear the soft whimper of a child's voice in the background. The stress of being a single mother had probably contributed to Janae's "come to Jesus" moment. It wasn't easy parenting a preteen on my own, and I couldn't imagine how it felt to be the sole provider for a toddler. Then again, maybe she had someone to help. I shook my head. Why did I care? I couldn't feel any remorse. I could just see her, looking at Santana like he wore a superhero cape. I wondered what she'd see if she could look at him right now. Had she been visiting him?

I think the only reason I stayed on the line and listened to her is because I was shell-shocked. Too numb to move.

"I have a letter I wrote to you," she told me next.

"I don't want to hear it," I said. "Truth be told, I don't want to talk to you. Ever again."

"I understand," Janae said. "If it's any consolation, I always thought you were the nicest person."

I disconnected the call, and before I could stop myself, I hurled the phone across the room. It slammed into the wall, making a dent in the Sheetrock, before falling safely to the carpet. I didn't get the dramatic reaction I was hoping to see—my cell phone crushed into a thousand pieces. My hard-shell, waterproof phone case had prevented that. The wall hadn't fared as well, and I knew I would have to pay to have the damage repaired.

The phone rang again. "I don't believe this," I said between gritted teeth. It wasn't until the third ring that I realized it was the cell phone I used for business. I glanced at the screen. The caller was Levi. I didn't answer. I couldn't answer. The moment was too raw. I was sure I would break down in tears to the first person I talked to, and the last thing I wanted was to run Levi off with my drama.

I picked up a throw pillow and tossed it across the room. That was the only plush item within reach. But it didn't help relieve any stress. It did, however, knock over the yogurt that I'd forgotten about, perched on the armrest of the love seat. A thick puddle of blackberry-pomegranate yogurt landed on the carpet and splattered the nearby wall. For whatever reason, that yogurt was my breaking point.

"God, why?" I cried, dropping to the floor. "Why this? A daughter? After all he did to me, he still got the daughter he wanted."

I never should've returned the call. I could've gone about my life with no knowledge of Santana's other child. *Devin's sister.* "My God," I moaned, "Devin has a sister." Saying it aloud made it even more real. "This is too much," I cried. "This is too much."

One day, I'd have to tell Devin that he was a big brother. I'd read every letter that Santana had sent to him, and there'd been no mention anywhere.

It was entirely possible that Santana wasn't even aware of his daughter's existence. Until it became an issue, I was going to try my best to pretend that she didn't exist.

A text message from Levi lit up my phone. Thought about u this a.m. Read Isaiah 26:3.

I didn't want to read the Bible. I didn't want to move. I didn't even want to face the world, but I had no choice. I flipped into autopilot. Survival mode. By eleven fifteen, I'd made it to Warehouse Fitness to put in my time on the elliptical before my class rather than after. I needed to burn extra calories and blow off stress. I vaguely remembered talking to Ginger before class, but the conversation was all a blur, like a bad hangover. I'd popped two aspirin on an empty stomach. I'd lost my appetite after the conversation with Janae, and that stupid yogurt was still dumped on the carpet and splattered on the walls.

I slid down to the floor after class and leaned against the mirrored wall.

"Are you okay?" Ginger asked, dropping to her knees. "You don't look that good. And I'm only saying that because I'm concerned."

"I've felt better. I'll be okay."

Ginger pulled a bottled sports beverage from the side compartment of her backpack. "Here," she said, twisting off the top. "Drink this. You look kind of pale."

"How can a black woman look pale?"

Ginger turned beet red.

"I'm kidding," I said. I took a small sip of the drink and was amazed at how parched I actually was. After a long gulp, I took a few deep breaths through my nose. "Thanks."

"No problem," Ginger said. Her natural color had returned to her face, so now it was only slightly flushed from the strenuous routine we'd completed today. "Is it that police officer you were seeing?"

"No," I said, taking another sip of the drink. "I got some disturbing news this morning, but life goes on."

Ginger nodded, then pulled out the white face towel she'd tucked in the waistband of her shorts and wiped it across the back of her neck. "Life will give you an uppercut to the jaw when you least expect it. But you have to get back up and keep fighting. What other choice do you have?"

"You don't," I said.

So I fought my way through the rest of the day, even though that upper-cut kept taking me down. My mind wouldn't stop replaying the conversation with Janae. As soon as I managed to distract myself awhile, it would hit the rewind button and start again.

"Leftovers are in the fridge," I told Devin when we returned home from his football practice. "Please clean up after yourself when you're done."

I went to hibernate in my room. If I could sleep away the rest of Monday, then perhaps Tuesday would be better. Levi had said I needed a new Sunday morning song, but all I wanted to do was push through this Monday mess. Barely ten minutes had passed when Devin knocked on my door.

"Ma?"

"What is it, Devin?" I asked.

"There's yogurt all over the floor in the living room."

I groaned. "I forgot about that. I'll get it later."

"Do you want me to clean it up?"

"No," I told him, meaning it. Devin's attempt at cleaning my mess would only make it spread.

The door opened, and Devin stepped into the room. "Are you okay?"

He'd asked me the same question twice when we were in the car. I'd thought I did a good job masking my mood by showing interest in the robotics team he'd signed up for school, and the accolades he'd received from Coach Johnson during practice. Evidently not.

"Did you eat already?" I asked him.

"Yes."

"That was fast. Do you have homework?"

"Just math."

"Go ahead and jump on it so you won't be up too late."

"Yes, ma'am. Do you need anything?"

"Sleep," I said.

"But it's only six o'clock," Devin said. "Do I need to call somebody?"

Somebody like who? I thought. We'd been abandoned on this island by ourselves for so long that there wasn't anyone for him to call if I truly needed help. The only help I needed right now was from God.

Thirty minutes. I'd give myself thirty more minutes to wallow, and then I'd get back in the fight. Besides, I had encrusted yogurt to clean up.

⌒

Thirty minutes and two snooze buttons later, I woke up with a clearer head. There was yogurt to be cleaned and a load of towels and linens to be washed, so I trudged down the hall to the living area.

Despite my objections, Devin had done a decent job at cleaning up my mess. He'd scrubbed the area with a kitchen sponge and even soaked it with carpet cleaner. There was only a hint of a stain on the soft beige carpet, but nothing that another round of elbow grease wouldn't get rid of. He'd left three dirty cloths in the sink that I figured he'd used to wipe the wall. I rinsed them and wrung them out, then headed to the laundry closet.

The smell of mildew hit my nose as soon as I opened the door. I didn't have to follow the odor very far when I noticed the bag Devin had taken to Coach Johnson's house. Wet swim trunks. I should've guessed. I loosened the drawstring, opened the bag, and flipped it over to shake out the smelly culprit. Out fell his pair of black swimming trunks, a soggy pair of dingy white athletic socks….and a condom.

16

I yanked the covers off Devin with such force that he probably thought the end of the world had arrived. He blinked, straining against the bright light of the room, then shielded his eyes with his arm. His math book lay open on the mattress beside him.

"What is it, Ma?"

I snatched the goose-down pillow from under his head and whacked him with it. I knew it wouldn't hurt him, but I had to do something.

"What *is* it?" I said, taking another swing with the pillow. This time, I missed him, but the breeze sent his unfinished math homework floating to the floor. Devin used his bare feet to propel himself back against the headboard.

"What's wrong, Ma?" He tried to reach for his sheet or his comforter to cover his boxer shorts, but there was nothing there. I'd pulled everything off the bed.

"That's what I want to know!" I screamed. "What's wrong with your bringing this"—I held the wrapped condom in the air—"into my house?"

The color drained from his face. I finally understood what Ginger had meant when she'd told me I looked pale.

His words babbled out of his mouth, bouncing all around, as he searched for an explanation.

"Somebody gave it to me when we were at the cookout."

"Somebody like who?" I demanded.

Devin looked around like he was searching for an escape route. But he was backed against the corner. Literally.

"If you don't tell me now, I promise you, I'll come with you to school first thing in the morning and have the principal pull every last player out of class."

"R.J."

I knew R.J. He was the shortest on the team and had ears that stuck out like satellite discs. They probably looked cute when he was three or four, but he still hadn't grown into them. If only I could get a grip on those ears right now and use them as handles.

"So why is R.J. passing out condoms? Is he the sex education teacher now? Did he teach you about STDs, too? Did he pass out anything about pregnancy and child support? Because you *do* know that you don't have a dime to your name, right?"

"Yes, ma'am," Devin squeaked.

"And what did you plan to do with this?" I held the silver wrapper in plain view.

Devin shrugged. He was not the kind of boy to ever be at a loss for words.

"Do you know what it's for?"

"I think so."

I had to collect my bearings before I asked my next question, because depending on how my son answered, he might have to call 9-1-1 after all. "Have you ever tried to use one?"

Devin looked horrified at the question. "No, ma'am. I don't even know *how.*"

Relief washed over me. I covered my eyes with the palm of my hand and took slow, deliberate breaths to calm my racing heart. I couldn't believe I was having this talk with him. Some people might have said that I shielded him too much, but this was exactly the kind of nonsense I was afraid of.

"Why did R.J. give this to *you?*"

He shrugged again. "I don't know. We were talking about stuff, and then he started talking about sex. He had a box of some of…those, and he asked me and some of the other boys if we wanted one. I didn't want to be the only one who didn't take it."

"Why not? You know right from wrong. I've told you a thousand times that if somebody is doing or saying something that you know isn't right, then get away from him. Plain and simple."

"Yes, ma'am."

"Don't give me lip service if you're not going to do what I tell you to. Show me you understand with your actions. One day, R.J. is giving you a condom; the next time, he might ask you to try some drugs. Are you going to do that, too?"

Devin shook his head.

I was doing it—the thing I'd said I'd never do but that every parent has done. I was talking like my own mother.

Devin was my baby. He'd always been the beat of my heart. Looking at his facial expression, I knew that peer pressure had made him take the condom. However, that didn't excuse his actions.

"I'm angry and I'm disappointed," I told Devin, lowering my voice to its normal tone. I'd never been a screamer when it came to disciplining him. My mother had acted as if she believed the only way I would hear her was if she yelled at the top of her lungs. In her house, I was guilty until proven innocent, but she never gave me a chance to clear my name. As far as I was concerned, this situation was bigger than anything I'd ever been caught doing.

"I'm sorry, Ma," Devin said, leaning down from the bed to pick up his notebook paper and toppled math book. He smoothed the pages and closed the book, using his homework as a bookmark.

"Apology accepted," I said. As I picked up his comforter and spread it back across the bed, I tried to think of a suitable punishment. I couldn't let Devin off without a penalty of some sort. He had to feel the sting of his actions. "In the meantime, you're off the football team."

"But—"

I held up my hand. "Don't go there. Don't even do it."

Devin wilted, and I felt sorry for him. But I couldn't change my mind.

I bent to retrieve the blunt pencil peeking out from under his bed. "Finish your math homework."

I left him to determine ratios and work with bases and exponents. I had an equation for him: What result do get when your mother is angry to the fifteenth power?

I padded back to my bedroom. Despite my feelings, I couldn't bury my head in the sand—not when things like condom distribution were going on around me. Needless to say, Devin wasn't naive about the reality of sex.

Kids talked. Boys bragged about what they'd done, whether or not it was true. Commercials inserted between family-friendly television programming introduced children to topics parents wanted to avoid. The world had its own agenda, so I had to stay on top of mine.

I walked into the bathroom and stared at myself in the mirror. "Girl, you've got to get it together," I said to my reflection. "Big-girl panties go on right now."

I had to take partial blame for Devin's folding under peer pressure. I should've approached the topic before that little R.J. character had the chance to broach a grown folks' topic with the football team. Now I'd have to do quality control.

This was one of those times when I wanted a man's input. Every now and then, Devin needed a slap on the back more than he needed a hug. His voice was cracking, his testosterone was rising, and he probably had no idea how to process his emotions and feelings. Of course he was curious about sex; that was part of growing up. But he obviously needed an outlet with a man before we both rammed heads and locked horns.

I opened the drawer where I kept my scissors, then promptly used them to cut the condom into four pieces before shoving it into my trash can. I crumpled up some tissues and threw them on top, as if they would make any difference.

"Lord Jesus," I murmured, "if I've never needed You before, I sure do need You now."

Levi's name came to mind, and I didn't hesitate in picking up the phone to call him. I needed to return his call; and besides, the man had wiped my toes clean of every trace of paint. He deserved a call.

"Hello?" Levi answered.

"Hey," I said. "Is it too late for me to call?"

"Of course not. I'm just lying here doing some reading. I checked out this book from the library a while ago, and I've reached my limit in renewals. I want to finish it in the next few days, before it's overdue."

"I won't hold you up, then," I said.

"You wanted something," Levi said. "I can tell. What's going on?"

"The question should be, 'What's *not* going on?'"

"Hmm. Financial problems? Car problems? Work problems?"

"Those are the easy ones," I said, going to sit inside my closet. I plopped down between my summertime sandals and the closed-toe shoes I'd pulled out for the fall weather. "I found a condom in one of Devin's bags. He said one of his teammates gave it to him."

"Do you believe him?"

"I do," I said. "Does that make me crazy?"

"No, that makes you human," Levi said. "We should believe the best of our children, especially if we've taught them right from wrong."

"And Devin knows. But this is all wrong."

"That's life," Levi said calmly. "I know you don't want to hear it, but it won't be the last time he's faced with a situation where he has to choose between his friends and his faith. All boys go through these rites of passage at his age. They think they know more than they do. He'll be alright."

"Yes, but will I?" I asked. "I don't understand why he'd take the condom in the first place."

"Because he's—how old is he?"

"Twelve."

"Because he's twelve," Levi said with a laugh. "You'd be surprised at some of the things I did when I was twelve."

"Don't tell me that," I said. Wasn't he supposed to be calming my fears?

"But I didn't have you as a mom, and I was living with my dad, who probably encouraged foolishness more than he did anything else. Even so, I turned out okay in the end. Devin's on the right track, so even if he veers off again in the future, he'll be back. You can't just read about training up a child in the way he should go; you have to believe it."

So, the man washed feet, read books, and could quote the Word of God without effort. If he had a flaw, I didn't want to see it anytime soon. I just wanted to relish this little piece of heaven on earth.

"The next time you see him, could you drop something in his ear?" I asked. "Nothing to let him know I talked to you, but a nugget to inspire him to make better decisions."

"I get the request from mothers all the time. Should I wear my uniform? Scare him straight?" Levi asked with a chuckle.

"I'll take whatever works," I said. I pulled out my bin of nail polish and searched for a neutral color.

"Did you see the text I sent you the other day?" Levi said.

"I did, but that day was so crazy, I have to admit that I didn't read the Scripture verse."

"You should," he said. "When I read it, I immediately thought about you, so it must've been for a reason."

I abandoned my search for a suitable nail polish and went to find the Scripture instead. "What was the reference again?" I asked, sliding my Bible out from beneath my pillow.

"Isaiah twenty-six, verse three," Levi said, then went ahead and quoted it from memory: "*You will keep him in perfect peace, whose mind is stayed on You, because he trusts in You.*"

I flipped the pages of my Bible until I found the Scripture. It was already highlighted and starred. This wasn't the first time I'd needed it, and it wouldn't be the last.

"Are you sure you're not hiding a cleric collar from me?" I teased.

"No," Levi said. "I just know the Word of God works."

"You couldn't be more right," I agreed.

There was a moment of comfortable silence between us before Levi spoke again.

"Would you and Devin like to come to a get-together at Roman and Zenja's house after church on Sunday?"

I was hesitant, only because Devin was a factor. I knew we'd recently discussed the possibility of my dating, but I feared it still might be too soon.

Levi must've sensed my hesitation.

"You can meet me there," Levi said. "I'm inviting both of you because there will be some other boys Devin can hang out with, including Roman and Zenja's son, Kyle."

I sighed. "The last time I let him hang out with other boys, he came home with a condom."

"I think the only thing he'll come home with this time is a full stomach," Levi said. "Plus, this will allow me to establish a relationship with him so I can be that voice in his ear. The guys and I usually toss a few balls, play some video games, and show the young'uns how to grill. Devin's not going to be open with me if we haven't kicked it a few times."

"True," I agreed, seriously considering it. After all, Zenja had taken a chance on inviting a stranger to the Friday Night Love event, and she'd welcomed me with open arms. And where Zenja was, Caprice was likely to be, as well.

And where Caprice was, her sister would probably be. Carmela was entertainment in her own right. My Sundays were getting better already.

"How many days are you going to take to think about it?" Levi asked, interrupting my thoughts.

"Why? Am I on the list?"

"You *are* the list," he said.

"Well, since I'm a VIP, I guess I should be there."

"Good," Levi said. "I'll catch up with you later this week."

"Perfect." I stifled a yawn.

"Be strong, beautiful," Levi said. "You're doing a great job with Devin."

"Thank you," I gushed. "Good night, Officer Gray."

As I drifted off to sleep, I tried to keep my mind on God, but every now and then, my thoughts detoured to those deep-set eyes and that almost-dimple of Leviticus Gray.

17

After an entire week secluded in the apartment with Devin, I was relieved that we would finally have a break from each other, even if was for just a few hours. We definitely needed it. I'd grown accustomed to having my late afternoons alone, but since I'd axed out Devin's middle-school football career, I had to pick him up as soon as school was dismissed. On Thursday, he'd holed himself up in the back of the classroom when he'd been forced to attend my "Rush-hour Step It Up" class. By Friday, I was counting down the hours until the get-together at the Maxwells' house.

I'd ignored Devin's entire week of moping. It was going to take more than a long face to change my mind and put him back on the football field. Because he'd had more time to study, he'd aced both his social studies test on the seven continents of the world and his pop quiz in science class.

"Are we there?" Devin asked, sitting up from the reclined passenger seat when he felt the car begin to slow down.

"I'm pretty sure this is it," I said.

The brick house was situated at the top of a hill. Two beautiful planters framed both sides of the front entryway, but what I loved most was the cushioned porch swing facing the street. I always wanted one at our house in Charlotte, but because Santana had been against it, I'd had to settle for my hammock in the backyard. He'd thought it looked old-fashioned, but I thought it added a certain charm to the house. Of course, his decision was the final one. But as soon as I was in a position to buy a house for Devin and myself, if it didn't already have a porch swing, that would be one of my first beautification projects.

There were several cars already parked in the Maxwells' driveway and three others lined up in front of the house. I drove to the end of the cul-de-sac and made a U-turn in front of a house that looked to be about halfway completed, which seemed strange. Although the other houses throughout the neighborhood were well maintained, it was obvious they'd been built some time ago. I inched up behind the last car in line.

"Hey, that's Mr. Levi's truck," Devin said as Levi drove past us, then turned around in the cul-de-sac. We both lived approximately twenty-minutes away, so I wasn't surprised to see his truck. He'd sent me a text message when he'd left his house. I was anxious, though. Butterflies flitted in my stomach. I stole a glance at my reflection in the visor mirror, and at the same time, I caught a glimpse of Levi.

"I didn't know he was going to be here," Devin said, looking over his headrest. "I like him. He seems nice."

"You think so?" I asked. "I do, too." *And nice-looking.*

"I know I don't have to tell you to be on your best behavior," I said, unlocking the doors. "Especially around Mr. and Mrs. Maxwell's son and daughter. Make sure to respect their property and keep your hands off anything that's expensive. I don't want to have to pay to replace anything that you break by accident."

"Yes, ma'am," he said.

The mommy in me couldn't help but add another warning. "And if there is any inappropriate talk, or if any inappropriate items are passed around, you make sure you remove yourself from the situation. Is that understood?"

Devin nodded his head so fast, I thought it would wobble right off his neck. He opened his car door but didn't set foot on the ground until I gave him a signal to go ahead. He went straight for Levi's truck, which was fine with me. The sooner they started talking, the better.

In the rearview mirror, I watched them slap hands, then Levi lightly tapped the top of Devin's head with his fist.

I stepped out of the car and headed over to join them.

"Happy Sunday," Levi said to me.

"Happy Sunday," I said back.

I could tell by the way Levi looked at me that he would've given me a compliment if Devin hadn't been standing two feet away. Instead, he complimented me with his eyes. And with my own eyes, I said a silent "*Thank you.*"

"We'd better get inside in case they're already standing in line for Duane's famous ribs," Levi said as he started for the house. "He has a secret sauce that he's going to bottle and sell one day, or so he says."

"Falls off the bone?" I asked.

"Falls off the bone."

I followed Levi up the driveway and onto the porch. Zenja must've seen us coming, because she answered immediately after Levi rang the doorbell.

"What a surprise!" she said when she saw Devin and me. She stepped back and welcomed us into the foyer. "I didn't know you all were coming."

I raised my eyebrows at Levi. He'd brought two more mouths to feed, and the lady of the house had no idea.

"I talked to Roman," Levi stepped in to say.

"Well, no wonder I didn't know. He never remembers to tell me anything."

"I don't want to intrude," I said apologetically.

"Intrude? Girl, please. If you're on Levi's arm, you're definitely not an intruder. We have more than enough food—and love—for fifty people." She turned to Devin. "The other kids are upstairs, second door to the left, if you want to go up."

Devin looked to me for approval.

"Go ahead."

Devin walked calmly up the first few steps, then took the rest of them two at a time.

Zenja turned her attention to Levi. "You're empty-handed. Something is wrong with this picture."

Levi snapped his fingers. "I left it in the car. It's still warm. Not too long out of the oven."

I figured Levi must have some cooking skills that he hadn't disclosed. And if he'd brought an item at special request, then I had to be one of the first to taste it, whatever it was.

"What did you make?" I asked him.

"You'll find out soon enough," Levi said. "I'll be back in a minute."

Zenja led me into the kitchen while Levi ran outside to retrieve his prized side dish.

"Caprice, look who's here," Zenja said. "She came with Levi."

The look on Caprice's face was just as shocked as Zenja's had been, but I couldn't tell if it was because she was surprised to see me or because I was Levi's guest. A smile spread across her face, accentuating her beautiful features and flawless skin.

"Hi, Quinn," she said. "I'd come to greet you, but Zenja has me slaving away, as you can see. I don't know why she acts like she can't put together a salad."

"Because your salads always look so much prettier," Zenja said. "So full of color and nutrition."

"Oh, is that what it is?" Caprice said. She was dicing tomatoes at lightning speed, and from the looks of the waxy green peels around her, she'd already sliced through a vine full of fresh cucumbers, as well.

"What can I do to help?" I asked.

"Not a thing," Zenja insisted. She pulled out a stool at the bar so I could sit down. "First-time guests are prohibited from helping. Next time, though, expect to be chopping and dicing, too."

"And she's very serious," Caprice said. She used her forearm to turn on the faucet, then rinsed her knife. There was still a spread of broccoli, carrots, and yellow bell peppers that she needed to tackle, but with the way her knife flew across the cutting board, it wouldn't take long.

"Now for my special tea," Zenja said. "Quinn, you're sworn to secrecy for every recipe that you may happen to witness while in the Maxwell kitchen."

I held up three fingers like I was taking a scout's honor pledge. "My lips are sealed."

Zenja went to work on a pitcher full of freshly brewed tea, poured in a large can of pineapple juice, and started adding sugar. That was one beverage I wouldn't be touching. I could feel my blood pressure rising just looking at it.

"Don't worry, Quinn," Zenja told me. "This is Roman's special tea. There's no way I'd feed my guests a glassful of sugar like he and his mama like to drink. I'll make another batch of the toned-down version."

"That's good to know," I said.

"So," Zenja said, opening the stainless-steel refrigerator door, "have you and Levi been working together since you connected at the church?"

I'd known the questions would come, and Zenja hadn't wasted any time.

"We haven't presented at another event together yet," I said, skirting over the question. "I have some things in the works, and I hope to bring Levi on board once they're more solidified." Levi had struck me as a private person, so I definitely wasn't about to share about the time we'd spent devouring the Mae sisters' food or paint-dancing at the park.

"I'm telling you, the two of you fed off each other's presentations like you'd planned it that way," Zenja said as she removed a second pitcher of tea from the fridge.

"Thank you. He's very easy to work with."

As if on cue, Levi walked into the kitchen. "Are you all talking about me?" he asked.

"Drop the pie and keep walking," Zenja said. She opened another can of pineapple juice and added to the tea only half the amount she'd poured in the first mixture.

"Did you say 'pie'?" I asked. It didn't take more than one whiff for me to figure out that it was apple pie.

"She did said 'pie.' *Homemade* pie," Levi stressed. "Mrs. Smith's has nothing on Mr. Gray's. But I'll let the dessert speak for itself. And it doesn't just talk, it sings." He winked at me, and I nearly melted. "It'll have you singing, too."

"Good-bye, Levi," Zenja said. She took the pie from him and set it on a side table where a fluffy pound cake and a pan of pudding waited.

"Don't let them bully you into answering their questions," Levi told me.

"You know we wouldn't do that, Levi," Caprice said innocently, hard at work on the carrots.

"I think you've left me in good hands," I said. "I'll be fine."

"Alright," Levi said. "If that's the case, I'll leave you ladies alone."

Levi disappeared out the patio door and joined a group of men circled around the grill. Caprice's husband, Duane, seemed to be manning the grill, but Roman, Zenja's husband, was only a step away, holding a Mason jar of orange liquid. That must be the secret sauce Levi had mentioned.

"I have just one thing to say, and then I'll leave you alone," Zenja said. The whir of the can opener filled the kitchen. "I've known Levi for a little over a year, and he has never—I repeat, never—brought a woman to a function or mentioned seeing anyone. I realize you haven't known him long, but he must see something special in you."

"Levi's a nice man," I said. "We're just getting to know each other."

"Well, you have to start somewhere," Zenja said with a gleam in her eye. I could tell she was a hopeless romantic.

"I should apologize for her," Caprice said.

Zenja opened the fridge again and slid the two pitchers of tea onto the first shelf. "I was simply making an observation."

Even though I'd already been advised not to assist, I couldn't help myself. When Caprice started to clean up the vegetable peelings for her salad, I got up to lend a hand.

"And, speaking of Levi," Zenja went on.

"We weren't speaking of Levi," Caprice said. "You were the only one doing that."

"Fine. Then I'll continue," Zenja said. She took a tower of paper cups out of her pantry and began filling them with ice. "Levi is solid. A good, solid man."

From the way she enunciated her words, I thought she was talking about his stature before she went on to explain herself.

"By 'solid,' I mean he has a good foundation in God, and he stands on what he believes. That man prays on the men's prayer call every morning, he serves the community faithfully, and he doesn't sweep one woman in here this week and another woman the next. On top of that, he can bake. Now, what man in uniform have you ever known to both pray and whip up an apple pie?"

"None that I know of," I said, eager to taste it already. If the flavor was anywhere near as good as the aroma, I was in for a treat.

"Keep your eye on him, girlfriend," Zenja said. "Don't let him get away."

"I have a feeling you should be telling him that," Caprice said.

Her eyes had zeroed in on me, and though I didn't feel uneasy, I could tell she was about to go in deep. Some people have that way about them. Others called it "intuition," but I called it the Holy Spirit.

"I know we don't know each other, but would you be open to hearing what I believe God is saying to me about you?"

"Sure," I replied.

Caprice used her foot to push the trash can out of the way, then extended both hands to me. I placed my hands in hers, and she gripped mine firmly. There was a surge that passed between us. I knew what that meant. God was about to speak.

18

Despite all you've been through, I believe God is saying that you're ready for love again. You don't have to worry about whether the next man will be like the last man, because God has put a hedge of protection around you. He has shielded you with His love, and only a man who loves and honors God will be able to approach you."

I nodded, unable to speak. I knew that if I swallowed the lump in my throat, it might unleash audible weeping. God knew my soul needed a good cleansing, but I preferred those to happen in private.

"You've cried more tears of pain than a woman of your heart and grace should, but God says He owes you tears of joy," Caprice continued. "He's going to pour more blessings on you than you've ever imagined because of your faithfulness. God says He's going to give you a new song."

Those prophetic words released the floodgates of my tears. Caprice was supposed to be spinning a salad, Zenja was supposed to be filling cups with ice, but instead they were comforting me.

"I apologize," I said, dabbing away the tears with the tissue Zenja had pressed into my palm. "This is embarrassing."

"Don't be embarrassed," Zenja said. "You have no idea how many tears have been shed in this kitchen."

"Tell me about it," Caprice said. "You could clean the floor with the number of tears I've dropped in this room alone. I could probably swim in the tears shed at my house. But God is faithful. You remember that, okay?"

I nodded. "I will."

"There's a powder room in this first hallway," Zenja told me. "Go get yourself together so Levi won't think we were in here harassing you."

"You *were* harassing her," Caprice said, slipping back into their cajoling.

I slipped away to the bathroom to dry my face and freshen my lipstick. When I walked out, I nearly ran into Carmela.

"Ooooh!" she exclaimed, clutching her chest. "You scared me to pieces."

"Sorry about that," I said.

"I thought I was going to have to pull one of those self-defense moves you taught us. Jab you in the throat or the eyes," she joked as she blew into the kitchen, her long skirt sailing behind her like a cape.

"What are you talking about now?" Caprice asked her.

"Self-defense. As a matter of fact, I almost had to use one of the moves the other day on the man at the dry cleaner's."

"Why?" both Zenja and Caprice chimed in at the same time.

"Because he thought he'd misplaced my new suit. I'd already gotten it tailored and everything, so you know I was about ten seconds from giving him a good piece of my mind."

"Why would that call for self-defense?" Caprice asked. She'd emptied several bags of kale, spinach, and romaine lettuce into a salad spinner and was now spinning away.

Carmela planted her hands on her hips. "Because he threatened my sense of fashion."

We shared a laugh.

Carmela emptied one of the grocery bags she was carrying and placed two cartons of ice cream on the counter—one gallon of butter pecan, the other of old-fashioned vanilla.

"Is that what I think it is?" she asked, lifting up a corner of the aluminum foil covering Levi's pie. "That's fate. Levi brought the pie, and I brought the ice cream. Pie just isn't right without ice cream."

Caprice twirled the salad spinner. "Let it go, sister. Try to hook another fish."

There was an awkward silence, and Carmela's eyes shot my way for half a second. "I'll stick these in the freezer," she said.

Zenja glanced at the other bag. "What's in there?"

"I'm glad you asked." After stuffing the cartons of ice cream in the freezer, Carmela reached in the other bag and pulled out several small plastic containers the size of baby-food jars. They were filled with something that looked like ground spice.

Carmela arranged the containers in a brown woven basket in the center of the table that Zenja had set up for the food.

"You all have *got* to try these spices. They are beyond delectable," she said, sounding like the voice on a commercial. She continued her enthusiastic spiel. "They're perfect on meats and veggies, and people will think you spent all day grinding these spices down yourself. I'm telling you, they're that good." Carmela cupped one of the containers in her hand and displayed it for us to see. "The first sample batch is on me, but after that, you'll have to place your orders exclusively through the Web site. By the time it's all said and done, these are going to be on the shelf of every grocery store in America."

"That's great," I said, though it seemed like I was the only one who shared her zeal. I twisted the top off one of the containers and took a sniff. It seemed to be heavy on the pepper, but I could smell other spices, as well. "I wish you the best," I said, using all of my willpower to hold back a sneeze.

"Thank you," Carmela said. She sat beside me like she wanted to adopt me as her new friend. "I think I saw you at church today, but I was seated too far away to be sure."

"It could have been me. I was there today and last week."

"So, how have you been enjoying our services?"

"I love them," I said. "Devin loves them, too. He was up and ready for church before me this morning."

Zenja leaned against the counter. "That makes a difference when your children are excited about going. I actually don't attend that church, but my kids love going with their godparents. Of course, I think Duane and Caprice also bribe them with food afterward. But if it works, I say, do it."

Caprice claimed the stool on my other side. "I hope you're not wondering what in the world you've gotten yourself into," she told me. "We're really good, sane people."

"Only by God's grace," Zenja laughed. "In all seriousness, we really do love God, and we're committed to seeing people healthy and whole. Not that we have it all together—trust me, we have our issues—but every day, we're pressing toward that mark. We try to hold each other accountable as much as we can. And we try to have fun doing it."

"Speaking of which," Caprice put in, "did you hear about the women's retreat we have coming up at the end of next month? We're leaving on Friday and coming back on Sunday. You should come and invite some of your girlfriends. When I tell you we have a blast, I am not exaggerating."

I'd stuffed the flyer I'd picked up in my glove compartment. Blue Ridge was probably beautiful at this time of year, with the leaves changing color.

"I picked up some information about it," I told her. "And I wouldn't mind going, but I don't have any girlfriends in the area. Devin is about the only friend I have."

"Well, we've got to change that," Zenja said. "Every woman needs a sister to lean on. That's why we have two shoulders."

"You should come with us," Caprice said. "Both of us reserved rooms with queen double beds just in case. You are our 'just in case.'"

It was tempting, but not having a sitter, friend, or family member available to watch Devin meant that I was tied to the city. I didn't have help or a backup plan for child care. I was Plan A *and* Plan Z.

Zenja drummed her fingers on the countertop. "I can sense your hesitation. It's Devin, isn't it?"

"Bingo," I admitted. "There's nobody I can leave him with."

"Things will work out," Zenja said. "I've been there before, after my first husband died. God knows that if I hadn't have had Caprice, I never would've left the house."

I never would have suspected Zenja to be a widow. Judging by the ages of her children, she'd been young when she'd lost her first love. And yet she'd found love again. God had given her a second chance at love, and from what I could tell, Zenja was living gracefully in every minute of it.

Levi slid open the patio door, bringing the smell of charcoal smoke inside. There was nothing like the whiff of a good barbecue. Roman followed him inside, carrying a foil pan full of ribs, and I had a quick flashback to Santana's grilling skills. He didn't mind throwing on salmon, ribs, or veggies, whether the ground was covered in spring flowers, fall leaves, or a winter snow. Once, when a blizzard had hit the city and knocked down the electricity on our side of town for two days, we'd still enjoyed full meals. Santana would fire up the grill and stand outside, dressed like he was hitting the ski slopes. Devin had been six at the time and wanted nothing more than to roll in the snow, romping around and making snow angels throughout the entire backyard. Even though the bad memories outweighed the good, there were special times that I wouldn't forget.

"Ooooohhhhhh." Carmela's voice brought me back to the here and now. Her face lit up when the men walked through the door. At first, I thought her extra beam was for Levi, but she skirted right by him and over to Duane, holding a container of her special spice blend.

"You're just the person I'm looking for," she said to Duane, popping off the top. "I want you to try some of this on the ribs."

Duane deflected her hand with his shoulder and pushed past her. "Sis, I promise you, if you put any of that on my ribs, you're going to draw back a nub." He looked at his wife. "Get your sister, baby."

"Don't drag me into this," Caprice said, shaking her head as she lined up an array of salad dressings on the table.

"I promise, this will take your sauce to another level," Carmela said, shaking the container in front of his face. "One little shake. Try it on one rib."

"Don't mess with perfection." Duane tore a sheet of aluminum foil off the bulk-sized roll and made a tight seal over his prized ribs.

Ceding, Carmela dropped the spice container back in the basket with the others. "Hi, Levi," she said.

"What's up, Carmela? Is this the famous spice blend you were telling me about?"

Her attitude perked up as soon as Levi showed interest in the product. "Yes. You'd love it. You could probably use a little spice in your life."

"I'll make sure I take one home to try."

"Thank you," she said. "And if you *love* it—which I know you will—be sure to tell all your friends at the police department and take some orders."

"I'll see what I can do," Levi said.

Carmela was trying, unsuccessfully, to hide her interest in Levi. They may not have been in a relationship, but I could tell that they'd been on at least one date. And if Levi had decided at that very moment that he wanted to leave with her on his arm instead of me, she'd kindly apologize and attach herself to his arm like a barnacle.

I couldn't blame her.

Levi walked over to me and leaned against the counter. "You okay?"

"I'm fine," I said.

"I didn't want you to think I'd abandoned you."

"The thought didn't even cross my mind."

"Is Devin having a good time?"

"Must be. I haven't seen him since he ran up those stairs."

"I'm about to head up there to challenge the boys to a Madden tournament. Don't be surprised if I send him back downstairs crying. He's going to have to take it like a man."

I shook my head. He didn't know my son. He could play almost any video game with his eyes closed. He consulted game magazines to figure out tricks and unlock secret codes. I didn't understand most of it, but I had to keep a parental eye on it, for no other reason than to make sure he knew he couldn't get anything past me. Madden NFL was one of his all-time favorites.

"I'll make sure I keep a box of Kleenex handy for *you*," I told him.

"Let's make a bet," Levi said, lowering his voice. "If I beat Devin, you'll let me take you out this weekend."

"How did I get pulled into this? Besides, I don't bet."

"You're just scared."

I smiled. "You're using me as a trophy."

"Not a trophy—a treasure." Levi rested his arm across the back of my stool.

"And what happens if you lose?"

"If I lose, then I have to take you out."

"Wait. That doesn't make any sense. You're taking me out whether you win or lose?"

"Right. So, either way, I'm still a winner."

"You're just full of compliments."

"That's a lot better than being full of something else," Levi said, pushing away from the counter. "I'll let you know how things work out."

"I haven't agreed to this proposal," I told him.

"I'll be upstairs," Levi said, purposefully ignoring me. I wanted to watch him walk away, but I knew there were at least two pairs of eyes on me.

I didn't see Levi or Devin again until almost twenty minutes later, when Roman called everyone down to eat. We circled in the kitchen, held hands—Devin on my right side, Levi on my left—and bowed our heads as the man of the house prayed over the food and thanked God for relationships old and new. Levi's hand squeezed mine a little tighter, and I returned the gesture. We were still finding ways to speak without words.

Roman ended his prayer with "Good food, good meat, good God, let's eat!"

Of course, that provoked a round of laughter, and Roman got a playful slap on the tush from his wife.

"Ladies first," Roman announced, eliciting a groan from the young boys.

"See, that's exactly why all y'all need to be at the Man Up Monday session they're having at the church tomorrow," Roman said. "Duane, you're going to have some work on your hands."

Duane pumped his fist in the air. "I'm up for it. I can do them like my daddy used to do me and take these young men to boot camp."

"What's Man Up Monday?" I asked Caprice as I scooped potato salad onto my plate, followed by a spoonful of baked beans. It was a waste of time to try counting calories with a spread like this.

"Once a month, the men from the church get together and discuss a topic or address some kind of community need. Tomorrow, some of the men who are free during the day are making themselves available for the young men, since the kids have off for a teachers' professional development day."

"I'd completely forgotten about that," I said. I'd been so immersed in generating leads this week that all the days had run together.

"You should bring Devin. Duane will be there, and so will Zenja's son. He'll have fun, and you won't have to worry about finding something for him to do other than sitting in front of the television all day."

"Please, Mom?" Devin said, stealing a potato chip from my plate. I hadn't even realized he'd been eavesdropping on our conversation. I offered him a celery stick off my plate, too—which he declined, of course.

"It's boring to be at home all day," he said. "The only thing I'll want to do is practice my Madden game, because Levi is spanking me right now."

Zenja's son, Kyle, playfully fell to one knee. "We'll beg if we have to."

"I think it should be okay," I decided, thinking about what Zenja and Caprice had said. I had to trust somebody. But if he came home with another condom or, God forbid, something worse, I was digging a fallout shelter for us to live in until he turned twenty-one.

"Yes!" Devin cheered, slapping hands with his younger video game mentee.

"Can he spend the night tonight since we don't have school," Kyle asked.

"Maybe another time," I said, topping off my plate with one of Duane's "Succulent, Slap-Your-Mama-and-Get-Slapped-Back Ribs," the term written on the yellow Post-it note he'd stuck to the front of the aluminum pan.

"Come on, little bro," Devin said, propping his elbow on Kyle's shoulder. "We can hang out tomorrow."

Younger boys tended to look up to Devin. He used to have a ring of followers at our church in Charlotte. Unlike many preteen guys, Devin never treated younger boys like babies, and he didn't tease or bully them. But I suspected his fast friendship with Kyle had an ulterior reason: Kyle's cute sister, Zariya. She padded into the kitchen in bare feet, her toe nails painted bubble-gum pink. At least I knew Zenja had some say so on what her daughter wore. I could tell she was beginning to develop the body of a young lady, so I bet Devin had noticed, too.

I ate until I was about to burst, and I wasn't the only one. But none of us was too full to find room in a corner of our stomach for a slice of Levi's apple pie. He insisted on warming it and serving it himself, complete with a scoop of Carmela's butter pecan ice cream on the side.

After delivering my slice, Levi watched me, waiting for my reaction as I cut the pie with my fork. I decided to take my first bite without the ice cream to see if it was all Levi claimed it to be.

19

LEVI

After watching Quinn take her first bite of his apple pie, Levi knew he could convince that woman to marry him just by the dessert alone. His love would just be the whipped cream on top. She smiled and gave him an approving thumbs-up. Man, if he served her some of his banana pudding, she'd be running to the courthouse by the end of the week.

Levi felt comfortable with Quinn being there. He liked that she melded easily with his friends and didn't need to be constantly by his side.

"I'm fine," she said every time he checked on her.

And fine she was, in more ways than one. Her looks in no way reflected what she'd been through. She easily could've been bitter toward any man who approached her, or could've turned into such a recluse that nobody wanted to be around her. But Levi did want to be around her, and he was having that feeling more and more.

It didn't make sense. He kept telling himself that he hadn't known her long enough to develop feelings for her, but there was definitely something going on. His uncle Ron had met and married his aunt Meredith within six months, and now, more than thirty years later, they were still happily married. Sometimes it happened like that. Levi wasn't about to expect his own story to play out just like that, but at least it helped him justify what he felt.

Quinn was strong, she had her own mind, and she stood on her morals. Despite how she'd questioned herself earlier this week, she was doing an amazing job raising Devin. He was mannerly and polite. A good kid. Levi could tell between the ones who were putting on a show and the ones who had home training. Of course, Devin's father had probably had something to do with it, but Levi couldn't give props to a man who was a good father yet abused his wife.

"Did you enjoy yourself?" he asked Quinn as he walked her and Devin to their car.

"Yes," Devin answered before Quinn could get a word out.

Levi and Quinn eyed each other in amusement. Devin was walking ahead of them, using his shoe to push along a loose piece of gravel that had found its way to the driveway.

"I did, too," Quinn said. Levi thought she said more than that with her eyes. *Those eyes.... That smile....* Man, those alone could make a brother want to come home to her every night.

Devin asked for the keys, then ran ahead to start the car. Levi slowed his pace so he could steal some extra moments of privacy with Quinn. Once Devin had the engine going, they could hear the radio playing. Levi nodded toward his truck, and Quinn followed him to the driver's door.

"It's not my business," he began, "and I don't want you to think I'm trying to overstep my boundaries, but I think you should let him get back on the football team. Boys need a sport."

"He has baseball."

"But he's not playing right now. I think the punishment was too tough for the crime."

"So, I should just wait until he gets some fast little girl pregnant, and then pull him off the team?"

"It was just a suggestion. I'll stay out of it." Levi leaned against his truck and stuffed his hands in his pockets. "Don't get mad at me. You still owe me a date."

"If you bake me a pie."

"Oh, so it's like that? That wasn't part of the original deal."

"I never agreed to the deal," Quinn said.

"I have no problem baking you a pie if that's what you want."

"It is what I want," Quinn said, "but save it for later. I'll let you know when. Maybe for my birthday. It's next month."

"Twenty-one already?" Levi said.

Quinn pushed a few loose stands of hair behind her ear. "Not until next year."

Levi knew that a woman wasn't supposed to tell her age, but he had already calculated Quinn's when he'd run her license through the system after pulling her over. She didn't look thirty-seven. He knew women younger than she who hadn't aged nearly as gracefully. He saw a lot patrolling the streets. Lifestyle had a lot to do with it. Alcohol and drugs had added years to, and stolen beauty from, a lot of women; but good genes and God's grace seemed to have preserved Quinn's.

Levi knew he didn't look his forty-one years. His baby face helped him. A man had to use what he had.

"We need to get going," Quinn said. "I didn't mean to stay this long."

"We were having a good time. Trust me, Zenja and Roman can throw some all-nighters. You see how they were acting when Caprice brought out the games."

"And I saw how you men were acting when we ladies beat you down."

"Aw, we let you win," Levi said. "It was our plan from the beginning."

"Okay," Quinn said with a nod. "Whatever makes you feel better."

Levi noticed how Quinn kept glancing at her car. He realized she might be uncomfortable carrying on such a long conversation while Devin waited.

"Do you know how to get out of the subdivision, or should I lead you out?" he asked her.

"I'm good," Quinn said. "And thank you again for the invite. Caprice and Zenja were wonderful. Carmela, too."

"I might use some other words for Carmela."

"Levi!"

"Nothing bad," he added hastily. "I was talking about something like 'resilient.'"

Quinn smirked. "Nice recovery."

Levi pulled his keys out of his pocket. "Carmela has a good heart."

"Okay, I'm nosey. What's your history with her?"

Levi laughed. "There is none, unless you call one dinner 'history.' I don't."

She wagged her forefinger at him. "I knew there was something. You baked her an apple pie for your first date, didn't you?"

"Do I look crazy to you? You've seen the effect my apple pie has on women. She would've started stalking me."

"I have to admit, it was *that* good," she said. "Better than any I've ever tasted."

Quinn held out her hand for Levi to shake. He obliged, even though he would've rather put his arms around her.

"I'll call you," Levi said.

"I hope you will," Quinn said before she turned and walked away.

20

When I turned into the church parking lot, there were several men and about twenty boys circled near one of the basketball hoops. I pulled into a space on the opposite end of the lot. Hopefully, Devin hadn't seen me arrive, and I wanted to keep it that way. I loved watching him when he wasn't aware of it.

Every day he looked more and more like his father. In the past two months, his voice had dropped another octave, and the mustache shadow above his upper lip was growing darker. I didn't tell him that even his sideburns were thickening. It was hard for me to imagine that ten years from now, I'd be looking into the face of a man with a full-blown mustache and beard. Make that looking *up* into his face.

After much thought and prayer, three phone conversations with an apologetic Coach Johnson, and plenty of encouragement from Levi, I had decided to let Devin back on the football team. Even though he'd accepted his fate, I could tell that he was still moping around the house. The only good thing about the time he'd spent off the team was that he hadn't needed to stay up late finishing his homework, and he'd had more than enough time to study for his tests.

When the circle parted, I finally saw what had them all riled up. It was Levi. On a motorcycle. Instead of his police uniform, he was wearing a pair of dark-wash denim jeans, a sleeveless gray T-shirt, and a pair of sunglasses like those worn by the police officers on a TV show my dad liked to watch when I was growing up. *CHiPS*, I think it was called. All Levi needed now was theme music.

Hands shot up in the air and Levi pointed to Kyle Maxwell. I could tell he was eager to jump on the back of the black and purple bike. Levi pushed a helmet into his hands, and once it was securely on his head, Kyle climbed on behind Levi and held on to his shoulders. Levi pulled away slowly, then picked up a moderate amount of speed as he maneuvered around the parking lot.

I knew there was no way Devin would let this opportunity pass him by. He'd never let me leave until he'd had a turn taking a spin. Levi's motorcycle was just another thing that would make Devin think he was one of the coolest people who walked the planet. On the ride home from the Maxwells' the night before, Devin had gone on and on about Levi—his video-gaming skills, the fact that he was friends with a real Major League Baseball player, and his promise to hit some balls with him at the batting cages.

Levi and Kyle were on their third loop around the parking lot when Zenja's car pulled into the space beside mine. We stepped out of our vehicles at the same time.

"Levi is like a hero on wheels whenever he comes around with that motorcycle," Zenja said. She shielded her eyes from the September sun and watched Kyle's final loop around the parking lot.

"I didn't even know he had a motorcycle."

"Yes, ma'am. And Kyle rides along every chance he gets."

As I would've guessed, Devin was next in line. He strapped on the helmet and, finally noticing me, gave me a thumbs-up.

"I can add to Devin's list of things he's going to get when he has a job. I promise you, that list grows daily."

"Until he realizes how much those things cost." Zenja winked. "Don't worry—that list will dwindle quickly."

We watched as one of the men set up a line of orange traffic cones in the middle of the lot. When Levi circled around for the second time, he weaved masterfully through the cones, then doubled back and did it again. Devin—who looked entirely too comfortable on that bike for my taste—was holding his arms out to the sides like an airplane. I shook my head.

"I'm not the only one with a daredevil son, I see," Zenja said.

"Devin would stand up on the back of the motorcycle if he thought I'd let him get away with it," I said. "He'll try almost anything. He loves to frazzle my nerves."

"He sounds like the kind that will ride every roller coaster at the amusement park," Zenja commented.

"*Every* one," I affirmed.

"And you won't?"

"Absolutely not. I don't trust physics like that anymore. When I was younger, yes. But once I got older, I came to my senses."

Like a fool in love, I'd headed to Disney World with Santana after our honeymoon cruise to the Bahamas. It was my first trip to the land of Mickey Mouse, and I didn't mind acting like a big kid. I paraded through the park wearing my white sequined Minnie Mouse ears with the bridal veil attached to the back. My ears and I unashamedly rode Dumbo the Flying Elephant, floated through It's a Small World, and spun around in those teacups, which made me queasy. I should've caught the hint hours later when we headed for the other side of the park to Space Mountain. If I'd only known those two words together spelled disaster. Let's just say that by the time I finished shooting through the man-made outer space, I knew why God hadn't called me to be an astronaut. I left the remains of breakfast, lunch, and my Mickey-Mouse-shaped ice-cream bar somewhere in the perfectly pruned bushes.

"Look at Levi handling that bike," Zenja said with a chuckle. "You know he's showboating for you."

I knew it, too. Forget the motorcycle—Levi really shouldn't have been showboating those arms all around church property. *Jesus, keep me near the cross.*

It was as if Levi had sensed my thinking about him, because he dropped Devin off in the crowd of waiting boys and then, instead of picking up another anxious passenger, rode over to me. He lifted the eye shield of his helmet.

"Get on," he said. "I'll take you for a spin."

"I pass," I said. "Go ahead with the boys."

"I'll get back to them," Levi said. "Come on."

Zenja nudged me with her shoulder. "Go ahead with that man."

Levi held out the extra helmet, and I strapped it on. The inside was hot and sweaty, and I wondered when he'd last disinfected this thing. I rested my hands on his shoulders, but he tapped my left hand and said over his shoulder, "Hold on to my waist."

I obeyed. But Levi didn't have a waist. He had abs. If I could've used my fingers to count them, I would guess he had a minimum of a six-pack. Was there such a thing as an eight-pack? My, my, my. I could scrub clothes on his washboard. This spin through the parking lot needed to be over quick. I hadn't thought about a man like this in a long, *long* time.

Levi gave the engine a loud rev, then purposefully jerked forward. I clutched him around the middle.

I felt his abs move as he laughed, so I punched him in the side. "Stop playing."

"You know I wouldn't let anything happen to you," he shouted over the roar of the bike.

He circled the parking lot slowly the first time but picked up speed the second time around. In the middle of our second round, he veered toward the lot's exit. He stopped briefly to check for traffic, then pulled out into the street.

"Hold on," Levi said.

"You'd better not," I warned him, though it didn't sound very threatening. There was little traffic on the street, and we miraculously made every green light.

"I think that's a sign that we should keep going," Levi said.

I knew the interstate was approaching, but I doubted he'd take me onto I-40. I was wrong.

"Highway looks good," he yelled back. "Hold on."

I was too stunned to object. At first, I was terrified because the only thing I could think about was being crunched like a matchbox car under an 18-wheeler. However, Levi was a cautious driver, and although I knew he could've hit higher speeds if he wanted to, he stayed with the slower flow of traffic in the right-hand lane.

It was a smoother road than anticipated. Either that, or Levi somehow managed to dodge all the dips and bumps. I allowed myself to relax partly and leaned forward until my chin was resting on his shoulder. I wondered what he was thinking. I really didn't care. All I wanted was for the wind to blow my cares away.

"You alright?" he asked once we'd gotten off the highway after traveling about three miles. He stopped at the yellow light at the top of the exit ramp.

"Fine." I flipped up the front of the helmet eye shield for a moment. "That was fun," I admitted. "I bet they're wondering where we are. Devin, especially."

"Who's the parent?" Levi asked.

"He might be worried about his mama. I'm all he's got right now."

"He knows his mama's in good hands," Levi said, easing forward to the white line as oncoming traffic began to slow. "Let's roll."

I snapped the eye shield down and hung on for the ride back to the church, this time holding more tightly than before. When we picked up speed on the highway, I dared to close my eyes. It was exhilarating, and if I hadn't known better, I would've lifted my arms out to the sides, like Devin had done, to see if I could soar like an eagle. I already felt like I was flying.

We arrived back at the church way too soon. The group of boys was still waiting outside, although some of them had chosen to pass the time by lobbing basketballs at the hoops. Levi delivered me back to where Zenja was still standing. She was chatting on the phone, but she ended the call when I pulled off the helmet. I smoothed my hair back.

"Special delivery," Levi said.

"I didn't know if you all were coming back or if you'd ridden off into the sunset."

"Maybe next time," Levi said.

Devin ran up with a basketball tucked under his arm. His brow was dotted with beads of sweat, and I could tell by his soft panting that he'd been running the court. "Wasn't that awesome? Did you go on the highway?"

"Yep," I boasted.

"And you know what? I finally figured out how I knew Mr. Levi."

"What do you mean?"

"When I saw him ride off with you on the motorcycle, I remembered him because he was on a motorcycle that night."

"That night?"

I didn't have to ask him what night he was referring to. The Sunday night he'd called the police on Santana had been "that night" to us ever since. No other words were necessary to explain. The term came with its own memories, visions, and sounds.

"He was there." He looked at Levi. "Weren't you, Mr. Levi? We threw my baseball outside. Now I remember."

Levi had dismounted his bike so that it leaned securely on the kickstand. His red helmet with the black lightning streak was balanced on the seat.

I turned to look at him. I could tell by the expression on his face that Devin was right, but I had to ask, anyway. "Is that true? Were you at my house in Charlotte when...." My words faded.

"I was," Levi admitted.

"Why didn't you say...?"

"I was going to bring it up when I thought the time was right," he said, taking a cautious step toward me.

I took a step back. "Bring up what? That I'm your charity case?" I looked at Devin. "Go get your stuff. It's time to go."

Devin looked from Levi to me. "Am I in trouble?"

"No, baby. You're not. We just need to head out."

Devin's feet pounded the asphalt as he sprinted to the gate where all the boys' belongings were lined up.

"Can we talk about this?" Levi asked.

"I don't think we have anything to talk about," I said, trying to smile. I reached in my side pocket for my keys and realized that I'd left them in the ignition.

"I don't view you as a charity case. At all. That's the farthest thing from my mind."

"You don't have to say anything," I said, stopping him. "Don't worry about it."

"But I'm worried about you and what you're thinking."

He didn't need to know what I was thinking, because those two words—"that night"—had flooded my mind with memories once again.

21

I strained my eyes to keep them open because I had to fight the darkness that was trying to snatch me in. *If I can keep my eyes open,* I thought, *I'll stay alive.* My throat burned from screaming, and my neck throbbed from the leather belt that had pelted my flesh.

I can't leave Devin, I kept telling myself. *I can't let him see me die this way.*

"Put the gun down, Devin," Santana said. His voice was low yet forceful, but it still made my head pound. I could see Devin's blurry silhouette, and the image of the gun held out in front of him. Despite my objections, Santana had shown him where we kept the gun under lock and key. He'd shown him how to use it, so Devin was adept at loading bullets and releasing the safety. I'm sure Santana never thought that he might be teaching his own son how to protect his mother from his father.

"It's okay, Son. Your mom and I were just having a disagreement, that's all. We're fine."

I swiveled my head slowly to the left and then to the right, hoping Devin would understand the signal that we weren't fine. His image began to fade. *Come back,* I told myself.

The other voice in my head was the only one of comfort. **Stay awake, Quinn. Live.**

"No." Devin's voice trembled. "No. You were killing her, Dad."

"We're okay," Santana said. His voice became more threatening. "Put. The gun. Down. Now."

"No!" Devin screamed defiantly.

"Devin," I said, my voice weak. I could barely hear myself. It may have been a whisper. I wasn't sure. I weakly lifted a hand and touched my neck. It was warm. Wet. I tried to swallow. It hurt even worse.

"Ma," Devin said.

I thought I was answering him, but his questions became more panicked. "Ma? Ma?"

I had to use every muscle in my body to say, "Devin." I tried to smile, even though the pain was excruciating.

There was a loud pounding on the front door. Devin screamed, then started crying. I felt tears begin to pour from my own eyes.

I heard sirens, though I wasn't sure how long they'd been going. Devin must have called the police.

Santana started to get up.

"No! No! No!"

Whose voice was that? Mine? Devin's? Santana's?

There were too many voices now. Too much pounding and banging. Screams. The crack of breaking wood. Footsteps running down the hallway. Arguments.

And my world faded to black.

⌒

I hadn't realized there were tears on my face until Zenja touched my hand and pressed a tissue into my palm.

"It's okay," she said. "Do you want to talk?"

"No, I'm fine," I said, though I wasn't. I fingered the raised scar tissue on my neck. It would've been larger if I hadn't been so persistent in rubbing it with vitamin E oil every night. It was barely visible now, and easy to cover with a pat or two of foundation, which I applied every day. The physical reminder would always be there, and I was beginning to wonder if the emotional wounds would ever fade. It had been months since I'd last relived the horror in such vivid detail.

"You have to be strong for Devin—I get that," Zenja said. "But for yourself, sometimes you have to cry. And that's okay."

"I've cried too much," I tried to explain. "At some point, the tears have to stop. At some point, I need to get over it." Zenja didn't know my story. It was about more than just an unfulfilling marriage and a messy divorce. My body and spirit had suffered abuse for years.

"You'll know when you've cried too much, because the tears will no longer come when you think about the situation," she told me. "You can't put a time constraint on your healing. Let God do His work in you, however He needs to do it, however long it takes. Remember what I said about shoulders?" Zenja tapped hers. "We have these because we need to lean on each other. You don't have to walk through your hardships and sorrows alone. You're trying to prove you can make it by yourself, but you don't have to."

"You must think I'm pitiful," I sighed. "I cried yesterday at your house, and now I'm crying out here in the church parking lot. I'm stronger than you think."

"You don't have to prove anything to me," Zenja said. "Maybe that's the problem. How can you draw on God's strength if you're trying to be so tough?"

"You're right," I said, looking for Devin. Of course, he'd gotten distracted, and although he'd grabbed his backpack and cooler, he was using his free hand to play a pickup game of basketball. He lobbed the ball at the net, and it swished in, setting off a thirty-second celebration.

"Where are you headed now?" Zenja asked me.

"Home," I said.

"Great. I'll follow you there."

"You really don't have to," I told her.

"Of course I don't *have* to, but I *want* to." Zenja smiled. "And I won't take no for an answer."

"Sure," I said, shrugging. "You shoulder looks like it could use some company."

"Good. Then I'll follow you there. Give me a minute so I can call Roman and have him come for Kyle."

Zenja walked a few paces away with her cell phone, then headed toward Levi, who stood in a far corner of the parking lot, near some recycling bins and a drop-off container for donated clothes.

He was looking in my direction. I turned away. I couldn't face him. He'd seen me at my worst and hadn't said a word.

Zenja trailed me on the fifteen-minute ride back to my apartment. She would be the first person to visit me, unless you counted the maintenance man who serviced the complex. Devin had invited a couple of his neighborhood friends over to play video games, but I'd never hosted any friends.

"Ma, are you alright?" Devin asked.

"I'm fine, baby."

"Then why are you crying?"

"I'm not," I said, trying to breathe through my stuffed-up nose.

"But you were. I can tell."

I bet he could. A single teardrop could transform my face, giving me puffy eyes and a swollen, red nose—like I'd been standing outside in sub-zero temperatures. "Sometimes it makes me sad when I think about that day," I said, deciding to be completely honest. "I'm sorry you had to see that, and that your life had to change so drastically. I know you miss your old friends and your old school and church." I swallowed the lump in my throat before adding, "I know you miss your dad."

"Yes, ma'am," he said. He was looking out the window. "But, like you always tell me, change can be good."

"Speaking of change," I said, since we needed a more lighthearted subject, "I talked to Coach Johnson and told him you were coming back to the team. That is, if you want to."

"Yes!" Devin pumped his fist in the air. "And I'm going to stay as far as away from R.J. as I can."

That was fine by me. I checked the rearview mirror to make sure I hadn't lost Zenja at the stoplight.

"Mrs. Maxwell is behind us," I told Devin. "She's coming over for a few minutes. You can grab something to eat and take it in your room while she and I talk."

"In my room?" Devin repeated, clearly shocked. I'd always prohibited him from eating anywhere but at the kitchen table.

"Yes. Just this one time. But pick up every crumb."

I entered the guest entry code at the gate and let Zenja enter the complex first. Then I trailed her until she pulled over, letting me pass so that I could lead her to our building.

"I didn't even know this neighborhood was back here," Zenja said as she climbed out of her car. "It's in its own quiet little nook."

"Just the way I like it," I said. "It's perfect." I'd specifically requested the apartment building that was nearest the man-made pond. Every morning, a flock of geese floated effortlessly across the water before setting out for the day, sometimes leaving some of their friends behind to strut around the property, grazing on the grass. I loved watching their daily routine from my balcony.

"Please tell me you're not on the third floor," Zenja said when we started up the first flight of steps.

"No, just the second. The third floor is too much, even for me. Can you imagine having to lug groceries up three flights?"

"That's what Devin's for," Zenja said. "Right, Devin?"

"Yes, ma'am. I always have to carry the groceries in."

"That's part of manning up," I reminded him.

When we entered the apartment, I kicked a pair of Devin's flip-flops out of the way. "Excuse any mess you may see," I told Zenja. "I had no idea I'd be having company."

"No need to apologize for your home," she said with a smile. "It's supposed to look lived in."

"Well, your house is spotless," I said.

She shrugged. "I'm a special case. I have OCD when it comes to cleaning up. It drives Roman and my children crazy. I've probably scarred Kyle and Zariya for life. I bet they'll live like slobs when they finally leave home."

"They'll be fine," I said. "Have a seat." I pointed to the couch. "Can I get you something to drink?"

"Water would be great," Zenja said.

I filled two glasses of chilled water that I'd infused with slices of lemon and cucumber, mint leaves, and fresh ginger.

"This tastes so refreshing...and so healthy," Zenja said, running one finger down the condensation that had formed on the glass. She opened her other palm to reveal two Dove dark chocolate Promises wrapped in silver foil. "And here I was about to offer you a piece of chocolate."

"I'll take one," I said, taking one. "Dark chocolate is good for you, or so I've heard. I don't know if that's a myth, but it sure helps me feel better."

"Me, too," Zenja said, unwrapping hers. "Of course, I eat it all—light, dark, with almonds, with peanut butter. It's always a problem solver. I keep a jar of chocolates on my desk at work, and by the end of most days, I have to go in my stash in the closet and refill it."

I savored the piece of chocolate, then held out my hand for another one. Zenja dug in her purse, pulled out a handful, and dropped them in the middle of the coffee table beside my picture book of coastal lighthouses. I took two.

Then I put two coasters on the coffee table. They were part of a personalized set that Santana had given me on my first Mother's Day. Although I'd donated, sold, or left behind most of the gifts I'd received from him, these were special. Sealed inside the glass coasters were four different pictures of me and a round, doughy baby Devin. It was the coasters that pushed me to tell my story.

"Santana—my ex-husband—always walked in the door on Monday evenings with the most expensive gifts. They were his way of apologizing for another busted lip or bruised arm. He'd bring me ginger tea when I had stomach problems because he thought I was having cramps. He told me it was probably some kind of digestive issue, but I knew it was my nerves. Living with him was literally making me sick. And it wasn't just my stomach. There were migraines, too."

I glanced toward Devin's closed bedroom door and paused to listen. Although he couldn't watch cable television in his room, he did have a TV for playing video games. He had one of his football games going now—I could tell from the background music and the roar of the fake crowd.

"I knew the day was coming when I'd leave him," I continued. "I just didn't know when. I didn't know how. But I knew it was coming." I tapped my heart. "I could feel it."

I reached for my glass and took a sip to quench my palate. Zenja waited patiently. She had settled back on the couch with a listening ear, and I knew by the expression on her face that she wasn't here to get an earful of juicy gossip. She was here to listen to my heart.

"One Sunday night, he pushed me into the wall when I'd been painting in our guest room. He claimed I'd disrespected him when we were at church that morning. He had this thing about always thinking I was stepping out of my place as a woman. I sprained my wrist trying to brace myself for the fall. The next day, he came home with a fancy digital camera. All the bells and whistles."

Devin opened his bedroom door and padded across the hall to his bathroom. I waited until I heard the click of the lock before continuing.

"I couldn't have cared less about the camera at the time, but it gave me an idea," I went on. "It was almost a month before I managed to sneak and buy a cheap digital camera, and that was only because the first lady at our church had given me a gift card and told me to buy something for myself. It was our little secret. I don't think she ever suspected anything. As far as she was concerned, it was a random act of kindness. But God knew."

"Why did you buy another camera?"

"To take pictures. Actually, I bought a camera and a jumbo box of tampons to hide it in. I knew Santana had no reason to touch my feminine products, and he wouldn't even if I asked him to. And from that day forward, I took a picture of every scrape, bruise, and mark he ever made on my body, keeping the date stamp turned on. See, I may have been weak when it came to Santana, but I wasn't stupid. Those pictures were the evidence that sent Santana to jail."

"For how long?"

Devin came out of the bathroom and returned to his bedroom.

"Twelve years. Turns out Santana had a criminal history that I'd had no idea about." I emptied my glass. "He'd opened and closed the linen closet thousands of times, never suspecting that I'd hidden my camera in the bottom of that tampon box. It was pushed behind the soap and the two bottles of rubbing alcohol that he liked to keep there. Always two bottles, never one."

Zenja shook her head. "I know it's a cliché people use all the time, but you don't look like you've been through what you have. Trust me when I tell you that God's grace is shining through you."

"That's all I've had," I admitted. "And it still gets rough."

"But it will get better," Zenja tried to assure me. "Don't let people rush you through your healing. Not everything is cured with twelve steps and a certificate of divorce."

I smiled. "You—and this chocolate—are just what I needed. I feel better already, not having to hold all that poison inside. I just wish it wasn't Levi who'd seen me that day."

"Evidently that hasn't changed his opinion about you."

I shrugged. I understood that Zenja was trying to comfort me, but, like she'd said, I couldn't be rushed through my healing.

"I can't explain it," I told her, but I tried anyway. "It's easier to say it, but when you have to live with it, it's not as easy to overlook. That was the lowest part of my life, and while he may have witnessed just a small portion of it, he's still part of the story. He'll always have that as a frame of reference as it relates to me."

"Only if you live in it, Quinn. It was your history; it's not your destiny."

I shook my head. "I have all this baggage that I don't want to drop at his feet."

Zenja laughed. "He can take it. You saw those steel-toed boots he was wearing today, didn't you?"

I grinned. "I liked those."

"I bet you did." Zenja slid to the edge of the couch. "And I like you, Quinn Montgomery. I have a feeling you're going to be around for a long time. In my life and in Levi's life."

"We'll see," I told her. "God's will."

"That's how we do it. We try to get real deep in His will so we won't get tripped up on our feelings," Zenja said. "I know how it is. I know the real reason you keep this cold water around." She shook her glass so the ice tinkled.

"You might be right about that," I told Zenja.

She stood up and enfolded me in the sisterly embrace I needed. When I felt tempted to pull away, she held me tighter. She circled me until I felt like God Himself had his arms around me. It was a familiar feeling. I'd felt the same way at the park with Levi, because back then, it had nothing to do with his being a man and my being a woman. It had everything to do with his arms being an extension of the arms of God.

"Thank you for coming by," I said. "I know you have to get back to your family."

"Not before I get my nails done," she said, fanning her fingers in the air. "Mommy time."

"We need to do this again. Under better circumstances, of course. I still have stories to tell."

"We can trade stories all night long," Zenja said. "In fact, we do. Seriously think about coming to the women's retreat. It's like a supersized slumber party. And you know how it goes down at slumber parties." She laughed.

"What happens in Blue Ridge stays in Blue Ridge?"

Zenja winked and threw her purse over her shoulder. "See? I knew I liked you. Call me."

"I will."

I'd give it a few days before I reconnected with Levi. He was a man, so he'd understand. Men needed their space on a regular basis. And this time, I'd take the liberty to have mine.

22

LEVI

Levi didn't understand why Quinn had shut him out. It was Thursday, and she hadn't returned his phone call yet, though she had sent him a text: **Call u later.**

Levi had figured she would need some time, but he hadn't expected it to take three days for her to get over whatever she was dealing with. He didn't know what she was feeling. She could be embarrassed, angry, sad—any or all of the above.

Women. He didn't have a clue. When he thought he was doing the right thing, it turned out he was doing the wrong thing. Levi had thought he was protecting Quinn, but his decision backfired on him. Levi had no choice but to wait for her to emerge from her shell. In the meantime, he wasn't going to stay in Greensboro, twiddling his thumbs and waiting to see how she felt. He was on his way to Maryland to attend the wedding of a college friend.

"Daddy, are you coming to see me?" L.J. asked him when he answered his cell phone.

"I sure am, boss man. But I'm going to hang out with some of my friends first. Is that alright?"

"I thought I was your friend." L.J. was pouting.

"You are. You're my best friend. But tonight I'm going to go with some of my other friends to a party for Uncle Phil. He's getting married tomorrow, you know."

"You need to get married, too."

Here we go again. "First I need to find a special lady," Levi said. "We'll talk about that when the time comes. Are you more worried about me getting married or about wearing a tux?"

"Wearing a tux," R.J. admitted.

"That's what I thought," Levi said, changing lanes to escape the tractor-trailer that had been riding his behind. He shifted the seat back to give his legs more space. Levi was still adjusting to the feel of the rental car. Any other time, he would've driven his truck, but with gas prices being what they were, he didn't want to drive the gas-guzzler on the nearly 300-mile trip.

"What do you want to do when I get there?" Levi asked. This conversation wouldn't last much longer. He was approaching the stretch of Virginia highway where the signal always dropped out for ten minutes.

"Let's go buy some toys."

"Is that always going to be your answer? We do that every time."

"I like to get new wrestling men," L.J. said. "And Mama says you're the one with the money."

Levi wasn't going to touch that topic. His child-support payments came directly out of his monthly pay, always on time but never early. Greensboro police weren't exactly sleeping on mattresses made of dollar bills.

"I'll think about it, L.J.," he said. "Maybe we can think of something else fun to do."

"We could go see the president. That would be fun."

"Why, did he call you?" Levi mused.

"The president doesn't have my number, but you can send him an e-mail and give it to him."

L.J. thought his dad could do anything. If it was that easy for Levi to take L.J. inside the doors of 1600 Pennsylvania Avenue, he'd make it happen. Someday. But not this weekend. He was going back to his old stomping grounds.

Levi had first heard of Bowie State University at a college fair during high school. He'd done his fair share of partying there. Maybe a little too much, since it had taken him five years plus one summer session to complete his degree in criminal justice. He'd lived his college years to the fullest, and he thanked God all the time that camera phones and social media hadn't existed when he was doing his dirt. Levi was sure he'd made it into some snapshots on 35-mm film, but who kept up with those over the years?

L.J. was still ranting about which wrestling figurines he still needed. Thanks to Levi's wallet, the boy already had a plastic bin overflowing with them, along with a two-story wrestling ring and a set of fake kid-sized championship belts.

L.J. didn't know about the real wrestling that Levi had been infatuated with at his age. Jake "The Snake" Roberts, Hulk Hogan, "Nature Boy" Ric Flair—they were all about the performance, the show, the technique. They were the legacy. If Levi had known better, he wouldn't have let his mama take those wrestling figurines to the donation bin when he'd stopped playing with him. They could be worth something now. Then again, if they were, Brandy might've sold them for the money. That woman was a trip. She wanted somebody who'd work two jobs, double shifts, so she could sit with her feet up all day eating chocolate bonbons.

"Boss man," Levi said, when the static interrupted L.J.'s every other word, "my phone is messing up. I'll call you back."

"Okay. Love you."

"I love you, too, man. I can't wait to see you. We'll get every wrestling figurine you want."

Levi checked his phone for text messages. Nothing. He'd changed his mind about coming up for Phil's wedding this weekend, even though he'd requested off from work months ago. He no longer liked the things the old crew liked or did the things they did. The rest of them got together fairly often, and from the stories they told, they'd raised the stakes on foolishness since their college years. Levi didn't judge them; after all, he'd once been the ring leader. That was then. This was now.

Phil was ready to tie the knot, and he'd called earlier that week to tell Levi that the party wouldn't be the same if he wasn't there. He promised they wouldn't harass Levi when he chose not to join in their extracurricular activities, but Levi didn't believe him. There was a bachelor party planned. Enough said.

The crew was usually thirsty for women and liquor. Levi hadn't had a hangover since the day he'd found out that Brandy was pregnant, and even then the beers he'd downed on that occasion had been consumed in the privacy of his own home.

Thirty minutes after Levi passed through the dead zone, his cell phone rang.

"No time for cold feet now, man," Levi said to Phil as soon as he answered his Bluetooth.

"Man, it's never too late to back out. But I'm not doing it. My lady and I are rock solid."

"That's good to hear. I never thought I'd see the day."

"Neither did I. Why do you think it took me four years to propose? Man, Robin planned that wedding in six months. She would've gone to the courthouse, but you know her mama and mine weren't having that."

Levi laughed. "That's because your mama probably thinks she's the bride."

Phil's mama had always been over the top. She'd rocked weaves and extensions before they were in style, and she wore her signature ruby-red nail polish no matter the occasion. Levi could have sworn the woman thought she was Tina Turner. All jokes aside, she had the legs for it, even in her sixties.

"Man, my mama is a straight Bridezilla, and she's not the one getting married. My pops is ready for this whole thing to be over so he can get his wife back." Phil unleashed a string of curse words. That was him. As polished as fine china, but with a sailor's mouth.

"Tomorrow your pops will be set free," Levi said with a chuckle.

"And I'll be chained."

"Man, you've been chained for four years, anyway. The wedding just makes it official."

"And I've got some official debt to pay off as a result."

"You can afford it," Levi said. Phil was a big-time attorney who was marrying another big-time attorney. When Levi had been deciding whether to move from D.C. to Charlotte, Phil had tried to convince him to stay, but D.C. had been too much for him at the time. He'd had too many skeletons in his closet.

"So, what's the big plan for tonight?" Levi asked.

"I have no idea. They haven't told me anything. But we can't get the party started until you get here."

"That's a lie if I've ever heard one. Man, you're the groom. You *are* the party."

"Bro, I'm chillin'. I let Dave and Kwame do all the work. All I'm doing is showing up."

"I'll be there as soon as I can," Levi assured him, "but I'm a law-abiding citizen. Don't expect me burn up the road trying to get there."

"Whatever, Officer Gray. Just get here, all right?"

Levi was making good travel time. As long as there were no accidents up ahead, and he managed to pass through the city before rush hour, he'd be at Dave's doorstep in another two and a half hours. Phil didn't know it, but that was where the party would begin. Levi hadn't asked where it would conclude. He didn't know. Most likely—if he knew his college boys—Levi would choose to go back and crash at the hotel instead of sticking it out till the end.

Dave, a man with the money but not the time, had hired a party planner to host a casino night. Levi wasn't a betting man anymore, but he enjoyed an occasional game of spades with his fellow police officers. They didn't put up any money, but they did bet with food. The losers brought in either bagels or doughnuts for breakfast or had lunch waiting at the end of the shift.

Just the thought of food made Levi's stomach growl. He ripped open the bag of trail mix he'd bought at a convenience store when he'd stopped at the Virginia state line for gas, and shook some into his mouth. It was salty. Too salty. Good thing he'd bought a 32-ounce drink to wash it down.

He tuned in to some political talk show using the satellite radio. The time passed quickly while he listened to the bickering back and forth between the lefts and the rights, the conservatives and the liberals, the haves and the have-nots. It was annoying yet entertaining at the same time. Levi couldn't believe the mind-set of some of these people. Everybody thought he was right, and it seemed no one was willing to compromise for the good of America. Every time he saw Phil and Dave, they ended up debating politics into the wee hours of the morning. But there wouldn't be any of that going on tonight.

By the time he pulled into Dave's driveway, Levi was convinced that the political system needed an overhaul. No wonder voter turnout was so low during the primaries and other elections. People were confused. But later for politics.

Dave opened the front door before Levi had the chance to shift the car into park. He stretched his legs, bending them back and forth at the knees, before he finally stood up.

"Come on, bro!" Dave shouted. "You move slower than my grandpa Nate."

"Your grandpa Nate is dead," Levi said.

"Exactly."

Levi reached behind his seat for his weekender bag. "Why do I need to be in a rush? I know you don't need my help. I thought you had people getting stuff together."

"I do. Do I look like a man dressed for manual labor? I did my job. I wrote the check."

And evidently it had been a big one. Levi stepped into the foyer, amazed at the transformation—billiard tables, blackjack tables, poker tables, a roulette wheel, and then the kicker: an area for an open bar. This place could prove dangerous. At least Levi wouldn't have to be the designated driver, since all the groomsmen and Phil's other friends planned to crash at Dave's tonight. He hoped Dave had hired a cleanup crew, too. He'd need it.

"You look scared," Dave said, punching Levi's arm. "It's just your old buddies. We're not going to hurt you. I promise."

"I know about your promises," Levi said as long-buried memories surfaced in his mind.

"Don't start that again," Dave said. "When are you going to let that go?"

"Never." Levi stretched to crack his back, then checked his watch. The party wouldn't start for another three hours. He still had time to catch up on some sleep.

"I need to shower and stretch out on one of your beds. Are your bathrooms clean?" Levi picked up his duffel and folded his garment bag over his arm.

"Naw. I left them nasty 'cause I knew you were coming." Dave laughed. "And don't wear your priest collar under your clothes tonight. The idea is to have a good time."

"Collar or not, somebody has to tame you wild animals."

Dave gave a wild growl. "Just call me 'king of the jungle.' And it's gonna get buck wild up in here tonight."

"You know what? I'm gonna have my collar *and* my Bible on me tonight. Somebody's gonna need it."

"I love you anyway, bro," Dave said, and they finally greeted each other like lifelong friends who together had seen and done the good, the bad, and the ugly.

"You look good, Leviticus," Dave said. "Not as good as me, but you look good." He flashed a smile with teeth that had been professionally whitened.

"Man, how does your wife deal with you?" Levi asked.

Dave just laughed.

He had been married to Latrese for about six years. He'd been the first of the crew to be bonded in holy matrimony and have children. Nine months later, they'd welcomed twins—honeymoon babies.

"Where is the family, anyway?" Levi asked before starting up the winding staircase.

"At my mother-in-law's in Baltimore. I kicked them out for the weekend. Trust me, they were happy to go."

"Does Latrese know what's about to go down?" Levi asked.

"She knows I'm throwing a party for my boy. That's all she needs to know."

"I'll keep my cell phone nearby in case I need to snap some blackmail photos."

Dave shook his head. "No, mi amigo. Somebody's going to collect all cell phones and other electronic devices at the door." A sly grin slid across his face.

That meant it was going to be more than just "casino night."

23

LEVI

Levi should've known things were headed south sooner rather than later when the all-female hosts and serving line walked in. They strutted, sashayed, and slinked their way through the growing crowd of men, holding silver trays of appetizers above their heads. They wore long-sleeved white tuxedo shirts, knotted tightly under their breasts, and miniscule black tuxedo shorts with a sequined stripe down either side.

Levi wiped away the sweat that had beaded on his nose. Was it hot, or was it just him?

"Shrimp?" asked one of the women, extending her tray toward him.

Levi tried to keep from eyeing her ample set of twins as he took one of the bite-sized appetizers and popped it in his mouth. He tried to distract himself with a Scripture verse, but he couldn't think of one to save his life. He should've stayed in Greensboro.

"I'm good, thanks," Levi said when the woman posed in front of him.

She pouted her red lips. "Just let me know if you need *anything* at all," she said before gliding away.

Levi resisted watching her go. He pulled a handkerchief out of his pocket and swept it across his brow. It felt like a jungle in here. Dave needed to check the thermostat.

Soon Dave walked by with an unlit cigar in mouth, his eyes slightly glazed over.

"It's hot up in here," Levi complained.

"That's not my house, that's you," Dave said, too loudly. "You need to stop hiding in the kitchen and come out and enjoy the night. I know I am."

"I'm good," Levi said.

"Suit yourself," Dave said. "You do you. I'll do me."

At least Levi could fully enjoy the food and the music without any guilt. The D.J. was dropping some beats that took him back to high school and college. Back then, music had been real—and you could actually understand what the singers were saying.

The food was the best he'd ever eaten in D.C. Dave had hired the mother of one of his former clients to lay out the spread. Levi would never admit it to the Mae sisters, but she gave them a run for their money.

Levi watched the clock, and at midnight, he slipped out the front door. Every member of his "crew" was too preoccupied to notice. Levi was glad he'd thought ahead and moved his truck to the street so he wouldn't get blocked in. Vehicles were parked up and down the entire block, and as soon as Levi abandoned his space, another car backed into it. The guy could have it. He just prayed none of his friends did anything he'd regret.

By the time Levi stretched out on the king-sized bed in his hotel suite, it was all he could do to keep his eyes open. Still, he checked out the Bible app on his phone so he could read the daily devotional that was posted there. He needed a Scripture or some holy thought to push out the images he'd seen tonight. Otherwise he'd go to bed with visions, and he didn't mean of sugarplums dancing in his head.

Before drifting off to sleep, Levi prayed for his friends, and also for the women who were probably still parading around the house, drinking up the attention and the money. They were the kind of woman that most men wanted to take home to their bed but would never take home to their mama. The kind of woman one would invite to a family reunion was a woman like Quinn. Her body was just as nice as any woman's there tonight, but she carried herself with modest poise. To Levi, that was more attractive than big breasts and an ample backside. When it came to Quinn and those women, there was no comparison.

Thoughts of marriage began to creep into his mind, not necessarily marriage to Quinn, but with the woman God would lead him to. It was time to settle down. He'd never been the kind of man to avoid marriage like the plague, it just so happened that none of the women he'd met made him want to spend the rest of his life with her. But the more time he hung around married couples like Roman and Zenja Maxwell and Duane and Caprice Mowry, the more he longed for what they had: love. Companionship. A helpmeet. Someone to disagree with. Someone to make up with.

Maybe Quinn was that woman. It was too early to tell, but that didn't mean he wasn't willing to try. Levi checked his phone. Still no calls. No messages.

Levi went sleep with thoughts of Quinn and woke up with those same thoughts. The only call he'd somehow missed was from L.J.

"Daddy!" L.J. screamed as soon as Levi called him back. "What time are you going to get here?"

Levi rolled over and squinted at the clock on the bedside table. "In about an hour and a half."

"How long is that?" L.J. asked.

"Enough time for you to watch three cartoons," Levi explained. "Did you eat breakfast?"

"Yes, sir. I had pancakes. I made them myself."

"You did?"

"Yes, sir. I take them out of the freezer, put them on a paper plate, and push the first button on the microwave. Mommy showed me how."

Mmmm. Nothing like a wholesome plate of rubbery bread with syrup. Levi hoped the continental breakfast at the hotel had more to offer.

"Let me speak to your mom."

"Hold on," L.J. said.

"Good morning," Brandy answered almost immediately. He'd expected L.J. to have to call her name once or twice, as he usually did when Levi asked him to summon her.

"What's up?" Levi asked. "I'll be over there to get L.J. around ten, if that's okay."

"Actually, I was going to bring him to you," Brandy told him. "We can meet at the park near the house."

"That's cool, too," Levi said. He wondered what was wrong. Maybe her husband, Rich, had a problem with him coming by, though he'd never had an issue with it before. Levi wouldn't worry about it. It wasn't his problem or his business. He never had to ask what was going on in the household because L.J.'s mouth ran like water.

"I'll see you shortly," Brandy said.

"Can you bring his swimming trunks and a spare change of clothes for him?" Levi asked.

"Sure thing."

Depending on how the day unfolded, Levi would bring L.J. back to the hotel to take a swim in the pool. And since L.J. loved spending the night at the hotel, he was thinking about picking him up after the wedding so his son could stay with him until he had to head home on Sunday evening.

Levi showered, threw on a pair of jeans and a T-shirt, and headed downstairs for breakfast. Thankfully, they had the hot breakfast spread he'd been hoping for, and he stuffed himself while reading the weekend edition of *USA Today*. He downed his last bit of coffee—he'd need the caffeine to handle L.J. all day—then grabbed a handful of mints from the registration desk on his way out.

"I'd like to take him to one of those rooms upstairs," he heard one of the receptionists whisper to her colleague as he passed by. She'd probably meant to be loud enough for him to hear. *See, that's what I'm talking about,* he thought. *No self-respect.*

Brandy and L.J. were waiting for him when he arrived at the park. Not surprisingly, L.J. was standing along the edge of the lake, tossing bread crumbs for the geese. The birds opened the span of their wings as they strutted after the little white delicacies, two steps behind L.J. He dropped his bag of bread crumbs when he saw Levi, leaving the birds to fight and grapple for them. Feathers flew behind him as he ran and jumped into his father's arms.

"I missed you, boss man," Levi said. He hadn't realized how much until he held his son. It almost made him want to cry. L.J. seemed a lot heavier and taller since the last time he'd seen him, even though it had been only four months. He set him down in the middle of the ankle-high grass.

"You've definitely gotten taller," Levi observed.

"And check this out," L.J. said. He looked up at Levi and stuck his tongue through the gap where his two top front teeth should've been.

"Who took your teeth?" Levi knelt to observe his pink gums. L.J. had lost the teeth last month, and there still wasn't any sign of his adult teeth coming in.

"I pulled them out myself," L.J. boasted. "And when I put them under my pillow, the tooth fairy brought me five dollars. Both times."

"That tooth fairy must've upped her rates," Levi said. "I never got that much money for a tooth."

"Inflation," Brandy said, walking up to join them.

She was dressed like she was headed for a girls' night out, makeup and all.

"Big plans?" Levi asked, even though he wasn't really curious. Just making small talk.

"Not really. I'm probably going back home. Rich had to fly out yesterday morning for a conference in Houston."

"How's he doing?"

"He's okay," Brandy said. There wasn't the least bit of thrill in her voice. She used to gush whenever she said his name or talked about him, like she wanted to make Levi believe that her husband could walk on water. Maybe he was starting to sink. Levi didn't ask.

L.J. grabbed Levi by the hand and pulled him toward the jungle gym. "Come watch what I can do, Daddy."

"I'm coming, buddy."

L.J. dropped his hand and ran over to the playground.

Maybe I should've had three cups of coffee, Levi thought.

"So what are you two getting into today?" Brandy asked.

"I hadn't really decided," Levi said, not wanting to disclose his possible plans. "Why? Do you need him back at a certain time? I was thinking I'd bring him back around four, on my way to the wedding."

"Which one of your friends is getting married, again?" Brandy asked.

"Phil."

Brandy had never met Phil; she'd just seen him in a blurry cell-phone photo. Since her relationship with Levi had never taken off, they weren't exactly privy to the intimate details of each other's lives. They made sure to know about each other's parents and siblings, but that was it. Levi paid child support and did his best to be an involved father. Brandy was cordial enough to take pictures of L.J.'s monumental moments and tried to make his quarterly visit with L.J. as hassle-free as possible. The only times Levi got grief from her was when she was ticked off with her own man.

"Do you guys want some company?" Brandy asked.

"What?" Levi was sure he'd heard wrong.

"I was thinking maybe the three of us could hang out today. There's nothing for me to do at home except clean up or watch TV. I don't want to waste such a beautiful day stuck inside when I could share it with two of my favorite men."

Levi looked around to see if Rich was walking somewhere in the park, because there was no way Brandy was talking about him.

"No," Levi said. "That's not a good idea. I wouldn't want my wife kicking it with her son's father, whether I was in town or not. That's disrespectful."

"We're two adults. I think we can handle ourselves." Brandy pushed her shades to the top of her head to hold back her bangs. Levi had noticed the last time he'd seen her that she was letting her hair grow out. He'd always known her to keep it cut short. "I mean, if we *want* to handle ourselves," she added.

What had happened to Levi when he'd crossed the line into D.C.? Was there some kind of pheromone floating in the environment that had attached itself to him? He knew a brother could look good sometimes, but this was getting ridiculous. Only one person could be responsible for this foolishness—Satan himself. And Levi knew why. The devil wanted to trip him up. He'd let that happen once and had ended up with that little guy swinging his way across the monkey bars.

Levi rubbed his hand across his freshly shaven head. "Don't go there, Brandy. It's not attractive, and I'm not interested."

"So you're seeing someone?"

"What difference does it make? You're married. There may be plenty of men who want it and can get it from you, but I'm not one of them."

Levi took off at a slow jog toward L.J. He could tell that the boy's arms were about to give out, three-fourths of the way across the monkey bars, and his only option would be to drop down to the dust below him. The last thing Levi needed was a trip to the hospital. He'd experienced a broken arm before, and there hadn't been anything fun about it.

"You ready to go, boss?'

"Yes," L.J. said, letting go of the bar and dropping into his dad's waiting arms. "I almost made it across. I've been practicing."

"Practice makes perfect."

"What's that mean?"

Levi chuckled. At least his day wouldn't be boring. He unclipped his cell phone from his belt and turned it off. Today was L.J.'s day, and his son milked it for every ounce of fun it was worth. Six hours later, Levi dropped him off in Brandy's driveway. After the way she'd acted that morning, there was no way he was going inside. Besides, a brother was feeling himself. He was looking good in his suit and the bow tie Roman had let him borrow. He wasn't a bow-tie kind of man, but he was feeling the different look.

Levi opened the back car door for L.J. His son had been on a sugar high ever since their outing for ice cream and doughnuts, as well as an excitement high ever since their trip to the toy store, until they'd spent two hours dunking each other in the hotel pool. Now L.J. was dog tired, to the extent that he had drool dripping from his lower lip.

Levi shook his son's shoulder. "Boss man, you're home."

A nice, long string of slobber had formed at the corner of L.J.'s lip. His head bobbed forward when Levi leaned in to unbuckle him from his booster seat.

"Are you coming back to get me after the funeral?"

"The wedding," Levi corrected him with a chuckle. "Yes, I'm coming back to get you." He hoped the mistaken word wasn't a sign. But if Phil and Dave's wives found out how it had gone down at the bachelor party, there might be a funeral today, after all.

L.J. wobbled up the driveway with two wrestling rings clutched in his hands. Levi honked the horn to summon Brandy to the front door.

"I'll be back at around nine, no later than ten," Levi called out.

She nodded. "I'll have him ready in his pajamas."

"Appreciate it," Levi said.

"You can always use the guest room if you'd rather not spend the money on another night at the hotel."

Levi didn't even answer. He left Brandy there to deal with her demons on her own.

24

Focusing all my attention on work had finally reaped its benefits. God was faithful. The week had started off rough after Man Up Monday, but things had finally taken an upswing, at least in my career-building efforts. All week, I'd been consumed with making follow-up phone calls, distributing brochures, and picking up extra classes to teach when instructors called in sick or had another conflict.

Staying busy helped keep my thoughts off Levi and the entire situation. I'd told myself I'd wait five days before calling him. Five was a random number, but my time was up. Yet each of the three calls I'd made had gone straight to his voice mail.

Crack! Crack!

I was always amazed at the force behind Devin's swing. The balls flew out of the machine with lightning speed, and his bat connected with every one of them. Football was a good way for him to pass the time away and stay conditioned, but baseball was his God-given gift. That much was obvious to anyone who witnessed his skills.

I flipped through the stack of mail that I'd brought from the house, along with the letter from Santana to Devin that I'd picked up from my alternate PO box, where Marvin's wife forwarded my mail from Charlotte. I slid my finger under the flap, feeling the usual sense of dread. Santana never mentioned me, other than his regular *"Tell your mother I said hello."*

Crack! Crack!

The content of Santana's letters didn't vary much. He dished out advice for Devin's newfound sport, asked him how he was staying in shape for the approaching baseball season, and encouraged him to excel in his schoolwork. I didn't expect to get teary-eyed when I read the next part of the letter.

However, I'd been an emotional wreck since the beginning of the week, so any small thing could have gotten me started again.

I want to thank you for what you did to stand up for your mother. It proves you are a man because you stood up for what is right. I'm sorry for what I did. You didn't deserve it, and neither did she. I've been going to a class for anger management so I can get help for the reasons behind why I did what I did. I believe God has changed me. One of these days, you'll see. I may have a bigger stomach on the outside (laugh), but I also have a bigger heart on the inside. Keep doing what is right, and don't give your mother any trouble. I know you won't.

I've made a lot of mistakes in my life. I pray to God that you won't make those same mistakes. One of those mistakes was being with another woman when I was married to your mother. That was wrong. But as a result, you have a little sister named Deja. I have seen a picture of her, and she has the cutest cheeks. She is a blessing to me, just like you are.

I caught my breath. I couldn't believe Santana had not only confessed his infidelity but then told Devin about his daughter. So, that was her name. *Deja.* I couldn't believe she'd been named something so close to Devin, like we were all one big, happy family.

Thankfully, Santana's confession was at the bottom of the page. I ripped it off, tore it into tiny pieces, and chucked them into a nearby trash can, where they belonged.

"Your son's got some real power behind that bat," I heard someone say behind me. I turned around. It was the man with the yellow shirt and gray sweatpants who'd been walking around the area the entire time.

"Thank you," I said.

"What league is he training with?"

"Right now he's playing football. We're fairly new to the area, so he played with a recreational team last year. Before we moved here from Charlotte, he played travel baseball."

"I'm sure they were disappointed to see him go," the man said.

I had no idea where he'd been hiding the toothpick that suddenly appeared between the gap in his front teeth. He reached in his pocket and pulled out a business card. It was the simplest one I'd ever seen, but it was straight and to the point, with only his name and a phone number that was underlined by a clip-art baseball bat.

"When you start looking, give me a call. He has a spot on my team, no tryout necessary."

"Thanks," I said. "I'll be sure to hold on to this."

I unzipped the front pocket of my mini backpack and tucked it inside with some of the promotional postcards for my self-defense classes. I'd planned to drop them off tonight at the gym before it closed so they would be there for the Sunday afternoon crowd. I'd texted and called the owner, Lance, within the last hour, but he hadn't returned either attempt at contact. He'd said he wanted to take a look at my materials before he let me leave a stack at the front desk.

"I'm ready, Ma," Devin said. He'd taken off his batter's helmet and replaced it with a cap from one of his favorite teams, the San Francisco Giants. That made me start thinking about him leaving home. He would graduate from high school in six years, and I was trying to figure out how that was possible, since it felt like I'd taught him to tie his shoes no more than three weeks ago. It made me feel all sentimental and mushy.

We headed for the gym, even though I hadn't heard back from Lance yet. I draped my arm around Devin's shoulders as we walked inside.

Devin swung the steel doors open for me and let me walk in ahead of him. I stole a kiss on his forehead as I walked by.

"I'll let you have that one for free," Devin said, turning his baseball cap visor to the back. His laid-back walk transformed as he strutted past the exercise machines and some of the scantily dressed women who were doing leg lifts and triceps raises.

He can't be serious, I mused. Right now, he had nothing to offer them but baseball dreams and a laundry basket of dirty socks and underwear. While I went to the back offices, Devin headed for the stationary bikes. I found Lance in his office, partially hidden by a stack of new exercise mats that were still wrapped in plastic.

"Hey, Lance," I said. "I tried to call you."

Lance stood up, but not before he did a set of squats and lunges. His legs were built like a horse's, and he knew it, too, because he always made sure to wear shorts that showcased them.

"You did?" He lifted some papers off his desk. "I have no idea where my phone is. Anyway, what's up, beautiful?"

Lance called everybody "beautiful." Or "love." Or "brick house." His attention made most women giddy, and I believed they showed more skin than usual just to reel in his compliments. Women flocked to Lance. And he flocked to them.

"Wow!" Lance said when his full attention was on me.

I looked behind me. "Wow, what?"

"Wow, look at you. I've never seen you wearing anything but workout gear."

"I do have other things in my closet," I told him.

"Maybe if I took you out, you could wear a dress that showed off those legs. You shouldn't put in all that hard work for nothing."

"I do it for my health," I said, ignoring his comments. He could have his choice of women from the ones in the gym that evening. *Take your pick*, I wanted to tell him.

"No, I'm serious. We should get to know each other outside of the gym. I think I'm a person you'd be interested in."

"You could really use a boost of self-confidence, huh?" I asked sarcastically. "I really think you should think more highly of yourself." I handed him my promotional materials. "I'm flattered, but I'll pass. I don't mix business and pleasure."

Lance sat on the edge of his desk and crossed his legs at the ankles. "If you change your mind, the offer always stands. But I can't say I blame you."

Then he looked over my materials. I guess it was protocol for him to review the information, but it wasn't as if he hadn't seen it before. He'd booked me to teach a self-defense class to the local agents at the insurance company he worked for in Charlotte the following week.

"These are fine," he finally said, handing the stack back to me. "So, you set to get with the insurance agents next week?"

"More than ready," I said. "If they're anything like you, I'm sure they'll be a fun group." *Fun and cocky*, I thought to myself.

"They'll keep you entertained, no doubt."

I was scheduled to teach nine agents at lunchtime on Tuesday. The insurance company was paying me—very nicely and above my usual fees—and also providing a catered lunch. On top of that, they'd preordered pocket-sized Tasers—pink for the women, black for the men.

Lance had a lot of irons in the fire, and I admired his hustle. On top of being a partner at the gym, he sold every kind of insurance imaginable and had recently started selling all-natural energy and weight-loss supplements. He was a go-getter. A goal-getter, to be more accurate. If one stream of income dried up, he had another one flowing right behind it.

"You know, you should really think about selling my weight-loss supplements."

I shook my head. "I don't think that's my kind of thing."

"Who cares? It makes money. Isn't that everyone's kind of thing? Believe me, you'll learn to love it."

"If I change my mind, I'll let you know."

"And let me know what you want to do about teaching these new classes we're adding. Take that flyer over there," Lance said, pointing to the printer. "If you get back to me by Thursday, I'll let you have first dibs. Your son looks bigger every time I see him. You'll need the extra money just to feed him."

"You're right about that. I'll get back with you," I said, heading out.

"Don't forget about that other offer," Lance added.

I ignored him and went to retrieve Devin from his fake workout. He hadn't even pretended to be working up a sweat. There were too many bouncing body parts in this section. I had to get him out of here.

"Let's go, Pooh Bear," I said.

"Ma," he hissed in embarrassment.

"Boy, please. Let's go. You need to go home and clean your room." I was hilarious. Devin was mortified, but it was all in good fun. If he thought that was bad, he had no idea what kinds of pictures I had stashed to give to his future wife.

"I need to go to the bathroom," Devin said.

"I'll meet you at the car." I was headed out the door when I caught a glance of a police uniform in my peripheral vision. I turned, hoping it was Levi. It wasn't. I checked my cell phone. Nothing. Maybe my plan to wait five days before calling him had backfired, because now I couldn't get in touch with him at all. And from the looks of things, he wasn't concerned about calling me, anyway.

I tried calling Levi but was sent directly to voice mail, same as every attempt I'd made earlier that day. This time, I decided to leave a message.

"Hi, Levi. This is Quinn. Just checking in to see how you're doing. I know I've been somewhat of a ghost this week, but I needed to get some things done." I paused. "And to get myself together." Another pause. "Call me when you get a chance."

That night, when I closed my eyes to go to sleep, Levi still hadn't called.

25

LEVI

The sea of single men parted once Phil launched his bride's garter over his head. Suddenly, Levi was standing alone in the middle of the ballroom dance floor with a garter looped over his fingers. He didn't remember reaching for it, but the lace-trimmed satin accessory was in his possession. The men who'd escaped his fate high-fived one another and wiped their hands across their brows in an exaggerated show of relief. It was all in good fun. Levi tossed the thing over his head and caught it behind his back without looking.

The photographer summoned the woman who'd caught the bridal bouquet to join Levi for a picture, and she seemed happy to oblige. Levi casually draped his arm over the woman's shoulders, but she leaned in close enough to put her head on his chest and lift one leg in the air. Everyone egged her on until she jumped into Levi's arms.

"See how easy it'll be to carry me over the threshold?" she asked.

It would've even been easy for L.J. to pick her up. She had the face of a grown woman and the body of a petite teenager. After posing for one last picture, Levi set her down on her tiny, high-heeled feet but couldn't get away without a dance.

"Just one," she pleaded, pulling him back to the center of the dance floor, where some of the members of the wedding party had already gathered. "It's good luck. You can't break the tradition."

Levi had never heard of that tradition. It probably looked as if he was dancing with the flower girl, but this woman had clearly perfected her moves in adult-only nightclubs—no doubt about it.

"I can't keep up with you," Levi said, his way of bowing out of swaying with her R-rated gyrations. "I'd better leave you with somebody who can handle your moves."

"Dave told me you were a police officer," she crooned, running a finger down the row of buttons on his shirt. "I'm pretty confident you can handle them."

There was no telling what else Dave had said to her. Levi would have to deal with him at a later date. For now, he was ready to scoop up L.J. and head back to the hotel. The reception was beginning to die down, anyway, especially since they were starting the soul train line for the umpteenth time.

"Congratulations, my brother," he told Phil when he was finally able to get to him. "You have a beautiful lady."

Phil looked like he'd already sipped a few too many glasses of champagne. Add that to what Levi had seen him drink at the bachelor party, and he was headed for a second hangover. "She is fine, ain't she?" Phil said, eyeing his wife in her strapless white gown. "I should've married her a long time ago."

"Yeah. You're lucky she waited around for your crazy behind," Levi joked. "But it's all good now. Today is the beginning of forever."

"Listen to you, sounding all sappy."

Levi slapped him on the back. "I think I'm getting out of here. I need to go pick up my little boss man."

"I understand. Tell L.J. I said hey. Next time you're up, we'll hang out."

"Make sure you get permission from your wife," Levi told him. "You're a married man now."

Phil puffed out his chest. "I run my house," he said, then looked around, as if to see if his new bride had heard him.

"I know you do," Levi said. "You run the dishwasher, the vacuum cleaner, the washing machine, and your mouth."

"Your time is coming," Phil said. "Go home and put that garter under your pillow so you'll have sweet dreams."

When Levi collapsed in bed that night, the only thing under his pillow was L.J.'s foot. "This is crazy," Levi said, pushing his son's leg away from his face again. He adjusted the sheets so that L.J. was completely covered. Levi liked to keep the room cold while he slept.

As promised, L.J. had been dressed in his pajamas when Levi had picked him up at Brandy's. He'd padded outside in flip-flops and a set of red boxers and matching shirt printed with yellow construction trucks and green bull-dozers. Levi hadn't given Brandy a heads-up when he was on his way. The last thing he'd wanted her to do was have time to scheme up some ridiculous plan, like opening the door dressed in red lingerie.

L.J. hadn't fallen asleep until almost one o'clock in the morning. The nap he'd taken earlier had given him some extra fuel, and he'd been on full blast, begging to return to the pool as soon as he'd walked in the hotel door and caught a whiff of chlorine. Levi had refused after peeking at the pool and spotting a group of college-aged kids occupying the entire deep end. Levi knew the drill—things were about to get rowdy. They were coupled off, playing a game of chicken, the girls balancing on the boys' muscular shoulders.

Levi picked up the remote control and muted the television. He'd for-gotten to brush L.J's teeth before bed, but there was no way he was waking him, even though he'd sucked down a big bag of gummy bears. One night without floss and fluoride wouldn't hurt.

Besides, it was time for Levi to catch some z's himself. He needed to get back to Greensboro tomorrow, and although he'd originally planned to return no later than nine o'clock in the morning, L.J. had tried to convince him that they needed to see a movie, go bowling, and visit the arcade, the skating rink, and the indoor jumping playhouse. *Scratch the skating rink.* Levi couldn't skate, so there'd be nothing he could do to keep L.J. on two feet.

Levi leaned over to listen and feel for the soft breathing of his son. He'd take him wherever he wanted to go. Brandy would appreciate that he'd worn him out before returning him to her care. Levi probably wouldn't see him again until the holidays, so he felt it was his duty to give his son something to remember. Levi spoiled him, but L.J. deserved it. Other than running his mouth every now and then in class, he was a good kid.

Levi reached for his phone in the inside pocket of his suit jacket. It was empty. He tossed the covers around, opened the drawer of the nightstand, and checked under L.J.'s body to see if his son had swiped it so he could play Pac-Man. No such luck. Levi retraced his steps in his mind and finally remembered that he'd turned it off that morning and stashed it in the glove compartment before heading to the wedding. It would have to stay there until morning.

The room was dark, other than the glare from the television and a shaft of light escaping from the bathroom door. Levi stretched across the bottom of the king-sized bed to keep away from L.J.'s flailing arms and legs. But it didn't matter. By morning, L.J. was perched on his father's chest.

"Good morning, boss man," Levi said when he awoke. He ran his hand across the crown of his son's head.

"I'm hungry, Daddy."

"Can I open my eyes first?" *All boy.* Levi frowned and turned away from his son's morning breath. Was a five-year-old's mouth supposed to smell like a garbage disposal? That's what Levi got for not making sure he brushed his teeth.

"Your eyes are open," L.J. said, using his fingers to pry Levi's eyelids open even wider.

This was a battle Levi wasn't going to win.

"Let's get washed up and dressed first," Levi said.

"We're just going downstairs. It doesn't matter."

"It does matter. Good hygiene always matters."

After Sunday breakfast and a good teeth-brushing and extra gargle for L.J., Levi buckled his son in his seat for their second day of bonding. First they headed to the cinema to see what kid-friendly film they could catch first.

In the car, Levi finally had a chance to check his phone. He listened to several voice mails from Dave, who wanted to hook him up with Felicity, the woman who'd caught the bouquet. Not happening. There was a message from his partner at work, and finally the message that made Levi wish he were back in Greensboro.

"Hi, Levi. This is Quinn. Just checking in to see how you're doing. I know I've been somewhat of a ghost this week, but I needed to get some things done." Pause. "And to get myself together." Another pause. "Call me when you get a chance."

Levi grabbed L.J. by the hand. The boy was too excited to bother watching for moving cars in the parking lot. "Come on, Daddy." Levi would have to put Quinn on the back burner until his visit with L.J. was over.

That didn't happen until nearly four o'clock that evening. Levi lifted L.J. out of the car, hoisted him onto his shoulders, and trudged toward the driveway of Brandy's house. He was relieved when Rich answered the door.

They slapped hands. "Good to see you, Rich. How are things going?"

"I'm tired, bro. My trip to Houston was nonstop. When they said we could leave early, I jumped on the first flight out this morning."

"No matter where you live, the hustle is real," Levi said.

Levi handed over L.J.'s Spiderman rolling travel bag.

"Thanks for looking out for my son," Levi said. He said it all the time. He'd never had any beef with Rich. As long as Rich kept stepping up to the plate, he was alright with Levi.

"My pleasure," Rich said. "I know you'd do the same if the situation were reversed."

L.J. had already attached himself to Levi's leg. No matter how many hours they spent together, it was always hard for L.J. to let his dad go. It was even harder for Levi to leave his son. Crying didn't make Levi any less of a man, but he always waited until he was alone in the car before he let the tears fall.

"I'll see you soon, Son," Levi said.

L.J. nodded but buried his head deeper into his father's side.

Levi knelt down and lifted his son's head until their eyes met. He wondered if L.J. knew he was looking at his future self. Of course, Levi knew he had no idea. They shared more than their physical looks alone. Levi could see his son's resilience. He had a brave heart, and God was going to take him more places than he could dream of. Levi kissed L.J.'s forehead.

"I love you, boss man. Behave and do your best in school, alright? I'm glad you're my son. You're the best I could've ever asked God for."

Levi meant every word. He swallowed the lump in his throat. He hated that L.J. couldn't grow up under his roof—at least, not yet. That was something he couldn't change right now. But someday, he'd be able to send for his son. Until then, he'd continue to be the best father he could, and he'd always make sure L.J. knew how much he loved him.

"Come on—let's take a picture," he suggested. "That way, when you call, I'll remember what you look like. I don't have any photos of you with your teeth missing." Levi tugged at L.J.'s shirt. "You might have to borrow your great-grandpa's false teeth the next time you go see him."

L.J. grimaced and stuck out his tongue. "Eeewwww. That's nasty." He giggled, then wiped his hands down his cheeks, leaving white, salty trails where his tears had been. He gave a wide, toothless grin while Rich took a picture of him and Levi using Levi's cell phone.

"Call me tomorrow night," Levi told him.

"Okay. We'll say our prayers together."

"We sure will." Levi looked at Rich. "Tell Brandy I said thanks."

"Will do. She's upstairs lying down. She said she wasn't feeling well."

Levi smirked as he walked away. *Evidently she's sick of your behind*, Levi thought.

Finally, he was Greensboro-bound. He worked his way through the streets until he was on a steady trajectory down the highway. After setting his car on cruise control, he called the woman whose voice he'd been wanting to hear for days.

"Hello?"

"How are you, Ms. Montgomery?"

"Fine. And how are you, Officer?"

Levi leaned back in his seat. It was amazing how her voice affected him. Those women at the bachelor party, and the ones who had ogled him at the wedding, had done nothing to move him. But the mere sound of Quinn's voice made him think of his future.

26

My heart pitter-pattered when I heard Levi's voice.

"What have you been up to?" Levi asked.

"Working. That's about it." I wanted to say, *And thinking about you,* but I was nowhere near that bold.

"That's what most of my week was about—until I went out of town, of course," Levi said. "I'm headed back in from D.C. At the last minute, I decided to attend a friend's wedding and also spend some time with L.J."

"That's nice. How was your weekend?" I wasn't sure I really wanted to know. Bachelor parties, hookups with old friends, weddings and receptions.... Levi had probably been a walking magnet for every woman with romance on her mind.

"Nice. Phil and Robin have been together forever. We knew it was coming sooner or later."

That was all the information he volunteered, and I wasn't going to press for more. He was a grown, godly man, and anything he'd done—or hadn't done—didn't involve me. If Levi was the man I thought he was, he'd kept his hands clean. There was a string of silence between us.

"I'm glad you finally called," he said. "It's good to hear your voice."

"It's good to hear your voice, too," I said. "I didn't know if you'd want to speak to me again."

"Why would you think that?" Levi asked.

"Because of Monday...how I flipped out a little."

"When I called, you texted me back and said you'd call me later. So I left it at that."

"I did, didn't I?"

"You did."

Five days. Me and my stupid five-day waiting period. I used the tip of a pair of scissors to slit open the sealing tape of the cardboard box that held my painting supplies. As I did, it felt like a breath of air being blown into my body, resuscitating my life and my spirit. I lifted out the bag containing my acrylic brush set and folded back the flap.

"How long will it take you to get back?" I finally asked him.

"I'm just heading out. Hopefully I'll be home around ten thirty."

Next I took out an eleven-by-fourteen-inch canvas. "That's too bad," I said. "Today is Sunday. You were supposed to take me out."

"I would've come back earlier if I'd known you wanted to go out with me."

"Stop playing," I said.

"I'm not playing. I'm a grown man. I don't have times for games."

My heart was doing those crazy flips again.

"I'd still like to see you tonight," Levi said. "But I understand if you think it'll be too late."

"No, I'd like that," I said. A sigh of relief moved through my body. I hadn't run Levi off.

Our conversation became easier, falling back into its usual rhythm, and before I knew it, an hour had passed. It felt like we were back eating breakfast with the Mae sisters. Levi told me about casino night, and how he'd opted to head back to the hotel before things got too out of hand. I told him about the call from Janae and how Santana had tried to break the news of Devin's half-sister in his latest letter. Another hour passed. I'd set up my easel and painting supplies near the patio door facing the lake, promising myself that the next morning, I'd paint life onto the blank canvas staring back at me.

"Ma," Devin said, "I can't find those jeans you just bought."

"I'll help you in a sec," I told him.

Once Devin was out of earshot, I gave Levi my address. He said he would call when he was about thirty minutes away.

I grappled with what to wear, then finally decided to put on my most comfortable pair of jeans and a green and yellow long-sleeved shirt from Devin's old baseball team that said "Devin's Mom" on the back. I nibbled on carrots and celery sticks while I worked on the jumbo book of puzzles

Devin had picked up in the grocery store checkout line. He loved Sudoku, logic games, and crossword puzzles, and he'd gotten me hooked on them, too. I could do them for hours. In fact, I did. It helped the time pass quickly.

It was Devin's responsibility to clean up the kitchen before he headed to bed, so he rinsed off the dirty dinner dishes, loaded them in the dishwasher, and wiped the counters. By nine o'clock, he was headed to his room with a notepad and pencil to write Santana another letter. When he asked me why his dad's latest letter was torn off at the bottom, I played dumb.

It was close to ten fifteen when Levi called. After freshening up, I peeped in on Devin about three times to make sure he was sound asleep. Finally Levi called and told me he was in the parking lot. I eased out of the door and locked it behind me.

Levi's truck dwarfed the cars parked on either side of him. He climbed out of the driver's side, and we shared a quick hug. I wished it would've lasted longer.

"How was the ride?" I asked.

"Felt shorter than usual. It helps when you have something to look forward to," Levi said.

"You drove this big monster all the way to D.C.? I bet it guzzled gas."

He shook his head. "I drove a rental. I stopped at home before I came over."

No wonder he smelled so good. And he looked as good as he smelled. Levi had parked under the streetlight, so I was able to see his face clearly.

He gestured to the truck. "Care to sit awhile?"

"Sure."

He opened the passenger door for me, then shut it after I'd gotten in.

Once he was seated beside me, I couldn't help but giggle. "Is it just me, or does it feel like we're two teenagers who snuck out to see each other?"

He chuckled. "What would happen if Devin found us out here?"

"Devin sleeps pretty soundly. Unless he has to get up to use the restroom, he won't be opening his eyes until morning."

Headlights approached us, then passed, the car continuing over the maze of speed bumps in the complex.

"Let's deal with the elephant in the truck, since we haven't talked about it," Levi said. "It was never my intent to hurt you. From the time I made the connection between you and that night in Charlotte, I never looked down on you. As far as I'm concerned, you're a woman to look up to. I want to apologize for not being up-front and forthright."

"And I apologize for overreacting," I said.

"Who says you were overacting? You're entitled to feel the way you do about that situation. I know it hasn't been an easy thing to deal with."

I nodded. "But it's getting better. One of these days, it won't hurt anymore when I think about that Sunday. It already doesn't hurt as much as it used to."

"One day at a time." He rested his hand on the steering wheel.

"One Sunday at a time," I added.

Levi looked at me with such intensity. "You're beautiful, you know that? Organically beautiful."

That made me smile. "Where'd you get that line?"

"You liked that, huh?" He flashed a grin, giving me a glimpse of that almost-dimple. "The truth is the truth. And the truth is that I've missed talking to you, Quinn. I've gotten used to hearing your voice almost every day. It doesn't seem right going to bed at night if I haven't spoken with you."

I couldn't believe Levi had exposed his feelings like that. Most of the men I knew were hesitant to express themselves in a personal way. Either Levi wasn't that kind of man, or he was deliriously tired from being on the road for so long and didn't realize what he was doing. I chose to believe the former. His honesty gave me no choice but to take the cloak off my feelings for him.

"I missed talking you, too, Levi. Meeting you has been a breath of fresh air for me."

I was finally able to exhale. Our words had moved us into a different place. I wasn't in a rush to be in a relationship. I wasn't in a rush to find love. But I did like that someone had missed me. It felt good to know that in the exact moments I'd been thinking about Levi, he might have been thinking about me.

"Both of us have a messy past, and some things we might be ashamed of. And while there's nothing we can do about that, we *can* control the choices in front of us, and I think we should take a chance and see where this goes." He waved his forefinger back and forth between us. "If it's not right, at least we can say we tried." He winked and added, "At least we'll know that you're crazy for not wanting a man like me."

"Oh, really?" I gave him a playful punch in the shoulder.

"Really."

"Well, if I'm crazy enough not to want a man like you, you'll still have to see me at church and whenever we ever cross paths sat Zenja and Roman's."

"I can handle it if you can," Levi said, raising the temperature in the truck. With a distinct chill in the air, it was finally starting to feel like fall— my favorite season of the year.

"I'm a big girl," I said. "You know what I've endured. I think I'll be okay."

I'd often wondered how it would feel if and when I started to develop feelings for another man. I hadn't known whether I'd feel exhilaration or anxiety, whether I'd be frightened or fearless. Now I knew: I felt them all. They rushed in at the same time. Yet I was ready to take the plunge.

"Can I kiss you?"

"Did you really just ask me that?" I said, hoping my lips weren't too dry because I definitely wanted that kiss.

"I don't want to overstep your boundaries. Or mine."

"Maybe you should write me a letter so I can check 'yes,' 'no,' or 'maybe.'"

Levi reached over, opened the glove compartment, and pulled out what looked like an old receipt and a ballpoint pen. He pressed the paper against the steering wheel and scribbled something on it, then handed it to me.

Can I kiss you? —Yes — No — Maybe

His handwriting was horrible.

I took the pen from him, shielded the paper from his view, and made my selection. Then I folded it into a tiny square before handing it back to him. "You do realize how ridiculous this is, don't you?"

"I'm a man of suspense," Levi said. He unfolded the paper slowly, never taking his eyes off me. Once the paper was open flat, he glanced down at it.

Levi didn't give me the chance to respond, object, or change my mind. He leaned forward and pressed his lips to mine. Softly, like a gentleman. I responded like a demure lady. A first kiss is always the hardest to figure out. You never know if it will be awkward, disappointing, or amazing. I'd never considered that it could be *beyond* amazing.

And it wasn't because it was long and salacious and drew us to a place we shouldn't dare go. It was because I knew we had a connection, and we'd sealed it with a sweet, closed-mouthed kiss.

"There will never be another first kiss with me," Levi said. "That was it."

"It was worth the wait," I told him.

"Oh, so you've been waiting for it?"

"That didn't come out right." In the light of a streetlamp, I could see the light shimmer of lip gloss I'd left on his mouth. I wiped it off with my thumb. "We should probably keep our lips to ourselves from now on."

I felt like he was looking at my lips when he said, "That's going to be hard to do. Your lips are the perfect shape. Like a heart."

I wagged my finger near his face. "No, no, no. You're just going in for round two." One of us had to exercise willpower. I guess it was my turn tonight.

"I'm saving this note," Levi said, refolding the paper and tucking it in his pocket.

"What for? A scrapbook?" I asked.

"No. As proof that you tried to seduce me." He grinned.

I rolled my eyes. "Whatever. Read it again. You're the guilty party."

Levi raised both his hands in the air. "Guilty as charged, your honor." He adjusted the heat to a lower temperature. What he probably needed was a cold shower.

Levi reached for my hand, and we let our palms rest together. I stared into the shadowed windows of the residents who shared my apartment building. I knew few of them by name. Amber and Parrish lived below me, but they'd been house-hunting, since Amber was four months pregnant with their first child. Caleb, my neighbor across the hallway, was in graduate school during the day and worked as a security guard at night, hence the reason I rarely saw him.

"I know we're trying us,'" I said, but "'us' doesn't include Devin right now."

"I understand," Levi said. "There's no rush. It'll happen when the time is right."

"Speaking of the time, I'd better get to bed. I have a long day tomorrow, and it starts as soon as I drop Devin off at school."

"You need your beauty rest."

"I'm not the one who's been on the road," I said, trying to stifle a yawn.

"This was the best part of the road trip," Levi said. "Coming home." Our fingers entwined.

"Go inside," Levi said after a minute had passed and I still hadn't budged. "I'll walk you to the door."

We walked closely, but not hand in hand. When we reached the top of the stairs, Levi pulled me into a tight embrace. I could've slept right there.

"Thanks for stopping by," I said. "Our Sunday tradition continues. You managed to get me out of the house again."

"Mission accomplished," he said, kissing the side of my hair. "Have a good night."

God, guard my heart, I thought to myself as I closed and locked the door. Because I had a feeling that Levi had the key.

27

Of course Devin can come over—that's no problem," Zenja said to me. "Trust me, it makes my life easier when I don't have to worry about Kyle complaining that he's bored. Devin is always welcome."

"I don't want to impose if you have other plans," I told her.

"What other plans? Unless Roman has a show somewhere, we're in relaxation mode on Sundays after church. The only thing we'll be doing is stuffing our faces at brunch and then sleeping. Every now and then, we watch a movie as a family."

"Thanks, Zenja. You're a lifesaver. Devin loves your entire family. He's taken on the official task of being Kyle's big brother."

"And that's helpful, because Zariya's at the age where she's horrified by everything her brother does. I'll be happy when these years of drama are over."

"It makes me grateful that I have a boy," I said.

I was sitting in my car, watching the gym parking lot fill as people showed up for the lunchtime workout. I noticed Ginger pull up in her yellow convertible Volkswagen Beetle. She was wearing a neon orange outfit that was as bright as the paint job on her car. She jumped out with a duffel bag slung over her shoulder and lifted out a black garment bag, along with a pair of heels. It was time for me to get inside.

"Exercise is calling," I said to Zenja.

"Get in a little extra workout for me," she said. "When I finish my lunch, I get to explore the fourth-grade classrooms at their 'Taste Around the World' event."

"That sounds fun," I said. I admired Zenja's career as an elementary-school principal. Her passion for education and for the students was always evident.

"Fun and fattening," Zenja said. "They don't make it easy to eat healthy around here. There's always some parent dropping off muffins or doughnuts in the office, and those kindergarteners are always having some kind of ice-cream celebration or Dr. Seuss party. Which means food, of course."

"Willpower," I said. "It's all about willpower."

"Will Power? I've never met him before," Zenja joked. "Well, carry on. I'm headed to Germany, Mexico, and France."

"Auf Wiedersehen, adios, and au revoir," I spouted.

"Pretty and smart, too. Levi had better stay on his toes."

I knew how to say hello and good-bye in about eight different languages. Amazing, the random things my mind remembered from my years of high-school chorus.

"We'll see you Sunday, Zenja. Probably around three o'clock," I told her. "I'll call you later in the week to confirm or to let you know if anything changes."

"No problem. And good luck on your workshops this week. God keeps opening doors for you, so keep walking through them."

"Thanks, Zenja. And I really mean that."

By the next day, I wished I had one of God's doors to slam in the face of a man named Marcus. The insurance agents Lance employed were an interesting crew, but none was as annoying as Marcus. He had a rebuttal, question, or smart-aleck remark for everything I said. He had an alternative move for every self-defense technique I taught. I wasn't sure how his colleagues endured him on a daily basis. I maintained my professional face, but I definitely had to say a few prayers of patience over the hour-long demonstration.

A sweet, mousy-looking lady had finally taken a stand for the sake of the entire office. "For goodness' sake, Marcus, will you please put a plug in it?" she'd said in a thick Southern drawl. "You are not the expert. Quinta is the expert."

Did she say "Quinta"? I'd thought.

"I didn't correct her," I told Levi later that evening. "Since she'd finally shut Marcus up, she could call me anything she wanted."

"Next time somebody gives you trouble, call me," Levi said. "I'll show up with my nightstick."

I chuckled. "I easily could've flipped him over if I wanted to, but I thought that might mess up my chances for referrals."

Even though I hadn't seen Levi since Sunday, we'd been talking at least twice a day—in the morning and again at bedtime. During the week, I'd found myself thinking about him more often and saying frequent prayers for his safety. I wasn't sure how long I could keep our growing friendship under wraps from Devin, because I wanted to see Levi more often, and evenings were the only times he was available.

On Friday, Levi must've wanted to see me as much as I wanted to see him. The fourth quarter of Devin's first football game had just started, and I was wishing that the foam stadium seat I'd brought had a little more cushion to shield my backside from the steel bleacher. The Mustangs were putting a pounding on the visiting team, but it wasn't just because we had home-field advantage. The poor visiting team needed some extra practices, in my opinion. The score was 49 to 6, and even some fans of the home team were starting to cheer on the opponents.

I was sitting at the end of the bleacher for easy access to the exit after the final buzzer. Besides, I didn't like sitting in the middle of a bunch of giggly middle-school girls and the boys who were trying to impress them. I was watching the cheerleaders perform a death-defying stunt when I felt a soft pull on my arm.

I turned, expecting to see Coach Johnson's wife, who had apologized to me about the condom fiasco exactly fifty-three times. But it wasn't Tricia Johnson. It was Levi.

I felt enough excitement to jump into his arms, but I had to contain myself. "What are you doing here?"

"I wanted to check Devin out. What number is he?"

"Fifty-two," I said. "He's a defensive end."

"So, you know a little about football."

"Only what Devin's taught me," I confessed. "But I'm learning." I slid over so he could sit down.

"No, I'm good," Levi said, propping his arm against the end rail. "I'm staying for just a few minutes."

"A few minutes" ended up being the rest of the fourth quarter. Levi became engrossed in the game, especially with gawking at the opposing team's coach and his poor calls and techniques. "No wonder they're losing the game," he said.

"You're getting pretty worked up," I observed.

"My bad. If I wasn't wearing this uniform, I'd really get rowdy. It's all in fun, though. We have to teach our children good sportsmanship."

When the final buzzer sounded, the Mustangs went wild. All the fans spilled onto the football field for a postgame celebration. The team's fight song blasted through the speaker system to accompany the jubilation. The players had crushed themselves so closely together that we couldn't tell who was who until they disbanded and went to give congratulatory handshakes to the other team.

"Do you see him?" I asked Levi.

"Yeah, I see him. He's on the left side near the cheerleader with the ponytail on top of her head. White ribbon."

It took me two seconds to spot Peyton. She was never more than two steps behind Devin. I'd watched them silently and spied on them after football practice. If Devin was interested in her beyond friendship, however, he didn't show it. Yet that didn't stop her flirtatious behavior. Aggressive girls usually grew up to be aggressive women. And aggressive women rarely knew their boundaries. The image of Janae Brown whisked through my head. I wouldn't let it stay. That thought, and any other that tried to steal my joy, was quickly arrested by Isaiah 26:3: *"You will keep him in perfect peace, whose mind is stayed on You, because he trusts in You."*

Devin finally spotted me and Levi. He ran over to us, pumping his football helmet in the air. "Mr. Levi, what are you doing here?" he asked excitedly. "Did you come to arrest somebody?"

Levi laughed. "I need to arrest your whole team for putting the beatdown on those other boys like that. I caught the last quarter. You guys are awesome."

"Did you see me?"

"I did," Levi said, slapping Devin on the back. "You've got skills, man."

I was glad there'd been a man there to witness at least part of Devin's first football game. I reached in my purse for my camera. I'd snapped some shots during the game, but Devin tended to shy away from posed pictures these days. So, while he talked to Levi, I captured the moment, focusing more on Devin's face than anything else. I was accustomed to seeing him riled up after baseball games, and this football-related jubilation was so different. His shoulder pads made him look broader and manlier than he was, and although the way he chewed his mouth guard was disgusting, it made for some interesting shots.

"Man, that move was crazy," Devin was saying. He handed me his sweaty helmet, and I gave him a partially frozen sports drink that had been thawing during the game. I still didn't understand how he refused to drink from the same beverage as his mother. During the game, he'd shared plenty of disgusting sports bottles with his teammates.

A whistle blew, and a crowd of blue and yellow swarmed toward the horse logo in the middle of the field. Devin ran back to circle up one last time so Coach Johnson could give the team his customary pep talk and final send-off.

"Thanks for stopping by," I told Levi. "That was a nice surprise. For both of us."

"I couldn't go another day without seeing you."

Levi and I walked together toward the exit gate. We kept a discreet distance from each other, although I felt like it would've been the perfect opportunity for me to reach out and graze his hand so he'd hold mine. Levi stopped and gave me two dollars to buy two promotional pom-poms from the booster fund-raising table.

"You never did tell me what we're going to do on Sunday," I said, pulling on the plastic strands of the pom-poms.

"I never meant to."

"Women have to know these things," I insisted. "How am I supposed to decide what to wear?"

"Jeans, a shirt, and a light jacket should be fine."

"A cute shirt? A T-shirt?"

"Wear what you would to a football game," he said. "Like what you have on right now."

I was finally starting to figure out the kind of man Levi was. He liked to do things that were laid-back, and I wondered if I would ever get to dress up to go out with him. I'd had a future date night in mind when I'd purchased a pair of shoes earlier that week. Having no outfit in my closet that would do them justice, I'd had to buy a new one of those, too. I guessed I'd have to debut it another Sunday. That was fine.

I knew Levi had said that I needed to ask God for a new Sunday morning song. Unbeknownst to him, my heart was already singing it.

28

"Ma'am, your registration is already paid in full," the woman at the women's ministry kiosk said to me. She handed me back my debit card, along with a purple and pink gift bag. "It seems that you didn't pick up your registration packet, though."

"There must've been a mistake," I said. "This is my first time coming to register."

She eyed her computer screen and correctly recited my address and phone number.

"That's me," I said. "But I promise you, I never registered.

"Well, thank the Lord for the blessing," the woman said. "You must have an angel in disguise, because you're definitely going to the Mountain High Retreat."

There was no disguise. I knew exactly what my angel looked like. He wore a black policeman's uniform and carried handcuffs and a revolver on his hip holster.

I made my way through the foyer toward the sanctuary doors. I'd already left Devin at his favorite place, "The Hangout," where the youth ministry conducted its worship services.

"Quinn," Levi called out. My angel in disguise was wearing a suit today.

"You clean up nice," I told him when he'd made his way over to me.

"I try." Levi shrugged. "You don't look so bad yourself."

"Thank you, times two—for the compliment and for taking care of my registration for the women's retreat. You really didn't have to do that."

"Who says I did?"

"So, we're going to play that game, are we?" I asked as I accepted a church bulletin from the usher by the door.

Levi didn't answer but followed me to a pew near the center of the sanctuary. We sat down together. We didn't discuss it or second-guess if it was the right thing to do. It just happened naturally. Or, as Levi would say, "organically."

When the worship service started, I nearly forgot Levi was by my side. I lost myself thinking about the goodness of God—how His face had been shining on me and how He had kept Devin and me in the safety of His arms. All was well with my soul. I was free to worship without fear of what would happen later that evening. I was free to worship without wondering who was eyeballing me from her seat. I rejoiced in 2 Corinthians 3:17: "Where the spirit of the Lord is, there is liberty."

During the message, Levi jotted notes in his Bible. It looked like it had seen better days, which told me that he actually read it rather than used it as a centerpiece for the coffee table in his living room. At one point during the service, he rested his arm behind me on the pew. If anyone had been entertaining questions about us, he'd answered them.

By three o'clock that afternoon, I'd dropped Devin off the Maxwells' house and was headed to Levi's townhome.

"Hey there," he said, holding the door open for me. "Right on time. I like that." His hand found the center of my back as he pecked my lips. "You can have a seat in here," he said, pushing a jacket and a remote control to the end of his sofa. "Give me about five minutes."

Levi had left the TV on for my entertainment, but I wasn't interested in watching the made-for-TV movie. I wanted to take in his home and see what it said about him. I could see the kitchen from where I was sitting. There was a bowl and an unfinished glass of something red perched on the side of the sink. The pub-sized table of maple wood was built for two. It looked as if he'd tried to dress it up with place mats and matching napkins, but one of the table settings was now covered by two stacks of opened mail, magazines, and handfuls of spare change.

Levi's home décor could be described in one word: bachelor.

The walls were bare, but at least they were painted a color other than eggshell white or beige. He could definitely benefit from a woman's touch here and there. The only pictures in the room were the two framed photos on the mantel of a little boy, no doubt his son. He was the spitting image of Levi, down to his almost-dimple. He was a cutie.

Levi returned with a small leather backpack.

"Did you find anything interesting?" he asked.

"Anything like what?" He'd sparked my curiosity.

He shrugged, then picked up the jacket on the couch and slid his arms through the sleeves. "I don't know. Some women like to snoop."

"I'm not a snooper. I observe, but I don't snoop. I didn't leave this spot."

"I'll see that when I play back the surveillance video footage."

"You don't have security cameras. Stop playing."

"You see the right-hand picture frame on the mantel? You might want to take a close look at it."

He can't be serious, I thought, but I checked it out anyway. I flipped it to the back and studied the sides, but I couldn't see where a camera or any other recording device could've been hidden.

"You're wrong for doing me like that," I said. "I'm going to get you back."

"Don't start what you can't finish, beautiful," Levi said. "I have all kinds of practical jokes up my sleeves." He unzipped his leather bag and told me to put my wallet and cell phone inside.

I eyed him warily. "Why?"

"Because we're taking the motorcycle."

"We're *what?*"

"Taking my bike," he said, avoiding my astonished face. The face that said, "*You must be crazy.*"

"You've ridden with me before. You know I'm a safe driver."

"It's not you I'm worried about. It's the other drivers. The only thing between us and the road is air."

"And our guardian angels." Levi held the leather bag open. "We're good."

"I can't believe I'm doing this," I said.

I dropped in my wallet, my cell phone, and a small makeup case. Levi turned off the television and the lights in the house but flicked on the porch light as we left. I guessed that meant we were going to be gone a while. We left his house via the door leading to the garage, which was wide enough to house both his vehicles, though his truck had only a hairline of space in front and behind. He hit a button, and the garage door slid open with a soft whir.

"Put this on." Levi handed me one of the helmets hanging from a hook on the wall, then assisted me with strapping it securely before putting on his own. There wasn't going to be any lip-locking while we were wearing these things.

Levi mounted the bike first, and I waited for him to start it before I climbed on behind him. Even though we'd taken a spin before, my heart was still in my throat. But once we were flying freely on the highway, I settled down. I felt my wings begin to spread like an eagle. *I could get used to this*, I thought as I tightened my grip around Levi's waist. I wasn't fearful; I just wanted to cling to him. Indeed, I felt safe with him—and with all those guardian angels encamped around us.

I didn't ask any questions about our destination. I wanted it to be a complete surprise.

Levi exited the highway, and our adventure continued through the streets.

"Are you okay back there?" Levi asked when we'd stopped at a red light on East Market Street. I could count the number of times I'd been on this side of town, the first being when I'd gotten lost on my way to an author discussion and book signing at Chavis Library.

Levi leaned the motorcycle into a left turn, taking us onto the campus of North Carolina A&T State University. He slowed down to the point that anyone out on a run easily could've kept pace with us. We didn't stop until we reached the football field.

To my surprise and delight, the marching band was in formation in full practice mode. I unstrapped my helmet, happy to let my entire head breathe.

"This is the Blue and Gold Marching Machine," Levi said.

Being young definitely has its advantages, I thought as I watched their synchronized high-step marching and the way they stayed together without losing their rhythm or the tightness of their formation. The drum major shimmed and shook his shoulders while he did a back bend. When the set was over, he was balancing on the top of his hat.

"You see how they got their name?" Levi asked. "They move like a well-oiled machine. And those are the Golden Delights," he said when a group of women with batons pranced off the field.

"Since you're in Greensboro, you're an honorary Aggie now," Levi said. "I'll make sure you experience the Aggie Pride sooner or later. Homecoming's almost here." He slid his helmet back on. "You ready?"

"That was quick," I said.

"We're on tour, sweetheart. Hit it and quit it. Don't worry, there are more than enough Sundays, Mondays, and Tuesdays in our future. We'll be back."

We'd barely started down the road before we stopped again, this time at the gates of Bennett College.

"The young ladies who attend here are known as the Bennett Belles. In the late eighteen hundreds, some emancipated slaves bought the location, but it didn't become a college for women until sometime in nineteen twenty. It's only one of two HBCUs for women only."

"Along with Spelman, right?"

"Right."

"You really know your stuff," I said.

Levi tapped the side of his helmet. "The mind is the most dangerous weapon of all if you use it right."

In ten minutes, we were cruising through the streets again on Levi's historical tour. I think he liked to impress me with facts like you might learn from watching *Jeopardy*. It became a game. He'd quiz me on facts he knew I had no clue about. I let him teach me everything he could, asking him questions, pumping up his ego. Every man needed that.

"Are we going to have a pop quiz at the end of the day?" I asked as we pulled away from the Carolina Theatre.

"If I told you, then it wouldn't be a surprise," he said. "Let's grab something to eat."

"Good. I'm starving."

"And I know the perfect place," Levi said. "Stamey's Barbecue."

"I'm not sure if I like the analogy of being stuffed like a pig."

Levi kissed my hand. "It'll be worth every bite."

This was by far the best Sunday afternoon I'd had in a long time. So much joy had seeped out of my spirit over the years, I hadn't realized how deflated a life I'd been living. Now I was learning to enjoy the simple things, to take pleasure in every minute of the day. Life wasn't perfect, but the God

I served was. I basked in His grace and presence, and I knew that not even a man like Levi could take the place of God in my life.

I clasped my arms around Levi's midsection and held on. Things in my life had definitely changed, and I was ready to hold on for the ride of my life.

29

LEVI

One day during the week, we'll get to the Civil Rights Museum downtown," Levi said, pushing his empty plate inside the brown bag. Quinn was still working on her coleslaw and hush puppies. She always took slow, deliberate bites of her food, while he tended to shove his meals in his mouth. He'd always gotten in trouble for that.

"You were right—there's more history in Greensboro than I realized," Quinn said.

Levi nodded. "Every city has a history, just like every person has a story."

"So what's next?" Quinn covered her leftovers with a napkin and handed her plate to Levi. "The day is still young."

"What's your curfew?" he asked. "There's nothing like taking a ride through the city at nighttime."

"I should probably pick up Devin by eight so he can get home and get ready for school," Quinn decided.

Levi detected a hint of disappointment in her voice. "Another time, then." He took her hand and helped her up from the picnic table bench. He'd found a quiet, secluded area in the park for them to enjoy their BBQ. Their private oasis had been interrupted only by the occasional runner.

"Let's take a walk," he suggested. "Then we'll get back on the bike and see where it takes us."

"Sounds good to me," Quinn said. She rested her head against his shoulder as they strolled toward the walking path that winded through the park. Though the sun had been out earlier, a curtain of clouds now blocked it.

After a minute, Quinn said, "Some people wouldn't approve of our jumping into a relationship so soon. We're practically strangers."

"I've washed between your toes," Levi pointed out. "I think we're more than strangers now."

"You know what I mean."

"What 'people' are you talking about? Whoever they are, I'm not concerned about what they think. I've prayed about this, and I'm trusting God on it," Levi told her.

"You've prayed about me?" Quinn asked, lifting her head to look at Levi.

"You sound surprised. Of course I have. And you should pray about me, too."

Quinn slowed her pace, forcing Levi to shorten his strides so they could stay in sync. "Levi, I pray *about* you and *for* you. I'm taking a huge chance with my heart."

Levi stopped. "Baby girl, I can't promise that I'll never hurt you, but I can promise that I would never do so intentionally. You're God's daughter, and I don't take that lightly. The only thing I want to be responsible for is making your life better, even if I'm in it only for a short time."

Quinn shook her head. "Don't say that."

"We said it was a chance we were willing to take, right?"

She nodded. "Relationships are for a reason, whether for a season or for a lifetime."

Levi had meant every word he'd said. Quinn made him want to be a better man. She was the kind of lady who made a man want to settle down. In a year or two. But Levi preferred to live in the moment, and his foremost concern was about today.

And the day had been a success. Levi could tell by the way Quinn had comfortably leaned into him as he'd showed her the city. She seemed to appreciate his quirky fascination with history.

They began to stroll again, following the directional signs along the trail. Soon they disappeared into the arboretum of overhanging trees. The curtain of night was beginning to fall. Hidden birds chirped above them.

Squirrels and chipmunks scurried brazenly across the walkway ahead of them. The crickets sang a welcoming chorus.

A rustle in the bushes made Levi turn. A deer, possibly. Definitely something bigger than a squirrel. There was a crunch of leaves and then a sudden rush of black toward them. Quinn's scream jolted him into action. A body rammed against Levi with such force that it knocked him down. As he hit the concrete path, he felt the skin scrape from his elbows as they broke his fall. He punched with the force of a madman, flipping the perpetrator off him. Even though he was still on his back, Levi managed to kick the guy in the stomach. He doubled over.

"Quinn!"

A second attacker had his arm around Quinn's neck, but when she gave one quick, forceful jab in his groin area, his grip loosened. With his guard down, she grabbed his arm and flipped him over to the ground. *Thud!* The coward scrambled to his feet, then ran in the opposite direction, leaving his companion to fend for himself.

"Levi!"

He knew better than to ever turn his back on an assailant, but he'd been so worried about Quinn that he'd lost focus. He turned just in time to duck, preventing a tree limb from connecting with his head. He caught it with one hand, tussling back and forth with his combatant as if involved in a tug-of-war. The man in black kicked Levi in the knees, causing him to fall to the ground again.

"Give me your wallet, fool!"

"Fool"? Nobody called Levi out of his name. He stayed low to the ground and charged into the man's midsection. The assailant's center of gravity faltered. Levi connected with his face, drawing blood from his nose. He hit him a second time, then a third. The fourth blow landed with such power that the man was knocked out cold.

"Quinn." He didn't see her. She must have backed away from the chaos.

Finally he spotted her. Her eyes darted back and forth before finally landing on him. She was in a fighting stance, ready to strike again, if necessary; yet there was terror in her eyes. Levi could see the rise and fall of her chest as she heaved each breath.

"It's okay, babe." Levi reached into his back pocket for his cell phone and held it out to her. He needed to keep both his hands free. "Call nine-one-one."

Quinn didn't move.

"It's going to be okay," Levi told her.

She nodded.

Levi didn't like the look in her eyes. She still seemed afraid—this time, of him. Levi held out his phone, and Quinn took two hesitant steps toward him. She reached out far enough to take it from his hands, then stepped back again.

Her hands trembled as she dialed the three numbers. "Yes, I'd like to report an assault," she said, and Levi thought he detected some strength in her voice.

Levi fed her the details of their location and told Quinn to give the dispatcher his name.

"They're on their way," she said when the call had ended.

At the first sign of movement from his attacker, Levi pushed his knees into the man's back and held him down with his body weight. The guy was too weak to fight back.

"This isn't a good day for you, homeboy," Levi said. "You need to make better choices with your life. And the next time you want to attack somebody, you might want to make sure it's not a cop and a self-defense expert."

The man groaned. Levi didn't know if it was from pain or from the realization that he'd chosen the wrong people. Less than five minutes after the call, Levi heard a siren in the distance. Quinn ran the short distance down the trail to lead the police to where Levi was holding the man. Levi's colleague, Officer Payne, immediately slapped handcuffs on the man's wrists, then yanked him to his feet. That was when Levi spotted two more officers jogging over. They snatched the assailant by the elbows and pushed him toward the patrol car.

"Evidently he didn't know who he was messing with," Officer Payne remarked.

"That's what I told him," Levi said. "There were two of them. The other one ran away like a little girl when my woman put the beatdown on him."

Officer Payne raised his eyebrows. "Your woman?" He looked over at Quinn, who was still keeping her distance. "About time, Levi. I was starting to wonder."

"Don't start with me. Sometimes it takes a while for a treasure to be discovered."

Office Payne lowered his voice. "She still looks shaken up. You might want to get her home."

That was already Levi's plan. They walked through the clearing to the parking lot. Quinn had started shivering, so Levi draped his jacket across her shoulders. He made sure she was comfortable on a park bench while he gave his colleagues a report and the best description that he could of the attacker who'd gotten away.

After Levi's work at the park was done, his next job was to make sure Quinn felt safe. He sat down beside her.

"Tell me what you're thinking," he said. He tried to take her hand, but Quinn didn't respond. "You look like you're still in shock."

"I am," Quinn said. She ran her hands up and down her arms.

"At least you know everything you teach actually works. You put a hurting on that guy who jumped you. Sent him running."

Quinn made a noise that was kind of like a laugh, but not really.

"This wasn't a good way to end our day," Levi said.

Quinn looked up at him. He was still trying to read the changing look in her eyes. Serious. Thoughtful.

"Talk to me, Quinn."

Quinn shook her head like she was trying to dismiss her thoughts, but Levi wouldn't accept it. He couldn't let her crawl back into her shell.

"You've got to be able to tell me what you're feeling."

Time passed slowly as Levi waited for Quinn to answer. She took a deep breath before she began. "There was such rage on your face. You didn't even look like the same man. I've seen that before. One minute, Santana would be calm, and the next minute, he would erupt."

Now Levi got it. Her ex-husband. The abuse. The flashbacks.

"I'm not Santana," Levi finally said. "I'm not perfect, but I'm not him. I've never put my hands on a woman that way, and by the grace of God, I never will."

"I'm ready to go home now," Quinn said. She gave Levi an unconvincing smile. "I'll be fine. Really."

"Alright," Levi said. He helped her put her helmet on, pulling the strap tightly, and then he mounted his bike. Quinn got on behind him and put her hands on his shoulders. He wanted her to cling to his waist, as she had before. He needed her to hold him tightly. *He* wanted to hold *her* tightly.

"Can I use your restroom?" Quinn asked when they finally arrived back at Levi's.

"First door on the left," Levi said. "Can I get you something to drink?"

"A glass of water and an aspirin, if you have one," she requested. "I'm starting to get a headache."

Levi went to the kitchen for a bottle of water from the fridge and an aspirin from the cabinet. He set them both on the coffee table, docked his cell phone at the nearby speaker station on the end table, and scrolled through his play list. There it was—one of his favorite instrumental pieces. "The Lord Is My Shepherd." He had it playing softly when Quinn returned from the restroom.

When she sat beside him, he touched her cheek. It was cool, affirming his assumption that she'd splashed her face with cold water. Levi smoothed her hair back. It was slightly tangled from being confined within the helmet.

Quinn twisted the top off the water bottle, tossed the pill in her mouth, and washed it down. Then she closed her eyes. Levi knew it wasn't just the music that soothed her. The Scripture, too, was playing its way through her soul.

"*The LORD is my shepherd; I shall not want.…He restores my soul.… Yea, though I walk through the valley of the shadow of death, I will fear no evil… surely goodness and mercy shall follow me all the days of my life; and I will dwell in the house of the LORD forever.*"

Quinn looked up, and Levi saw a genuine smile for the first time that evening. "I did kick his butt, didn't I?"

"I knew you had it in you," Levi said. "And you definitely don't have to worry about me falling out of line. I like to have all my body parts working in order. Homeboy didn't run away; he limped."

They chuckled together.

"I'm not going to let the day end like this," Quinn said, perking up. "You did so much to make it special."

Inside, Levi breathed a sigh of relief. He stood and held out his hand. "Let's dance."

"Are you serious? To this music?"

"Yes. Haven't you read in the book of Psalms about how David danced until his clothes fell off?" He paused. "Wait—that's doesn't sound right. Let me rewind it."

"Please do," Quinn said, standing up. She took his hand in one of hers and rested the other one on his shoulder.

"There's only one rule," Levi told her. "We have to dance like we did back in middle school. There has to be twelve inches of space between us. The chaperones used to carry around rulers to check."

Quinn laughed. "That's a good idea, and right on time." She started to sway with the music. "Schools should probably enforce that standard today, too. I think I'll take my ruler along when I chaperone Devin's autumn dance next month."

"Poor Devin," Levi said.

"Poor me," Quinn rebutted. "I'm the one dealing with a preteen boy."

"Before you know it, that boy will be a man." Levi lifted her hand so that he could twirl her.

"I'll be more than blessed if he ends up being a man like you."

30

You've got to be kidding me," Zenja said after I'd related the attack in the park. "That's crazy."

"Tell me about it. It was like something out of a movie. I heard some rustling in the brush, and then, all of a sudden, they ran out at us. One targeted me, and the other, Levi."

Zenja had just brewed a pot of her favorite raspberry tea, and she poured me a cup. I cautiously sipped the steaming liquid. It was delicious.

"Levi unleashed his counterattack like a madman."

Zenja gave a little chuckle. "What did you expect him to do—scream like a little girl and pass out? You should be grateful he beat that thug down. And you?" Zenja wagged her finger at me. "You're a bad chick yourself."

"I hope that's the first and last time I have to use what I've learned in a real-life scenario," I said. "Thank God my training kicked in."

"It kicked in, and you kicked butt. But, barring that situation, it seemed like you had a great time on Sunday."

I could have sworn I saw hearts in Zenja's eyes. "I had a fabulous time," I conceded, putting those two idiots behind me and remembering how I'd felt holding on to Levi as we rode through the streets of Greensboro. I would never see the city the same way again. I was holding tight to that memory—the feeling of the wind in my face and the scent of Levi's cologne on his shirt as we leaned into the turns together.

"Did you ever imagine this would happen on that Friday night when you gave the safety presentation together?" Zenja cradled her cup in her hands and blew softly over the liquid.

"I wasn't thinking about a relationship at all," I admitted. "My mind was on business and Devin, that's it."

"Isn't that when the best men arrive? When you're not thinking about them, and they sort of pop up into your life?"

"Or pull you over for speeding," I added.

"Arrest me, boo," Zenja laughed. She held her wrists together like they were shackled with handcuffs.

"I can already tell what kind of weekend it's going to be in Blue Ridge," I said. I didn't tell her that Levi had taken care of my registration, though he still wouldn't confess to it. It was our little secret.

"You're going to love it," Zenja assured me. "I've never regretted getting away with the ladies. It'll be my fourth time going. After the first year, I locked it in on my calendar. Barring a family emergency, I will always be in attendance."

"I can't wait. Sometimes I feel like I'm running on a hamster's wheel trying to keep it all together. I need the time to step back, breathe, and enjoy where I am in life."

"You'll do that and more," Zenja said. "We pack a lot into the weekend, but we still manage to get some much-needed rest and alone time with God. If you're listening, He'll speak."

Roman had graciously offered to let Devin stay with him and Kyle for the weekend. It would be just the boys, since they were shipping Zariya off to her cousin's house in Burlington.

"Are you sure you didn't have to pressure Roman into hosting Devin while we're gone?" I asked.

Zenja put her hands on her hips. "Let me tell you something about Roman Maxwell. He doesn't do anything he doesn't want to do. Trust me on that. They'll probably order takeout every day, go shoot some hoops, and catch a movie. And when Roman wants to hide away in the garage and get away with all those instruments of his, Devin will be there to keep Kyle company. If you ask me one more time, I'll be tempted to use one of those moves you taught me. The only problem is that if I flip you over, I might end up on the ground myself."

I laughed. "We don't want that to happen." I was already starting to feel as if I had strained a muscle in my back from the superhero flip I'd done. It was going to be a night of sleeping with ice packs.

The Mountain High Retreat was only three weeks away, but I began to look forward to it as much as I looked forward to my Sundays with Levi.

"Do you remember what Caprice said the first time you came over?" Zenja asked. "She said God was going to put a new song in your heart. That's just what is happening now with Levi. He's helping God write that song. You said yourself that Sundays with your ex-husband were your worst days."

"And now Sundays are my best days," I said.

"Did you know that Devin has been helping Kyle with his fractions when he comes over here?"

"I had no idea," I confessed.

"I've tried twenty different ways to teach him about mixed numbers and decomposing fractions. I'm an elementary school principal, for goodness' sake, and I couldn't make him get it. It wouldn't stick until Devin helped him. Then, all of a sudden, the light came on—the glorious light," Zenja sang. "I'm at the point that I would pay you to let Devin come over. He's so pleasant and well-behaved."

"Thank you," I said. "I have to admit, he is a joy to be around. Every now and then, he has his issues, as all children do; but, given what he's been through over the past couple of years, he's my proof that prayer can hold things together."

"Amen to that," Zenja said. "Where are you and Levi headed tomorrow?"

"To a dinner theater," I said.

⌒

For the last eight weeks, Cassie Winters had become Ethel Waters during her one-woman show at a local dinner theater. I didn't mention to Levi that although I knew Waters sang "Stormy Weather," I had absolutely no clue about any details of her life. He, on the other hand, had probably researched her thoroughly, including the time period in which she lived. But when that woman took the stage, I felt like I knew Ethel Waters. She embodied her spirit and brought her back to life. She made me laugh, stirred my soul, and even brought tears to my eyes.

"She was phenomenal," I said as we walked back to the car after the performance. "I don't even have the words to describe it. To be able to capture and hold a crowd like she did is truly a gift from God."

"Cassie is a retired drama teacher," Levi explained. She was also married to one of Levi's superiors on the police force. "Whenever there's a performance in town, you can be sure she had a hand in either writing it, directing it, or acting in it."

"She should be on Broadway," I said. "She's that good."

"I've told her the same thing, but she said she never wanted to. She prefers the local community stage. Twice a year, she takes her former drama students, and anyone else who wants to go, on a bus trip to New York City to see a Broadway show. Next spring, they're going to see *A Raisin in the Sun*."

"Let me know when registration rolls around," I told him. "I want to be on that bus. I've never seen a play on Broadway."

"Have you been to New York?"

"No," I admitted. "I've never taken a bite out of the Big Apple."

"I can't believe it. I thought every woman had taken at least one shopping trip to NYC."

"Not this woman," I said. "There are many things I want to do that I've never done, or that I want to do again. But that's about to change."

Levi helped me into the passenger seat of his truck. "Things like what?"

"Giving blood. Going on a cruise. Traveling overseas—though I don't know I'll pull that off, since I'm scared to fly. Running a 5K. Growing a garden. Falling in love. The list goes on and on."

"I think you'll cross off those items one of these days," Levi said.

It wasn't my first time sharing my dreams with Levi. We'd peeled away so many layers of ourselves as we'd shared with each other the deep things. The heart-to-heart conversations. The kinds of things that would make a shallow man or woman reconsider the relationship. But we were still here, growing together. Sunday afternoons, and now Monday mornings, too, were our special times. Other than Devin, Levi's was the first voice I heard in the morning and the last one I heard at night.

Levi started the truck. "Maybe we can work on your list together."

I unwrapped a peppermint and popped it in my mouth. Dinner had satisfied every taste bud on my tongue—a complete feast from the buffet—but something had left an aftertaste of garlic. Maybe the green beans. Whatever the case, fresh, minty breath was better than what I had now.

I wasn't expecting a kiss tonight from Levi, even though God knew I wanted one. Levi's lips had started to awaken feelings and desires that I'd been able to hold at bay thus far. We couldn't pretend that our physical desires didn't exist, and acknowledging them was the first step we took in controlling them. We committed to no lip-to-lip contact. Since we truly believed it was God who'd brought us together, we prayed that our relationship would honor Him. And pray we did. Every day.

"You use the word 'we' so freely," I observed, since I'd noticed him doing it more and more.

"I didn't realize it," Levi said. "Does it bother you?"

"No, it doesn't bother me, but it can be strange to hear another man including me in his life. Sometimes the mind has to catch up with what the heart already knows."

It was getting close to eight o'clock, the time I usually picked up Devin from the Maxwells' house. As always, I'd met Levi at his house, so we drove back there so that I could get my car.

While he backed his truck expertly into the garage, I popped the trunk of my car to get the gifts I wanted to give to him before I left for the retreat later that week. I'd wanted to present Levi with something thoughtful and creative, since every outing Levi had planned for us had been done with me in mind.

I lifted out the two frames, wrapped individually in brown paper with navy blue bows, and carried them inside the house.

"What're those for?" Levi asked as he peeled off of his coat and tossed it over the back of the couch.

"They're for you.

"For me?" He looked genuinely surprised.

"It's nothing big," I rushed to say. "Just a thank-you. And some décor for your place."

"You don't like my style?" Levi joked. "It's called 'bachelor bland.'"

"Oh, I can tell. Everything is brown, navy, or black."

"Did you notice the rug in the living room? You have to give me credit for that, at least."

The brown rug had slight hints of red threading that ran from end to end. It would be a huge stretch to consider it a "pop of color."

"It'll do for now," I said. "We'll let it stay."

"You said 'We'll,'" Levi pointed out as he helped me out of my sweater.

"No, I didn't."

"Yes, you did," Levi insisted. "Your mind is catching up with your heart already."

Maybe I had said it. Maybe he was right. Of course, he was.

Levi clicked on the hallway light and emptied everything from his pockets into the catchall basket near the door—spare change, crumpled receipts, several packs of spearmint gum, and some butterscotch candies. If there was something he needed to find, that basket was the first place he checked.

Then he turned and glanced at the two packages leaning against the coffee table. "Let's see what I have here," he said.

I followed him into the living room and sat down beside him on the couch.

For a moment, he just gazed at the gifts, still in their wrapping.

"Well, what are you waiting for?" I prodded.

"I'm just relishing the moment. Nobody ever gives me anything."

"What about your son?" I asked.

"He's six. The only things he ever gives me are lists of the things he wants. Which, of course, I expect him to do."

"Oh, right." That was a pretty dumb question. Levi had said that L.J.'s mother routinely sent him pictures of his son and made sure that he was available whenever Levi came to town, but that was about it. Levi had added that, truthfully, that was all he wanted. L.J. *was* his greatest gift.

"Will you open them, please?" I said, my nervousness mounting. The idea for the gifts had seemed like a sweet thought, but I was beginning to feel less sure of my attempt to make memories.

Levi peeled the brown paper off at a painstakingly slow pace, but when he finally saw the framed canvases, I knew he recognized them immediately.

I'd cut out four swatches from the canvas we'd painted with our feet when we danced at the park on our first Sunday outing. Our footprints had mingled in a wonderful array of colors, giving it the feel of abstract art. The swatches were large enough to be bordered in a 16 x 20 mat, encased behind the glass of dark walnut frames. I'd framed four in all—two for him, two for me.

Levi leaned down closer to the prints to read the small script I'd added to each corner: "Sole to Soul."

He turned to me with amazement in his eyes. "I could kiss you right now."

"You could, but you won't," I said, almost daring him. "We have to keep all that intimate stuff under wraps."

"That was your idea, not mine," Levi said. His eyes spoke volumes. I looked away. "I guess it was because you felt you couldn't control yourself around all this manhood."

He flexed his arm muscles, showcasing two boulder-sized biceps. I tapped one of them with my fingers. *Rock solid.*

"All that manhood had better stay away from me," I said. "Don't start none, won't be none." I pushed my hair over my shoulders. I'd worn it down tonight, cascading in curls, because I knew Levi liked it that way. I still hadn't made up my mind about a haircut. I wanted something different, but not as short as Caprice's. Changing my look was long overdue. Levi had said that he didn't have a preference when it came to a woman's hair length, but, regardless of his opinion, I'd be doing what I liked for a change.

"Since you think I need help with my decorating, where should I hang these?" he asked.

I turned around and looked at the wall. "Right here over the couch. They're the perfect size."

"Works for me," Levi said. He set them on top of the couch, propped against the wall. "We could take these to a museum in Italy or somewhere and make a couple million."

"I'd let you be the salesman," I told him. "Italian women would love you."

"More than the American women."

"I can't speak for all American women, but I know one who's pretty enamored of you."

"Oui oui, ma chérie," Levi said in his best French accent.

"That's not Italian," I laughed.

"I like French things, too. French fries, French horns, French poodles, French toast, French kisses…."

"You don't make things easy," I said. "You're such a flirt."

"I'll do better," Levi said. "I'm supposed to be a man of God; but, at the same time, God made me this way. He shouldn't have made you so alluring and so beautiful, with such a magnetic smile, and smelling all good and peachy." Levi pointed a finger at me. "You need to stop wearing that lotion. You know what you're doing."

"That's been my favorite scent for forever," I said. "I can't help that it has that effect on you. What do you want me to wear?"

"Bug spray."

I rolled my eyes. "You're so silly."

"And you're so gorgeous." Levi pulled me toward him, and I willingly fell against his chest.

I leaned my head back and let him kiss me. And no, it wasn't the French kind. It was the sweetest, simplest act of love. On the cheek. I pulled away before our mouths could find their way to each other.

"I need to go now," I said. "I have to pick up Devin." I gathered my sweater and wrapped it around my shoulders.

Levi nodded. "That's best." He walked me out to my car, where he wrapped his arms around me, shielding me from the brisk fall breeze. "This is the perfect night for that motorcycle ride," he said into the side of my hair.

"I'd love to, but you know I can't. Devin's waiting for me."

"I know."

I turned my head so that it wasn't buried under Levi's armpit. "This time next week, I'll just be coming back from the mountains."

"I'll miss you," Levi said.

"I'll call you," I told him.

"You can't. It's against the rules of the women's retreat, or at least that's what Zenja told me."

"Zenja was giving you a hard time. If anybody could get a call through, it would be you. But I'm not sure how good the reception will be up there."

"As long as your airwaves to God are clear, that's all that matters."

"You're right," I said. "That's all that matters."

31

You didn't have to come and see me off," I told Levi, when in fact I was thrilled to see him. I'd been preoccupied with sliding my weekender bag into the luggage compartment of one of the two charter buses that would transport us up to the mountains. We'd already prayed for safe travels and divided the 113 ladies into groups based on who would be rooming together in the cabins. With approximately twenty women in each three-story cabin, I wasn't sure what was in store.

"Quinn, I think you have a visitor," Carmela had said, carrying her clipboard, as usual. "Either that or you've been a very naughty girl."

The second I turned around, Levi activated the flashing blue light on top of his police cruiser and let the siren blare for a few moments. *No, he didn't.* Of course, everyone looked his way.

He stepped out of the vehicle carrying a single red rose.

"Did you have to make such an entrance?" I asked, slightly embarrassed as the gazes now shifted to me.

"That's what happens when you're in the presence of a queen," Levi said. "You blow the trumpets."

"Is that what you call your siren?"

He shrugged. "It was my only option. Next time, I'll bring Roman along to play you a serenade." He handed me the rose.

"Thank you," I said. I was typically a private person, and while I wouldn't necessarily have called Levi's arrival a "public display of affection," it may as well have been one. He'd pretty much made it known to everyone gathered that there was something going on between us. Most of the women barely knew my name, let alone any details about me, so I wasn't worried about gossip making its way back to Devin. Right about now, his head was probably buried in his social studies test, anyway.

"So there you have it," I said. "Now everybody knows your business."

"I'm a grown man," Levi said. That seemed to be his answer for everything. "People *think* they know my business already, so I might as well give them something to talk about."

"You definitely did that," I told him. "At least you gave them something good to say."

"Always." Levi paused to listen to the mic mounted near his shoulder as the dispatcher's voice came through. "I was hoping I'd catch you before the buses rolled out," he told me when the mic went silent. "It looks like you guys are about ready to get out of here."

"According to Carmela's clipboard, we're should depart at nine thirty so we won't be thrown off schedule for this afternoon's activities."

"What's on the itinerary?" Levi asked.

"Why?"

"No reason. Just curious. What's the big secret?"

"It's no secret, but I'm still not telling you. It's a for-women-only weekend."

Levi looked over my head at the crowd of ladies milling around. "Zenja's brainwashed you already."

Less than thirty minutes prior, Zenja had said her good-byes to Roman. He'd assured me that Devin was in good hands and that they planned on living it up since there weren't going to be any females in the house. Devin could've flown over the moon when I told him that he'd be spending the weekend with Roman and Kyle.

I noticed the women beginning to move to their assigned bus. A few stragglers were still unloading items from the trunks of their cars, and a devastated toddler was screaming at the top of her lungs as her mother tried to peel her off her neck. I felt sorry for the mom. She looked like she was about to cry herself for having to leave her child behind.

"I guess that means we're ready to roll," I said.

"Enjoy yourself," Levi said. "And behave."

I laughed. "I'm going on a retreat to the mountains with a bunch of church ladies. What kind of trouble could we possibly get in to?"

"You never know. There's a wild one in every bunch."

Carmela approached us, having just buzzed through the parking lot to corral everyone toward the buses. "I promise she'll be back on Sunday," she told Levi. "Do you think you can survive until then?"

Levi squeezed my shoulder. "It'll be hard, but I'll try."

I wanted to get one last hug, but since Carmela was standing there staring at us as if we were a museum exhibit, I simply gave Levi a wink and headed for the bus.

Caprice and Zenja were seated at the front of the bus on either side of the aisle, holding the spots beside them for me and Carmela.

"I don't know what you've done to that man, but Levi is smitten," Zenja said as I lowered myself into the seat next to her.

I propped my purse on my lap, rose in hand. "That makes two of us," I said, my voice low. "Isn't he sweet?"

"I've never known him to be any other way."

"I know he's bound to do something that will crawl under my skin."

"Of course he will. He's a man. And likewise you'll do something that'll make him look at you cross-eyed, too. But that's part of every relationship between two imperfect people."

Our driver released the air brake, and our bus bounced to a start.

"Everything's moving so fast," I admitted.

"That's because it's new," Zenja said. "It feels like a whirlwind romance."

"Exactly. It's exciting and scary at the same time. I've had a whirlwind romance before, with my ex-husband. And you know how that went. I'm not getting stuck in my past, but I also don't want to repeat my mistakes."

Zenja opened a bag of dried apricots and offered me one. I passed. "I didn't get to eat breakfast," she said. "Meals on the run—the story of my life." She popped one in her mouth. "But, back to you and Levi, I think it's wise to spend at least a year dating somebody before you consider marriage. Issues have a tendency to surface by the time you've made it through all four seasons. You'll see how the other person handles conflict and stress. You'll find out if he's portraying somebody he really isn't."

"That's a good rule of thumb," I said. "Of course, we vowed to keep physical intimacy out of the equation."

Zenja shook her head. "I remember those days with Roman. Other than burying my first husband, that was the hardest thing I had to do in my life—and I'm not exaggerating." She laughed. "Sometimes you'll have to lock that police officer out of your house. Don't even let him in."

I could see it now—me looking through the peephole and refusing to let Levi inside my apartment. It may have sounded crazy, but it was practical. Our best dates might end with a wooden door between us.

Caprice leaned over across the aisle. "What are you two whispering about over there? It must be about a man. An officer and a gentleman."

"And you talk about me putting people's personal business in the streets?" Zenja said.

"I think Levi took care of that when he swooped in like a knight in shining armor back there," Caprice retorted. "The man showed up in a patrol car and turned on his lights *and* siren for you. He might not want to admit it, but the man is officially in love. If not love, it's a whole lot of like."

I had a whole lot of like for him, too, but I didn't want Levi to be my primary thought during the retreat. I had been drinking in God's grace and mercy like cold water on a scorching hot day. He had shown me such kindness that my greatest desire now was to please Him. I'd finally begun to realize what it meant to cast my cares on Him. God was my Father, my Counselor, and my closest Friend. When it was time to leave the Blue Ridge Mountains on Sunday afternoon, I wanted to go home a different woman.

Carmela wouldn't let the women on our bus rest until we had participated in the two icebreaker games she'd planned, after which Caprice threatened to throw her clipboard out on the highway if she didn't stop harassing us. I pretended not to hear when she also warned her little sister not to make any sales pitches for spice blends, makeup products, weight-loss pills, or tourism services during the trip. Carmela hesitantly agreed.

We were an hour into the three-hour ride when I decided to catch a nap. If the rest of the women on the bus felt anything like I did, they were exhausted. I'd been running errands for myself and Devin all week, had picked up a few extra evening exercise classes, and had found myself painting late into the night when I should've been asleep. The more I created colors and experimented with different brushstrokes, the more I wanted to. A wellspring of ideas and visions had flooded my mind, and I couldn't shut it off. I didn't want to.

"Wake up, sleepyhead," Zenja said. She shook my arm.

The scene in front of me could've been painted only by God Himself. The trees were dressed in shades of red, orange, and gold, and they brushed against a cloudless sky. From the front row of the bus, I would have had the perfect view of our ascent into nature, and I'd slept through the whole thing.

"Are we here?" I asked.

"Almost," Zenja said, pointing out the window. "The buses are going to stop here so we can transfer to those passenger vans, which will take turns transporting us up the mountain. The buses are too long and too wide to make the curve."

That should've been a warning.

Soon I was sandwiched between Caprice and Zenja, praying for my life. Although I wanted to meet Jesus face-to-face someday, I hoped this wasn't the day. The winding dirt road leading to the camp was so narrow and steep that when I looked out the window, the only thing I could see was the edge of the cliff. It seemed to be a straight drop-off into the rocks and trees below.

"Tell me when it's over," I begged them.

"Open your eyes," Zenja coaxed me. "It's beautiful."

"I'm sure it is," I said. "But I'll use my imagination."

By my watch, the ride up to our cabin took less than five minutes, but it felt like five hours.

"That wasn't so bad, was it?" the van driver said as he opened the door. He assisted each of us out of the van and into the crisp, cool air. Our five cabins were tucked within a cove of trees, visible from one another yet separated by gravel trails. The view from the top was breathtaking, and although the ride had rattled my nerves, I would have taken it again, knowing what awaited at the peak.

"Let's get settled while the driver gets the rest of the ladies," Caprice suggested. "He has to make a few more trips to get everyone up here." She set down her bags, looked up at the sky, and inhaled slowly, deeply. Then she exhaled, held her arms out to the sides, and filled her lungs again. "My God," she said, "I am so thankful to be here. I feel Your presence."

We all stood together, temporarily silenced by Caprice's words. I, for one, wanted to take in the moment. I desired to receive all God had for me for the weekend. I prayed that my time away from Greensboro—away from the routine of life, away from Devin and Levi—would be worth every second.

One lady moved. Then another. Then yet another, until we were all standing in a circle, our hands joined, our heads bowed.

"Father, thank You for our safe travels," Zenja began. "Thank You for allowing us to spend another day with You and to be about Your business. We ask that You would touch the heart of every lady on this retreat. Only You know our deepest hopes and darkest regrets. Only You know the true desires of our heart. Search us, God, and know our hearts; try us and know our thoughts. Allow us to be a blessing to one another during this Mountain High Retreat. We're here for only a short time, but let the impact last forever. In Jesus' name, amen."

"Amen," we all sang out, following it with thunderous applause and cheering.

"Let's not wake the bears and other wild animals," Carmela said. "Y'all can praise God out here, but I'll get my praise on inside that cabin." She tilted her bag on its wheels and bumped it across the gravel toward the first cabin.

"I'm with you, girlfriend," I laughed.

It didn't take us long to get settled in our assigned rooms. Afterward, we convened in the common area. There was a kitchen, but we wouldn't need to use it, as Caprice had arranged for a local catering company to handle all the meals for the women in our cabin.

"It feels nice to have somebody else cook for a change," Zenja said. She'd changed out of her ankle boots into a pair of fuzzy socks.

"Tell me about it," one lady agreed. "I have four boys, and I spend more time in the kitchen than anywhere else. And let me tell you, I hate to cook."

Carmela flitted down from the loft area, her clipboard in hand. "Ladies, ladies," she chirped. "I have your agenda. I didn't make copies, so I'm just going to post one on the refrigerator. I'll keep one for myself, in case you have any questions."

"What do we have planned, Carmela?" Zenja asked. "I know you can't wait to tell us all about it."

Carmela's face lit up. Zenja had given her the boost she needed. "Well, since you're begggggiiiinnngggg me," she teased. "I know it's been a long week, so for the rest of the afternoon and evening, we'll be observing 'Rest in Jesus.' We'll take time to get to know one another, unwind, read, go for walks, pray. Whatever it is you want to do, it's all about you." She snapped her fingers. "Tomorrow, the fun begins. We're going to start with 'Prayer and Pastries' in the morning, 'Tell-It-like-It-Is Testimonies' after that, 'My-Mama-Should've-Told-Me Moments' in the early afternoon, and then, after our break, we'll end with our 'Dance like David' talent extravaganza." Carmela threw her hands in the air as if she were waiting for a standing ovation.

I couldn't fault the woman for her excitement. From the little I knew about her, Carmela did seem to have an enthusiastic outlook on everything.

"Thanks to my little sissy, there shouldn't be a dull moment," Caprice said as she emerged from the kitchen, where she'd been talking with the head chef from the catering company. "Now, I don't think I have to remind you ladies how I dominated at the talent show last year. So if you plan on winning, you'll need to bring your A game."

Zenja rolled her eyes. "Here we go again."

"Should I ask?" I said.

"My bestie thinks she can sing, and these ladies here have pumped that notion into her head. A few years ago, we went on a cruise together, and she somehow won a thousand-dollar prize in karaoke. They might as well have given her a Grammy."

"I can't wait to hear her sing," I said.

Zenja stuck playfully stuck her fingers in her ears. "Let's see what you say after tomorrow night."

I chatted with Zenja for a while, then made it a point to mill around and introduce myself to the other women. Everyone was so inviting and welcomed me into the fold. There were a few questions about Levi, but I didn't mind. We found a small vase under one of the kitchen sinks for me to put my rose in, and I used it to adorn the center of the dining table.

I was sitting in a rocking chair on the porch with a woman named Iris when the van driver, Julian, pulled up outside the cabin and rolled down his window.

"Is there a woman named Quinn Montgomery in this cabin?" he asked us.

"That's me," I said, standing up. My first thought was of Devin. Had something happened, and Roman hadn't been able to reach me on my cell phone? I'd left every emergency contact number I could come up with, including the number of the cabin rental company. But when Julian smiled, my fears were allayed. Maybe I'd dropped something from one of my bags.

Julian got out of the van, came around to the front passenger door, and swung it open. He reached inside and pulled out a glass vase holding a bouquet of a dozen red roses.

"No, he didn't," I said.

Iris shook her head. "Oh, yes he did."

Julian placed the bouquet in my arms. "Be careful. It's heavy," he said.

When I carried it into the cabin, the ladies nearest the kitchen gathered around in admiration.

"Those are beautiful."

"I bet he's thinking about you right now."

"The only thing my man ever gives me is a hard time."

I opened the card attached to it.

Here's the other eleven. Love, Levi

Zenja walked up and smelled the roses. "How does that man expect you to keep your mind on God if he's still trying to romance you from Greensboro? I was joking when I told him not to call you, so I guess he wanted to get to you any way he could."

"I'll call him tonight," I said, taking the single rose from the small vase and adding it to the larger bouquet. I slid the showpiece to the middle of the table and went back outside, where my rocking chair was still waiting.

Iris smiled at me, although the light in her eyes was dim. "I used to have that kind of love," she said.

And I knew at that moment why I was there.

32

LEVI

Roses delivered, the text message read. Levi had asked that the driver send him a notification when the roses had been delivered to Quinn. He could almost give himself a pat on the back. He'd thought that his showing up that morning to see her off would be unexpected, but he knew for certain she would never expect him to send the rest of the bouquet to her at the retreat. He couldn't help it; despite his tough-looking exterior, he was a romantic. He'd been told as much, plenty of times, but he always liked to see his lady smile. And Quinn was his lady.

Quinn may have been the one at the retreat, but she wasn't the only one who'd be doing some serious praying over the weekend. Levi needed it, too—no doubt about it. The more time he spent with Quinn, the more he wanted to be with her in the way that a husband was with a wife. He kept telling himself that. A *husband* and a *wife*.

Fighting his flesh had become an everyday battle. It was a good thing Quinn could be strong; otherwise, things might go where they weren't supposed to. It was easier for Levi to be celibate when he wasn't attracted to anyone. Before Quinn, he'd been content to keep busy at work, picking up extra security assignments, and also volunteering at the church. But Quinn had invaded his routine. She'd become an integral part of his life. When he wanted to see a movie, he checked the Sunday schedule to see if they could fit it in. And breakfast on Mondays with the Mae sisters wasn't the same if she couldn't join him.

"How are you holding it down, bro?" Levi asked Roman when he picked up the phone. "You ready to have Daddy Day Care open for the weekend?"

"You know it," Roman said. "The boys won't be any trouble at all. Zenja stocked up on snacks; I'll get them pizza and wings tonight, maybe rent a few video games, and we're set. It won't take much to keep them happy."

"Boys are easy to please," Levi conceded. "I don't know what I'd be doing if I had a little girl."

"High maintenance," Roman said. "And the older they are, the worse it gets. They always have their hands out for something. They want to wear all the clothes they're too young for, and makeup and all that crap. Zariya keeps my blood pressure high, man. I'm telling ya, girls are no joke."

"My prayers and my sentiments go out to you," Levi joked. "But you'll survive."

"No choice," Roman said. "With all these busters around, I have to show my daughter what a real man looks like. She spends most of her time mad at me, but one day she'll appreciate it."

"No doubt about that," Levi said. He'd stopped at home during his lunch break to grab something to eat, and now he gazed at the framed canvases Quinn had given him. Hanging them on the wall had seemed like such a small addition at the time, but whenever Levi walked in the room, he realized what an impact they made on his space. They brightened it. A woman's touch—there wasn't anything else like it. When she came back to town, he'd take her out on a shopping trip for some other items to spruce up his place. Maybe some pillows for the couch, an accent rug, or something like that. He didn't know what he needed, but she would.

"You should come by and hang out with us," Roman told him. "You know me—I'll let the boys stay up all night, so they'll sleep late."

"I don't know if Devin can hang," Levi said. "You know Quinn doesn't play around about his bedtime. He'll be asleep by the time the clock strikes twelve."

"He'll be straight," Roman said. "There'll be too much going on for him to sleep. And I already told Quinn I do things differently than she does, and she was fine with it. She didn't care. Like all those women, she was just happy to be getting away for some peace and quiet."

"I'll come by after I get off work and hang for a while, then," Levi told him.

"Yeah, come spend some time with you future stepson," Roman teased.

"You're really going to play me like that?" Levi opened the refrigerator and pulled out some two-day-old shepherd's pie he'd ordered from a restaurant down the street. He didn't know how it was possible, but it tasted better the older it got.

"You can't fault me for speaking the truth," Roman said. "But that's the future. You have time."

Levi set the microwave to two minutes to get the food piping hot, the way he liked it. "Man, we're not rushing anything. We're enjoying each other. She's been through a lot, so I know she'll check me out for a minute before she completely puts her heart out there. I can't blame her for that. I think her ex-husband was the devil's brother."

"It was that bad?"

"Unfortunately. For real, though, pray for Quinn. And I'm not just saying that 'cause I'm feeling her. Whether or not our relationship goes to the next level, she deserves to be healed and whole."

"I've got nothing but respect for you, Levi," Roman told him. "You're a good man. Carmela might run your name through the mud since you kicked her to the curb, but I'll always stand up for you."

"So, you're full of jokes. I can take it," Levi said. When he heard the dish start to pop and splatter, he opened the microwave door and pulled it out.

"In all seriousness, both of you have my prayers," Roman told him.

"I appreciate it," Levi said. "See you tonight."

He pushed his unopened mail to one side of the table so he could eat without the clutter surrounding him. Roman was right—any time with Devin would be time well spent. Quinn had even suggested it herself. And it would take a while for him to establish a relationship and build higher and higher levels of confidence. Levi wouldn't try to replace Devin's father, but he knew that every boy needed a father figure, especially at that age. Devin seemed cool with him now, but if he saw Levi getting too close to his mother, he might put up a wall. He was older than Levi's son. He'd seen and experienced things that would influence what he thought of any man in Quinn's life.

Too bad he wasn't like L.J., ready to attach himself to anybody who'd buy him a wrestling figurine or a pack of potato chips. To gain Quinn's heart, Levi would have to win over Devin's heart, too.

33

Iris had a caramel complexion with freckles dotting her nose. She stood before us, wringing her hands, as she shared her testimony. I felt every deep breath she inhaled. I could relate to every tear she shed. I wanted to stand up, pull her into a strong embrace, and assure her that things would be okay.

So I did.

Iris clearly hadn't expected that, and it wasn't something I normally would have done. But this wasn't a normal day, and my prayer had been for God to bring me out of my comfort zone. I knew this was His doing, because, when I saw my sister in Christ hurting like I'd hurt and weeping because she wasn't sure how she could start over, I couldn't bear for her to stand there alone. Zenja and Caprice had extended the arms of Jesus to me, and it was only by God's grace that I could do the same to Iris. There would be a day, I told Iris, when her testimony wouldn't provoke tears of sorrow but tears of joy from the trials she'd overcome.

"And do you know how I know?" I asked her. "Because I've been there. I'm two years out of an abusive marriage, and God has restored the ten years that the enemy tried to steal from me. The devil thought he'd taken my happiness, but God replaced it with an even greater joy. The devil thought he could torment my life, but God gave me the peace that surpasses all understanding. So you'll make it. If I can make it, you can, too."

"And if I survived, you can too," said Evelyn, the woman who'd sat beside me at dinner the night before and also during "Prayer and Pastries" that morning. There's one thing I know for sure: With God, there is no such thing as coincidences. She stood up and joined me. Evelyn joined me at the front of the room and took Iris's right hand, while I kept squeezing her left.

Iris was overcome with tears. She tried to speak, but her weeping was so intense that she couldn't manage any words. The whispered prayers of her sisters rose above her sobs.

"Strengthen her, Lord God."

"Pour out Your grace on her, Jesus."

"Give her the people she needs in her life."

"Heal every hurt. Calm every fear."

Though she'd been slumped over before, with every prayer of encouragement, Iris straightened, as if pulled upright by a puppeteer's string. She clasped her hands, placed them over her heart, and then, with the clearest, melodic alto voice I'd ever heard, began to sing. "Amazing Grace, how sweet the sound, that saved a wretch like me. I once was lost but now am found, was blind, but now I see."

Before I realized what was happening, my voice had joined with hers. I'm not a singer by any stretch of the imagination, but the joy I felt it my heart at the time couldn't be contained. After the first verse, Evelyn added her voice to ours. And though my eyes were closed, I could smell Zenja's perfume when she came to stand beside me. I felt her clutch my hand. Soon, an entire chorus of women's voices filled the crowded cabin. All one hundred thirteen of us had stuffed ourselves into the small space—seated on couches, chairs, the floors, the stairs, and the loft overlooking the common area—so that we could participate in the "Tell-It-like-It-Is Testimony" session that Carmela had scheduled.

And now we were one hundred thirteen women singing with one voice, praising the only true and living God.

"Through many dangers, toils and snares I have already come; 'tis Grace that brought me safe thus far and Grace will lead me home."

~

"Ma!" Devin ran toward me when I climbed off the charter bus. I could tell that he was trying hard to contain his excitement, but I knew my son had missed me as immensely as I had missed him. For the past two years, we hadn't been away from each other for more than a few hours—certainly not overnight.

Devin nearly knocked me over when he plunged into me for a hug. For once in his preteen years, he didn't seem to care who was watching.

I squeezed him so tight that I could've meshed his body into mine. "I missed you," I said, pecking a kiss on his temple.

He pulled away and studied me. "I missed you, too. You look different."

"Different? It hasn't been *that* long, Devin."

"I know, but you still look different. Like you've been at the beach or something."

It was better than that. I'd been in the presence of the Lord. He'd made His face to shine upon me, and if being kissed by the Son had given me a sun-kissed glow, I'd accept that compliment over any other.

We joined the line of women waiting to retrieve their bags from the luggage compartment under the bus. There were excited shrieks and tight hugs as husbands and children found their wives and mothers. You'd think we'd been away on a monthlong sabbatical. I guess they realized how much their women were crucial to the flow of their days. One poor husband—God bless his soul—looked like he hadn't slept in a week. As he hastily handed over his infant son to his wife, it was obvious he hadn't bothered to iron his clothes before leaving home.

"So, did you have a good time with Kyle and Mr. Roman?" I asked Devin.

"Yes! We did so much. It's like we had one big man cave to ourselves all weekend, doing man stuff."

"Man cave. Man stuff," I repeated. "Alright, whatever you say." I grabbed his arm and shook it. "You look like you're still in one piece, so the 'man stuff' couldn't have been that bad."

"We played video games, went bowling, and went to band practice with Mr. Roman. Did you know he could play every instrument ever made?"

"I've heard he's pretty good."

"No, Ma," Devin said, taking a step as the line inched forward. "He's better than good. He's amazing. You know how you say that God gives people certain gifts? Music is definitely Mr. Roman's gift."

Now I was more anxious than ever to attend a performance of Roman's group. If the venue was kid-friendly event, I'd consider letting Devin come along.

"Did you guys go to church today?" I asked him.

"Yes. Mr. Roman said no matter how late we stayed up on Saturday night, we still had to go to church. So we met Mr. Levi there, then went to the batting cages afterward."

"You did? That was nice."

I wondered where Levi was now. Since he'd seen me off before the retreat and had surprised me with the bouquet of roses, I'd assumed that I would see him soon after stepping off the bus. I glanced around quickly so I wouldn't seem uninterested in Devin as he continued rattling off the highlights of his weekend.

"Mr. Levi was supposed to come over on Friday night, but something came up, so he met us at church instead. After we left the batting cages, we went back to the house to shower so we wouldn't be smelling all funky when we got here to pick up you and Ms. Zenja."

"Where did Mr. Levi go?" I asked.

Devin shrugged and averted his gaze. "Home, I guess."

The bus driver handed my bag to Devin. I easily could've rolled it myself, but I let him be the gentleman. I looked around again, still hoping to see Levi, but he was nowhere in sight. *What's up with that?* I wanted to know. Sunday was our day. And I hadn't spoken to him since Friday night, when I'd called to thank him for the roses. I'd decided they were too cumbersome to bring back on the ride home, so I'd left them with the lady who manned the front desk at the cabin rental facility. I knew Levi wouldn't mind. Just because I was leaving the arrangement behind didn't mean I was leaving behind the smile it had brought to my face.

"Do you know how long it's been since I've had roses?" the receptionist had exclaimed. She'd set them on her desk and shoved her face in the middle of the bouquet to inhale the scent. "I swear, I'm keeping these till every last one of these here petals falls off."

I followed Devin to where Roman was parked. He'd already loaded Zenja's bag in the trunk of their car and was waiting for her to return from inside the church building with Caprice.

"He's good," Roman told me. "No scrapes, no bruises, no nothing. Devin was a joy to have around. No trouble at all."

Devin lifted my bag into the trunk of the Maxwells'.

"Thanks again for letting him stay with you. He thoroughly enjoyed himself."

"He's welcome anytime," Roman told me. "All it takes is a phone call."

"I'll keep that in mind," I said.

Iris had been one of the first to jump off the bus so she could make a beeline to the ladies' room, but I spotted her exiting the side door of the building. I waved to get her attention, then headed in her direction.

"You have my number," I told her. "Please use it."

"I will, I promise," she said. "You've blessed me this weekend—more than you know. Thank you for being so open and transparent with your life."

"I can't lie—there was a time when I wouldn't have shared my story. But I know that I have nothing to be ashamed of. I have victory in Jesus Christ. *We* have victory in Jesus Christ."

"Don't do that. Don't make me start crying again," she said, pulling a handkerchief out of the pocket of her slacks.

"God's counted all those tears, sister. You'd better believe that."

"And I count my blessings."

We hugged. Not one of those hugs for a person you barely know, but an embrace that said, *"I'll be here for you."*

I noticed Zenja had returned to her car, so I went to join my carpool with a promise to Iris that we'd speak to each other during the upcoming week. It was a short ride to our apartment complex, and from the way Zenja and Roman were ogling each other, I could tell it was going to be an even faster ride back to their side of town. I could almost hear the latch of their bedroom door turn and lock.

When we reached our apartment, Devin opened the door and dragged my bag inside behind him. On another day, I might've cautioned him to be more careful, but I was so glad to be home that I didn't mind if he added extra scuff marks to the bottom of my suitcase. Besides, my spirit was still soaring high over the Blue Ridge Mountains.

"There's no place like home," I said as I plopped down on the sofa in the living room. I covered my legs with the throw that I kept draped over the arm of the couch. Devin and I had wrapped ourselves up in it during many of our Friday stay-at-home movie nights.

Devin sat beside me, then turned so he could stretch his long legs across my lap. He slid his feet under the throw and wiggled his toes inside his socks. "I was thinking, Ma."

"About what?"

Devin picked at the cuticle on his left thumb, then turned his hands over to study his palms. They were smooth now, but during baseball season, they turned rough with calluses formed from the strong grip on his baseball bat.

"About Mr. Levi," he finally said.

That piqued my interest. "What about Mr. Levi?"

"He's a pretty cool man. And he's not married. He does have a kid, though. A son named L.J."

"He told me," I said. I pulled off the light V-neck cardigan I'd been wearing over my tank top. "I think Mr. Levi's nice, too. Did he talk to you about something you wanted to tell me about?" I wondered if Levi had hinted that we'd been spending time together. I doubted it, but I figured it didn't hurt to ask.

"Not really. We mostly talked about sports and school." Devin paused. "And making wise choices."

Bingo, I thought. *Point for Levi.*

"That's good," I said, trying not to sound like I was making a big deal out of it. I doubted everything Levi had drilled into Devin's head could be summarized in two short sentences. I wished he would tell me more, but I wouldn't push him. Not right now. "Sometimes boys need other men to talk to—men they can trust. Because, as much as I'd like to think I know it all, there are some things I can't teach you."

Devin nodded. "Mr. Levi said I could come hang with him sometimes. Is that okay?"

"Sure," I said.

"I think you should hang out with him, too. I mean, not all of us together. Just you and him."

I swallowed, then coughed to clear the lump in my throat. I was speechless.

"I told him that if he wanted to ask you out, it would be okay."

"Oh, you did, did you?" I thumped Devin gently on the head. "Since when did you start giving men permission to ask me out?"

"Well, Mr. Levi's the first one I've said that to," Devin went on. "I can tell by the way he looks at you when he sees you that he must think you're kinda hot."

"Really? Well, that's interesting to know." I guess the covert glances that passed between me and Levi hadn't been so inconspicuous after all.

"Trust me, Ma. I'm a young man. I know these kinds of things."

Devin had been to one session of Man Up Mondays and spent one weekend at the Maxwells', and now he'd all but dubbed himself a relationship expert. At least he had a good hunch when it came to Levi. I lifted Devin's feet, pushed the throw off my legs, then stood to go get a drink of water. This entire conversation with Devin was dehydrating.

Then a thought crossed my mind. I hoped he hadn't taken a sudden interest in my dating life because he wanted one of his own. *Not happening.*

Someone rapped on our door as I opened the cabinet in search of a super-sized glass. I figured it was probably Caleb from across the way. He'd been having trouble with his car battery over the past week and likely needed another jump start.

"That's Mr. Levi," Devin said, ending my guessing. He stepped into the kitchen and glanced at the clock. "He's five minutes early. I told him to come over at seven. You should get the door. I'm going to my room."

"Devin Scott Montgomery," I said as he scuttled away.

"It's all good, Ma. Like I need somebody, you need somebody, too."

I watched Devin with both amusement and astonishment as he scooted down the hallway. He stopped briefly and turned around, and when he looked at me, I could see a glimpse of his future. Undoubtedly, he would become the man God had fashioned him to be. Yes, we would have to figure out the raging hormones thing. Yes, sooner or later, Devin would have to learn about his little sister, and he'd have to visit his father. Yes, the two of us would have to navigate the waters of Levi—or whomever God sent to be in my life. But we'd be okay. If there was one thing I knew for sure, it was that God wants His best for us.

Devin ran back over to me, kissed my cheek, then raced back to his room and closed his door. I touched my hand to my face. Had my son really arranged a date for Levi and me? On the way to the door, I smoothed the top of my hair, which I'd wound in a tight knot at the crown of my head.

Levi. His deep-set eyes. His almost-dimple. *My man.* Could I say that?

"I was told to be here at seven," he said when I opened the door, looking over my shoulder before he kissed me on my other cheek. The two men in my life had made my face happy.

"I *just* heard you were coming over, maybe thirty seconds ago," I told him.

"The whole idea was Devin's," he said as he stepped inside. "I must've impressed him with my batting skills at the cages today."

"That quite possibly could've done it," I conceded as I closed the door behind me. An adult male other than the maintenance man was inside my four walls, and I felt safe. I felt loved.

Levi followed me into the kitchen and handed me the navy blue insulated bag he was carrying. Heat radiated from the bottom. I unzipped it the bag and knew from the first whiff what it was.

"You're not playing fair," I said. "I think this is a bribe." I slid the apple pie out of the bag and didn't waste any time finding a knife in my cutlery drawer.

"I'm not against bribing you with an apple pie if it means this officially makes you my lady."

Little did Levi know, but it was already official in my mind.

"With a pie? Really?" I joked.

"Don't forget, I've been preapproved by Devin. That has to count for something."

"How long do I have to think about it?" I asked flirtatiously.

Levi reached into his back pocket and pulled out a small square of folded paper. "While you think about it, take care of this for me."

I accepted the paper because I really wanted to slice into my treat while it was still warm. "What is this? A bill for your baking services?"

"Yes," Levi said, with a smile that said much more than his words. "With payment due in full—immediately."

I unfolded the page and immediately had a flashback to our first kiss. He'd actually kept the note he'd given me in his truck on the night he returned from D.C.

Can I kiss you? ___ Yes ___ No ___ Maybe

"This bill has been paid already," I said, spreading the paper out on the counter. We instinctively leaned into each other until we could feel each other's breath on our faces.

"So, Quinn Montgomery," Levi said. "The answer is still yes?"

I answered with my lips pressed to his. The kiss was soft. Tender. Perfect. This kind of kiss couldn't happen often, but for now, I was enjoying it. *God, please help me—help us*, I thought as I pulled away.

"Well, Officer Leviticus Gray, I think this means I can see you on more days than just Sundays," I told him.

"We should find chaperones," Levi said, smoothing back a stray hair that had been tickling my forehead.

"Devin would make a great one," I said.

With his thumb, Levi gently brushed the scar that Santana had left on my neck. I barely thought about it anymore, but Levi's reminder made me marvel at how blessed I was that my past did not define me.

"Your chaperone is missing in action right now," Levi said.

And then, right there in my kitchen, with Devin's video game blaring in the background and the scent of warm apple pie wafting under my nose, I let Levi kiss me again. And I kissed him, because I knew his lips tasted better than any homemade pie I'd ever had.

About the Author

Tia McCollors used to dream of being a television news anchor, but her destiny led her behind the pages instead of in front of the cameras. After earning a degree in journalism and mass communications from UNC–Chapel Hill, she went on to build a successful career in the public relations industry. In 1999, a job layoff prompted her to explore writing and pursue a career as an author. Following the birth of her son in 2006, she left the corporate arena to focus on her family and her expanding writing and speaking business.

Tia's first novel, *A Heart of Devotion*, was an *Essence* magazine best seller. She followed her popular debut with four other inspirational novels: *Zora's Cry*, *The Truth about Love*, *The Last Woman Standing*, and *Steppin' Into the Good Life*. In 2012, she released her first devotional book, *If These Shoes Could Talk: Devotional Messages for a Woman's Daily Walk*. Tia's seventh novel, *Sunday Morning Song*, follows *Friday Night Love* in Days of Grace, her first series with Whitaker House.

In addition to being an author, Tia is an inspirational speaker, as well as an instructor for writing workshops. She particularly enjoys coaching women of faith, female entrepreneurs, and stay-at-home mothers. Her speaking engagements and literary works have been spotlighted in a growing number of publications, including *Black Enterprise* magazine, *Who's Who in Black Atlanta*, *The Good Life* magazine, and the *Atlanta Journal-Constitution*.

Tia currently resides in the Atlanta, Georgia, area with her husband and their three children. Readers can learn more about Tia at www.TiaMcCollors.com or connect with her on social media at www.facebook.com/FansOfTia or via Twitter @tiamccollors.

Welcome to Our House!

We Have a Special Gift for You ...

It is our privilege and pleasure to share in your love of Christian fiction by publishing books that enrich your life and encourage your faith.

To show our appreciation, we invite you to sign up to receive a specially selected **Reader Appreciation Gift**, with our compliments. Just go to the Web address at the bottom of this page.

God bless you as you seek a deeper walk with Him!

WE HAVE A GIFT FOR YOU. VISIT:

whpub.me/fictionthx

WHITAKER
HOUSE